SAILING TO
BYZANTIUM

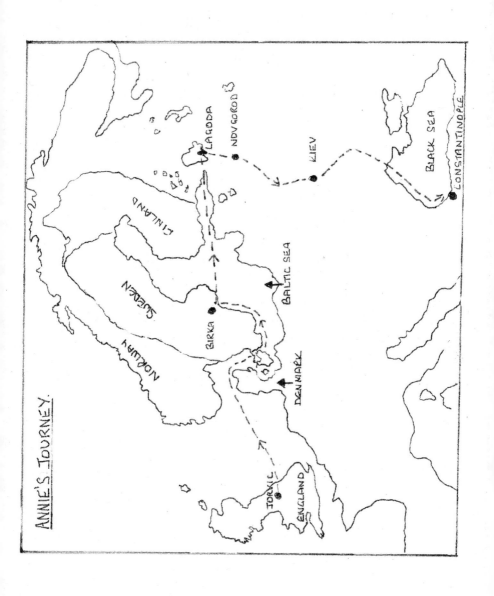

ANNIE'S JOURNEY.

Enjoy the Journey!
Maureen Thorpe

SAILING TO
BYZANTIUM

Maureen Thorpe

Ekstasis Editions

Published in 2020 by:
Ekstasis Editions Canada Ltd.
Box 8474, Main Postal Outlet
Victoria, B.C. V8W 3S1

Ekstasis Editions
Box 571
Banff, Alberta T1L 1E3

LIBRARY AND ARCHIVES CANADA CATALOGUING IN PUBLICATION

Title: Sailing to Byzantium / Maureen Thorpe.
Names: Thorpe, Maureen, author.
Identifiers: Canadiana (print) 20200223895 | Canadiana (ebook) 20200223909 | ISBN 9781771713849
   (softcover) | ISBN 9781771713856 (ebook)
Classification: LCC PS8639.H6745 S25 2020 | DDC C813/.6—dc23

Canada Council   Conseil des Arts   Funded by the   Canada
for the Arts   du Canada   Government
                                    of Canada

Ekstasis Editions acknowledges financial support for the publication of *Sailing to Byzantium* from the government of Canada through the Canada Book Fund and the Canada Council for the Arts, and from the Province of British Columbia through the Book Publishing Tax Credit.

Printed and bound in Canada.

For our Grandchildren
Jade, Will, Chelsea
Simon, Justin, Tristan, and Marlowe

Viking: one who lurks in a 'vik' or bay = pirate, raider.

So times were pleasant for the people there
until finally one, a fiend out of hell,
began to work his evil in the world.

~ *Beowulf* (99-101)

"Wed to the Wand" – The Völva, a Norse Witch.

And therefore I have sailed the seas and come to the holy city of
Byzantium.

~ William Butler Yeats

Glossary

This glossary may assist those readers unfamiliar with Yorkshire dialect.

asn't	have not
ad	I had
babbies	babies
bairns	children
cum	come
dus	does
dunt	does not
midden	dump
nivver	never
nowt	nothing
owt	anything
summat	something
teken	taken
sum	some
telled	told
tha	thou, you
t'	the
un	one
wimmin	women

1

Annie opened her eyes as she clutched a protesting Rosamund closely to her chest. Lightning flashed and thunder rumbled overhead.

What was that awful smell? Looking around, she appeared to be sitting in the centre of a midden, surrounded by, amongst various other murky objects, shards of pottery, bones and a whiff of excrement. I hope they're not human bones, she thought.

"Be still, Rosamund! Well, Aunt Meg, you've really done it this time. Where am I, and more importantly, where are you?" Annie Thornton's voice rose sharply at the end of the sentence.

"I'm here, Annie, I'm here!"

An apparition, emerging from the gathering dusk and waving its arms like a helicopter rotor, rushed across the stinking ground and clasped Annie to its breast. This creature from the bog became recognizable as Mistress Meg Wistowe, Annie's ancestral aunt and a practising witch. Annie had last seen her last year in the village of Hallamby, Yorkshire, in the Year of our Lord, 1415.

"I am so sorry, my sweeting, I became distracted on the last part of the spell. You were supposed to arrive at my friend's house. By The Goddess, Rosamund, do not jump down! Let's get you both out of here and cleaned up."

Aunt, niece and cat made their way out of the malodorous dump, feet sinking into the mire. When they reached the edge, Annie stopped and faced her aunt.

"So, where are we?"

"York—or should I say Jorvik: the Vikings are in charge. Let's get you to Gytha's home and cleaned up, then I'll tell you all."

2

Reflecting back on her first impressions of Jorvik, Annie's memory offered a jumble of reactions. She remembered following her aunt through dark, narrow, empty streets with small, long houses clustered together. Her strongest impression though—smells, coming in layers, not just of her soiled clothes, but also of wood smoke, the rank odour of polluted water, a damp earthy smell, a sharp, rancid, stale urine smell, and occasionally the salty tang of the sea on the soft breeze.

Aunt Meg opened the door of one of the narrow houses and they stepped in to a long room, dimly lit. Two women sat at the far end, the soft light from a small oil lamp illuminating them. The older of the two came forward.

"Tha found 'er, did tha? That's quite a smell she's brought in with 'er. Lord bless us; get 'er out of them stinkin' clothes. A'll warm sum water so t'lass can wash."

Now Annie, fresh smelling, in clean clothes, her tumble of black curls still wet, looked around and absorbed her first impressions of a real Viking home in Jorvik. The air was hazy. Smoke from a fire in the central hearth slowly found its way up to a hole in the roof.

"Impressive with how women organize such a compact living area." Meg pointed out the benches lining the walls, which provided a place for sitting, eating, working, and sleeping. Sheepskins, furs, and woolen blankets covered their surface. Baskets woven with dried reeds hung from rafters containing various household objects. A large square loom leaned against one wall. Stones attached to the warp threads aiding gravity gave the impression of a collection of gigantic Neolithic earrings. Dried rushes lay scattered on a hard-packed earth floor.

Annie fondly looked on as, Rosamund, her familiar or spirit guide, groomed herself by the hearth fire. Bea, Aunt Meg's cat and familiar, a mirror image of Rosamund, sat beside her, purring with happiness at seeing her friend again. Annie knew Rosamund was smart but it wasn't until Aunt Meg had told her that both cats were spirit guides and telepathic, that she realized their power. Like her aunt, Annie was also a witch, but still on a steep learning curve, suspended when back in the twenty-first century.

Annie's ruined jeans and running shoes had been abandoned somewhere, probably in another midden. Annie smiled, thinking of archaeologists digging in the twenty-first century, wondering how a Viking midden, circa 950, happened to contain metal buttons with Diesel imprinted on them and rubber soles stamped Nike.

Still disorientated after the unexpected time travel; Annie cast her mind back to the previous few hours. She had completed her shift as a community midwife in rural Yorkshire and returned to Hallamby village, on a pleasant evening in late May. She remembered pausing at her garden gate to enjoy the display of late spring blooms in the soft evening light.

Changing out of uniform into jeans and a tee, Annie made a pot of Earl Grey tea and sat back in the overstuffed armchair with Rosamund perched on her lap. As Annie sipped her tea, inhaling the aroma of bergamot, Rosamund's high voice pierced her consciousness.

"Aunt Meg is looking for you!"

In the next instant, both Annie and Rosamund were sitting in a stinky midden.

Annie looked fondly at her aunt. She had not changed at all since their adventures together last year. Steady grey eyes, so similar to Annie's, looked out from a face as yet unlined. Annie could see the wisdom accrued over centuries reflected there. Aunt Meg normally lived in the same village as Annie, but in the fifteenth century, not the twenty-first. Like Annie, she delivered babies and tended to the sick using her extensive knowledge of herbs.

Annie remembered the story her aunt had shared last year: of growing up in York, not being fully conscious of her hereditary power as a witch. When her betrothed went to fight in the French Wars with King Richard and died at the Battle of Najera, young Meg moved to Hallamby village. Over the years, she had honed her skills, both as a midwife and, as self-awareness grew, as a witch. Witch-hunting was a new sport in fifteenth century England, so Meg only used sorcery in unobtrusive ways, helping neighbours as they journeyed through lives made arduous by the feudal system. On the other hand, she also had become an expert in travelling through time, visiting old friends in need.

Last year, Meg had become concerned about the change in her village of Hallamby. People appeared fearful. Unexplained accidents occurred; the manor bailiff ruled through two bullies. Unable to persuade villagers to talk to her, Meg anticipated her niece, Annie, might bring skills from the twenty-first century to solve the problems. The fact that her niece was a fledgling witch and needed guidance was an added incentive. The Mistress Wistowe Detective Agency unintentionally came into being.

Annie ceased her musings and looked curiously at the two women at the far end of the room, the older one having given Annie the clothes she was now wearing, a long linen shift and a woolen overdress, secured by straps over the shoulders. Once she had seen that Annie had what she needed, the old woman returned to her task of grinding grain on a quern-stone, holding the wooden handle protruding from the top stone and turning the stone around and around. The work looked heavy and she struggled. Her companion, a younger woman with similar facial features, had a large ball of raw wool at her feet and a spindle in her hand, ready to spin yarn, but her hands lay idle as she stared down at the floor.

"The younger woman is my friend, Gytha," Meg spoke quietly. "Her husband, Ivar Ivarsson, is a fisherman, so he is often away from home. He fishes in the Ouse estuary and the North Sea. He is a Viking from Denmark and she is of English stock. They have two beautiful children: twin girls, Eydis and Eyia. I assisted at their birth seven years ago. The woman who helped us with your clothing is the twins' grandmother. Grandfather is out in the yard, preparing herring for smoking. It's traditional here for all family members to live under one roof." Meg stopped talking and took a deep breath. She lowered her voice even more. "That's the problem. It's the reason I sent for you."

"What, they live under one roof? That's the problem?"

Annie looked back at the woman who stared at the floor, Meg's friend, Gytha. The young woman looked up and turned to regard Annie. The look on her face made Annie want to cry. What could have happened to cause such an expression of raw grief?

"The twins are images of each other, only Gytha can tell them apart. They are healthy, lively children, admired for their happy nature and bouncing curls the colour of gleaming silver. Vikings think highly of blonde hair and will often bleach their own hair using lye soap but the twins come by their colour naturally. The twins were playing outside the house two days ago. Grandfather was watching them and had to leave urgently to go to the privy out back. Gytha was working at her loom, yet keeping her ears open for their chatter and laughter. The sounds stopped abruptly so she ran outside. They had disappeared. The street was empty. No one saw anything."

"How horrible. No wonder she looks so sad. Does her husband know?"

"He is due back anytime, so no, he doesn't know. Gytha hoped she would hear something before he comes home."

"Do you have any idea what might have happened? Do children disappear here often?"

"No." Meg paused. "Of course, this is 953 and Vikings are as much involved in the lucrative slave trade as any other culture, but slaves are usually taken during raids on other peoples and certainly not on the streets like this. When we go outside tomorrow, you will see how close together the houses are situated. There are always people going about their business. It is so hard to believe no one saw anything."

An elderly man came into the room, small in stature and owner of the bushiest, wiry, grey eyebrows Annie had ever seen. A straggly, grey beard adorned his chin, and, when he removed his wooly hat, he displayed a shining dome bereft of any hair. A strong odour of fish accompanied him so he must be the grandfather. He bowed to Annie.

"Tha's cum to 'elp us. We thank thee. Mistress Wistowe says tha's a powerful völva and will use tha magic to find our babbies."

Annie turned to Meg, "What's a völva?"

"It's the Viking name for a witch or sorcerer. We'll talk about it later."

The grandfather reached out and gently took hold of Annie's hand. "Am named Aeldred; me wife is Lioba. We 'old our little girls closely in our 'earts. It's my fault they're gone." His eyes filled with tears. "Tell us what to do and we'll do it."

Aeldred walked with Meg and Annie to the far end of the room. His wife and daughter looked up at them and began sobbing. Annie wrapped her arms around Gytha.

"I pledge this to you—we will do whatever we can—and use whatever skills we have to find your children."

Meg comforted Lioba, a tiny woman, already bowed from years of hard work. "I told you my niece is a powerful witch. Between the two of us, we will bring back your babies."

Lioba sniffed firmly, rinsed her face in water from a wooden bucket, made an obvious effort to straighten her shoulders and began preparing the *náttmál,* the night meal.

Annie watched with interest as Lioba selected carrots and a turnip from one basket and a sharp looking knife and wooden board from another container. She briskly skinned, boned and chopped up a large fish her husband brought from outside (bream, Aeldred explained, fished from the Ouse estuary), and soon had a stew simmering in a soapstone pot hanging on a trivet over the hearth fire, the steam finding the hole in the roof.

When the old woman took small clay containers from yet another basket and added dried parsley and thyme to the stew, Meg smiled at the expression on her niece's face. "Vikings are quite sophisticated in their knowledge and use of herbs."

Rosamund and Bea quickly devoured the skin, head and tail of the fish and proceeded to perform their evening grooming. The stew pot soon stood empty with Annie full of stew and guilt after downing two full bowls, in comparison to the others having eaten sparingly. When Annie offered a jaw-cracking yawn, Lioba showed her guests to a place on the benches laid with furs.

"Tomorrow, Aunt, you can explain this 'powerful witch' theory you have. Remember how you had to teach me to perform even simple spells?"

Annie arranged her furs to create a mattress and a pillow. Rosamund curled up beside her and both promptly fell asleep. They had travelled a long way from Annie's twenty-first century cottage in Hallamby, Yorkshire, not in distance but in time, aided and abetted in their time travel by clever Aunt Meg.

3

The next morning found Meg and Annie exploring the capital city of the Scandinavian Kingdom of Northumbria: Jorvik.

Annie grew up in twenty-first century York so knew her city well and had walked the walls many times. Last year she visited York, as it existed in 1514, on her first unplanned time-travel detective assignment and so became familiar with the state of the walls in late medieval times. Typically, as a local, she had not yet visited the Jorvik Centre in modern York, a re-creation of part of the city in its Viking era. Now she would experience the real thing.

The two women walked along the earth embankments now partially covering the dilapidated Roman stone walls, raised higher by the addition of a timber fence. Blue skies and a soft breeze blessed Jorvik.

"Sunny for a change," Meg commented as she worked her way around a large puddle. "Aeldred told me of relentless rain for two months."

An earthy odour combined with the stink of polluted water remained strong. Annie remarked on it.

"Part of it is from the tannery across the river, when the breeze is blowing this way; it's bad, isn't it? Tanners soak skins in urine. The river is quite smelly too: the Ouse is tidal, lots of mud flats, and everything finds its way into the water. But you would know that, born in York."

Annie wrinkled her nose. "The Ouse is clean now; it certainly doesn't smell like this anymore."

They wandered through the streets lined with long, narrow timber built houses with thatched roofs. The building material was the same for all: withies, or twigs, of willow or hazel woven between upright posts, which provided the base for a clay-like daub.

"You can see for yourself how the houses are built so closely together and how the narrow streets wind around them," Meg stood still for a second. "On the one hand, I can't believe no one saw the twins being taken. On the other hand, you could turn a corner here and be out of sight. Whoever took the twins had to work fast and not seem out of place; otherwise, people would have seen something."

It was evident that Viking administration favoured order and well planned communities. They crossed a new bridge built over the malodourous River Ouse and both expressed surprise at the number of churches they passed, made apparent by the stone crosses in front of the wooden buildings. Clearly, the Vikings had adopted the Christian religion.

As they walked along arm in arm, Annie brought her aunt up to date on her life since they saw each other last year, particularly her relationship in her own century with Adam Boucher.

"I'm really fond of Adam. We have fun together, but I don't love him as I loved Will. I know it's weird; Adam is a descendant of Will Boucher and is the landlord of the same inn, 'The King's Glove' that Will bought when I was visiting you in the fifteenth century. Perhaps I see something of Will in him. Our love was impossible, separated by the centuries. I must say, you have made my life complicated, Aunt Meg." She squeezed her aunt's arm, showing she was teasing.

"Will hasn't married, Annie; he is still running the inn. His friend Jack is steward of Hallamby Manor and Jen, his wife, is expecting another baby."

"Oh, I miss them all. Part of me is still in medieval Hallamby."

Wandering through Coppergate, Annie was impressed by the goods on display at the many shops and stalls they passed. They admired elaborate broaches made of metal; smoothly turned wooden bowls and cups, combs made from bone and necklaces made from beads of amber, jet and glass. Skilled artisans, both men and women, Viking and English, proudly showed their wares. Meg purchased two lengths of soft wool cloth at a shop where women worked at looms like the one Annie had seen at Gytha's home.

"Gytha and Lioba can turn this material into those overdresses women seem to favour. They will enjoy having cloth already woven and the resulting gowns will replace these dresses loaned to us."

As they moved closer to the docks, food sellers and fishwives vied with the other merchants and good-natured banter raised the noise level. A tantalizing smell of frying fish and onions briefly overwhelmed the fetid smell of the River Ouse and the rank odour of the tannery. Seagulls wheeled overhead, adding their voices to the clamour. Annie became aware of some individuals among the bustling throng who stood out by the absence of ornaments and bright clothing, pointing them out to her aunt.

"Why do these people look so different?"

"They're slaves. Viking society is quite rigid. Slaves, or thralls, wear undyed homespun clothing and a slave collar. Free yeomen are called *bondi* and the aristocrats are the *jarls* who support and fight for the king. Slaves can be freed, though, by their owners."

The concept of slaves shocked Annie; she had experienced the medieval feudal system last year, where serfs were in bondage to the local Lord of the Manor, but slaves…

Upon arriving at the docks, Annie gazed in awe at the variety of Viking ships. Only one had the ferocious dragon's head on the sweeping prow, familiar in every Viking story she had ever read. The ship measured at least thirty-five metres long and had room for over thirty pairs of oars.

"This majestic dragonship belongs to the king of Jorvik," Meg gestured at the longship, taking on the role of guide. "It is a warship. Interestingly, if the ship sails into friendly shores, they remove the dragon so people know the Vikings come in peace. The other ships are built for different purposes. The one with the higher gunwale and rounder hull is a trader. It has more room to store goods. Jorvik has become a huge international trading centre, with contacts and routes across our world. Those smaller ones with two or three sets of oars are used for fishing, like Gytha's husband's boat."

"I didn't know you're an expert on ships."

"There are lots of things you don't know about me yet. I'm sure you will discover more as we go along." Meg had a twinkle in her grey eyes.

"Speaking of discovering more," Annie asked, "what's all this about 'powerful witches?' You know I'm not powerful; I'm just a novice, still learning my craft."

When Annie's mother, on her eighteenth birthday, had revealed 'the family curse'—that Annie was the latest in a long line of witches—Annie felt both relief and frustration. Relief that now she knew why she felt different from her friends: their interests being boys, diets and avoidance of pimples. She loved studying herbs and following the phases of the moon. Frustration grew as to how to be a witch in more than name.

Aunt Meg patted her niece on her arm. "You're a good student and will learn much on this visit. I have a feeling we'll need all the help we can conjure up."

Annie looked again at the king's dragonship. She recognized the wood as her favourite, oak, and admired the intricate carvings along the dragon prow. Clinker built, each plank overlapped the one below and was overlapped by the next one above, like all Viking ships, forming a graceful and sleek hull.

"Who is the king here? I can remember some of the names from my history classes."

"It's a little confusing. York and Northumbria have had a number of kings over the last few years. Eiric Bloodaxe came to The Kingdom of Jorvik as king in 947 but the Northumbrians expelled him in order to appease the English king. He came back into favour in 952. He is married to Queen Gunnhild, although I have also heard rumours of a Scottish wife. There are so many stories about Gunnhild. She is a powerful völva. Apparently, she lived for a while with two Finnish sorcerers who shared their craft with her. She thanked them by having them killed! She has the reputation of being a forbidding woman who dominates her husband."

"This all seems way out of our league, Aunt Meg. We are midwives and herbalists. Okay, we're witches as well but not so powerful to mix with this company."

Meg began to shake her head.

"Sorry, Aunt Meg, I know you're really good at time travel, you've nailed that skill—except for landing me in the midden. And I know we solved the murder and got rid of the bad guys last year but kidnapping —I just don't know."

The women began to retrace their footsteps to Gytha's house. Meg wrapped her arm around Annie's shoulder. "I believe the people who snatched those precious girls are rich and powerful and coveted them for themselves or for the slave market. The twins have enormous value due to their uniqueness, not just the fact of looking exactly like each other, but topped with those silver curls.

"You can see how the houses are crowded together. So when the neighbours say they saw nothing I do *not* believe them. I think they may feel threatened. Avarice and corruption lie behind this deed, I am sure of it. You and I have the ability to expose whoever is responsible and bring the children back to their mother. Your skills worked well last year."

Annie remembered the manor steward of Hallamby branding her as a witch and of how close she came to burning at the stake, but forbore to mention this. She sighed and said only, "I trust your judgement, Aunt Meg."

4

When Meg and Annie arrived back at Gytha's house, they found the place in an uproar. Neighbours crowded around the open door listening to the disturbance. Rosamund and Bea looked like two bookends, each on either side of the door, tails curled primly around their feet. Ivar had arrived back from his fishing trip. His voice bounced off the walls of the small house; Annie pictured Gytha and her parents cowering before his anger.

"By all of the Gods, how could tha 'ave teken thy eyes off 'em? Tha knows how special they are, and thee, old man, what were tha doin' to let this 'appen. Children don't just disappear. Sumbody must 'ave seen summat."

Ivar appeared at the open door and began shouting at his neighbours. A big man, dressed in the Viking manner of loose pants with his lower legs bound with strips of cloth, soft leather shoes and a long tunic ending above his knees. His hair and beard were long and red, still snarled from his fishing trip.

"Tha's all standin' 'ere, listening. Tha's all supposed t'be me friends. Tha watched these bairns grow from babbies. Did anybody see or 'ear anythin'?"

Annie and Meg observed the crowd carefully. No one looked at Ivar. They just stared at the dirt road. One gangly boy, well on his way to becoming a man, was conspicuous because he stared at Meg and Annie rather than at angry Ivar.

"Keep an eye on the young man with the red hair and the beginnings of a beard," Meg muttered to Annie. "We'll have a word with him later. He's not dressed as a slave, but as a freeman and, come to think of it. I think we saw him down at the docks just now."

As shouting stopped in the Ivarsson household, neighbours dispersed. Meg and Annie moved tentatively into the long room followed by their cats. Ivar had run out of energy and sat on a bench, resembling a body lacking bones. He looked up tiredly as the women entered.

"*Kveðja:* greetings, Mistress Wistowe, I suppose tha's 'ere 'cos of this mess? Who's that wi' thee?"

Gytha's face showed the relief she felt now her husband's tirade had ended. She clutched her mother's hand tightly as she looked appealingly at her friend Meg.

"This is Annie, my niece. She is, like me, a powerful völva and, like me, she's travelled a great distance from another time to be here in order to find your children. Your wife asked me to come as soon as she discovered they were missing."

"Aye, thank Thor she did summat reight. A'll nivver get me 'ead around yon weird travel stuff, but tha's 'ere, that's the main thing. A'll eat and change then am off t'palace to see our king. I've fought by 'is side enough times in t'past. 'E or 'is jarls know everythin' that goes on 'round 'ere. If there's bin any raiders, 'e'll know about it. An' 'e'll listen to me cos 'e looks after 'is own."

Meg made a quick decision. "We'll accompany you if we may, Ivar. We need to decide how we will portray ourselves." She turned to Annie, "I'm thinking we must show ourselves as witches."

"Aunt Meg, are you trying to get us burned at the stake?"

"All that Church witch-hunting won't start for another four hundred years and certainly won't happen here. Attitudes toward witches changed around the time of the Pestilence: the Black Death. Before that, people respected and consulted us. The Church and the people began to blame witches, along with other 'so-called enemies,' for spreading disease and working against Christianity; that's when it became common to charge any one they thought was a witch with heresy.

"On the other hand, the Vikings have a great respect for sorcery and highly value the services of a völva who travels from town to town offering assistance and people treat her with respect. She practices many types of magic such as prophesy, creating illusions in people's minds and shapeshifting. We will become völvas; Norse witches, and must also become braggarts. Vikings appreciate a first-rate boaster. We walk a fine line, though. We are English yet we must be able to compete with the most powerful Viking völvas so we will dress as they do and match our skills with theirs. Both the Viking God Odin and the Goddess Freyja are the divine models of völvas—that's how much respect Vikings have for magic."

Annie's mind whirled as she attempted to absorb this fascinating information. She was sure they were outside of their league when it came to Viking völvas as well as Viking kings and queens.

Meg went over to Gytha and her mother, both still drained from Ivar's outburst. When she explained what she needed they looked less stressed: any effort toward finding the twins acted as a panacea. Digging deep into the clothing chests, they pulled out woollens and belts, pouches and beads. Grandma Lioba announced she was going to a neighbour's house for some articles.

Annie sat with a desolate Aeldred and held his hand. "We *will* find them and bring them back. Help us to prepare to go to the palace. Ivar is over his rage. We'll all work together. Your wife and daughter need your support." On hearing this, Aeldred sat up taller, offered Annie a weak smile and walked over to his daughter.

Lioba came back into the longhouse with her arms full of garments. She even had a hint of colour in her cheeks.

"A think we've got all we need," she cried. "Mistress Adamssen next door 'as a big chest full of stuff."

When Gytha and Lioba finished fussing, sorting and then dressing them, Meg and Annie looked at each other in wonder. As the 'senior völva', Meg looked impressive in a long blue robe. Glass beads hung around her neck and a belt secured her robe with a black pouch attached to it. Covering her head was a black hood made from animal skin and a wooden staff sat in her gloved hand.

Meg had sent Aeldred out to forage for two long pieces of wood suitable for staffs and instructed him on how to shape and polish them. While the women were dressing, Aeldred worked furiously on the staffs. At the head of Meg's staff, following instructions, he had created a knob and decorated it with rope and small stones.

"Aeldred, these staffs are magnificent. I am sure you have invested them with the power of a völva's wand."

Annie dressed similarly to her aunt but with much less decoration as she was a lowly apprentice attending her mistress. A woolen hood hid her black curls and covered much of her face. Meg instructed Gytha to find two woven baskets with handles for carrying, and skins to cover their contents.

"What'll be inside t'baskets?" Gytha asked.

"The most important items of all," Meg smiled. "The cats."

Meg then rustled around in her own belongings and placed some small objects inside her pouch without explanation to her interested audience.

"We are ready," she called to Ivar who had eaten, washed, changed and combed his hair and beard while the women fussed. He paced restlessly at the other end of the room.

Meg turned to Gytha and her mother. "While we are away I want you both to go to your loom and weave a wish into the warp and the weft. I believe you know what the wish will be." She swept out of the door with Annie and Ivar scrambling to keep up.

5

Ivar, familiar with the route to the palace, took the lead of a small procession. Behind him marched regal-looking Meg with her apprentice, while a group of neighbours, both Viking and English, followed, chattering excitedly amongst themselves.

The *Konungsgurtha*, the King's Court, sat by the southwest gate of the defensive circuit of the Viking city, occupying the site of the *porta principalis sinistra*, the west gatehouse of the ancient Roman encampment.

Along the way, Meg coached Ivar on what she wanted him to say when they arrived and Ivar shared information about his king.

The *Konungsgurtha* housed King Eiric's private rooms and, more importantly, his mead hall. Here he ruled supreme and rewarded his jarls for their support. He entertained guests from many countries in this hall and made his presence known as King of Northumberland, supported by King Eadred of England. His valuable position provided a buffer between the warring Scots in the north and the English to the south.

The gathering approached the large, impressive building. Solid, ancient Roman stones supported its base and the palace's wooden walls rose high and curved inward, topped by a huge thatched roof. Two wooden carvings of dragon heads reared upwards and outwards from the central peak of the structure. Ivar paused before warriors guarding a heavy wooden door, decorated with elaborate carvings of intertwined dragons and snakes.

"Your name and business?" demanded one of the large, hairy men who appeared to be as wide as he was tall. He wore the ubiquitous

Viking tunic and baggy trousers, his lower legs bound with strips of leather. His metal helmet hugged his head and the nosepiece protruded well beyond his nose. A large sword at his side and a battle-axe secured in a broad leather belt completed his armour. The other men, dressed identically, regarded them with interest but did not speak.

"Am Ivar Ivarsson of Jorvik. A've come to speak with me king about a crime so 'orrible it shames us all." Ivar spoke strongly, his shoulders braced. His bearing said he may be a fisherman now, but he had done his share of raiding and would not let this man intimidate him.

"These women with thee; who are they and what is their purpose?"

"This woman is a powerful völva, attended by 'er apprentice. She comes to Jorvik to 'elp me in me *kanna*, me search. She is famous in 'er...in 'er country."

Ivar could not quite get his head around this tangle of time.

"What's in those baskets? I need to examine them." The guard stepped forward and reached out to remove the skin covering Bea. Meg said nothing but the warrior suddenly pulled his hand back with a curse.

"*Helvete!* What was that? It felt like a knife stabbing me!"

"I am a völva, as you have been told. We bring gifts for the eyes of the king only. I mean him no harm."

The guard looked at his hand; two puncture marks oozed blood. He looked at her with narrowed eyes. "You will be watched closely. It had better be as you speak, you who say you are völva."

The warrior looked beyond Ivar and the women. "Who are these other people? What do they have to do with your crime? Are they witnesses?"

"They're friends, 'ere to support me."

"They must remain out here. Enter."

Ivar and his two collaborators entered the mead hall: the lifeblood and centre of Viking life.

It took a moment for Annie's eyes to adjust to the darkness and the warm, close atmosphere. She looked around in amazement at the huge space. A little natural light came from openings way up near the roof but torches and oil lamps positioned around the room provided the main illumination. Smoke drifted upwards to the opening in the roof from a central hearth and from the torches, adding to the surreal effect. Warriors, like the ones who opened the door to them, stood at attention around the room. Tall wooden columns, carved with writhing dragons and other mythical creatures, reached up to the heavy rafters supporting the roof. Looking down at the floor, she was surprised to see, not hard packed earth, but stones of different shapes and colours. Smells then jarred her senses; smoke, roasting meats, sweat, and—what Annie finally recognized as—testosterone— a distinctive odour identified by many visits to rugby games. Adam! She had to let him know she was away. Filing that thought away, Annie brought her attention back to her surroundings.

There was a party going on in the central part of the great hall. Men sat on long benches engrossed in various activities. Some played board games. A group sat around one man who was animatedly telling a story. Ivar whispered that these were the mead-benches.

"Like a said, our king 'as a duty to provide food and drink to 'is jarls as long as they fight for 'im."

"Which one is the king?" It was challenging to see over the heads of a room full of large men.

"Ee, lass, it's 'ard t'miss King Eiric. Look over there." Ivar pointed to the back wall.

Annie looked. King Eiric sat slightly higher than his jarls on a raised dais, accompanied on either side by his consorts. She could not make out their features from where they stood but the view soon improved. As the trio stood gawping like tourists in modern-day York, another large, hairy man came over to them – he, however, did not wear a helmet and no weapons showed.

"You have business here?"

"We want to speak with our king," replied Ivar. "I'm Ivar Ivarsson of Jorvik, son of Ivar Eiric Ivarsson of Denmark. Now am a fisherman in Jorvik but a used t'be a raider and seaman. 'Ave fought wi' King Eiric many times against them Scots and Irish. A must report a shameful crime to 'im. This woman, Margarette of Wessex," he inclined his head toward Meg "is a powerful völva and cums to pay 'er respect." He nodded at Annie. "This un 'ere is 'er servant."

The emissary examined the threesome closely from head to toe and asked them what the baskets contained. Meg peeled back the cover and the guard saw a roll of thick black fur. "It is a small gift for the queen," Meg told him.

"There are two queens in this hall," the emissary pointed out. "Do you have a gift for both?"

Annie turned back the cover of her basket, showing a similar roll of fur. Appearing satisfied, he led them through the mead-benches. A fight broke out close by and a game board and all its pieces went flying through the air. The two combatants threw wild blows at each other and their companions began cheering them on. Quickly, two guards came between them and restored order. Meg bent down and scooped something from the floor, dropping it into her pouch, moving so swiftly Annie only saw a blur.

As they grew closer to the royal dais Annie's heart beat faster. She remembered King Eiric's exploits from school history lessons. He had earned the reputation of being a brutal raider for a decade around Scotland and the Irish Sea, taking many slaves. He was the son of King Harald Fairhair of Norway and one of many sons. King Harald's small kingdom would not suffice for so many sons to inherit a piece. Eiric solved that problem by killing a number of his brothers, thereby increasing his odds of inheritance, hence his nickname 'Bloodaxe'.

"He certainly fills the space around him," she muttered to her aunt, "his size matches his reputation."

Eiric's huge throne, built of oak, displayed carvings of serpents and dragons winding their way up the chair legs. He sat on a thick white fur: a polar bear skin. It was the only pale item. Eiric clearly loved colour. He wore a red tunic over blue pants and a richly embroidered cloak adorned his shoulders. Pale red hair and moustaches hung in braids and a gold band with a dragon in the centre circled his forehead. An attendant stood behind the king, also dressed in an embroidered tunic and loosely draped pants. On his forearm rested a falcon with a hood over its eyes. Annie marvelled at the sheer theatre presented to the king's subjects.

On either side of the monarch, on smaller, similarly carved chairs also draped with furs, sat two women, each beautiful in her own way: one with fair braids; the other with black braids; both with gold circlets around their foreheads. Each wore colourfully and richly embroidered dresses secured by straps over their shoulders with fine linen gowns showing beneath. Many necklaces hung around their necks. Elaborate broaches secured the straps on the dresses and miniature scissors, combs, knives and ear spoons hung from the broaches, apparently a sign of status and wealth. Their gold mesh belts held carved leather purses.

"Bow your heads before King Eiric, Lord of Northumberland, his Queen Gunnhild and his Queen Iseabail." The emissary's voice boomed out, above the background noise in the hall, speaking the language of the court: Norse.

Ivar translated quietly to Meg and Annie.

"Gracious Lord, may I present to you Ivar Ivarsson of Jorvik, son of Ivar Eiric Ivarsson of Denmark, now a fisherman in Jorvik but formerly a proud raider and seaman. He has fought under your banner against the Scots and the Irish."

Ivar knelt, his head bowed. King Eiric nodded to acknowledge his former raider-in-arms.

Both the king and his wives now looked with curiosity at Meg. Annie stood a pace behind her aunt and, whereas Meg looked squarely at the king, Annie looked demurely at the ground, according to her lower station.

The emissary spoke again. "I present Margarette of Wessex. She is a powerful völva and, as she is in Jorvik visiting with her friends, wishes to pay her respects to you, Lord."

A harsh female voice broke the silence. "You dare call yourself völva?" The sound reverberated around the large room. The jarls paused from their games and storytelling, beginning to take an interest in the new visitors. Chatter petered out as men manoeuvred their way toward the dais forming a large semi-circle behind the visitors. Annie shivered in anticipation. The stage was set.

6

Meg spoke, her voice carrying clearly through the suddenly silent hall. "Who speaks to me in such an accusing voice?" Meg was no longer Aunt Meg. She appeared larger, grander and projected a commanding energy.

"*I* speak to you, woman. *I* am Queen Gunnhild, wife to King Eiric, mother of his eight sons, and daughter of *Gorm inn Gamli*: King Gorm of Denmark." The dark queen glared at the emissary; clearly, he had failed miserably in his introduction of her. "Why do you say you are a völva, a wand-carrier?"

"I am not here to argue about who I am. I am here to pay my respects and to help my *félagi*: my companion, in his anguish. I ask you to listen to him."

King Eiric shifted uneasily on his throne. Annie's heart rate speeded up. The powerful energy moving between these two strong women caused the very air to pulse.

"I do believe I may be able to help," a gentle voice broke into the silence. The fair-haired queen leaned forward. "It is meet and right we hear Ivar Ivarsson's story first. As the völva says, she is here to help." Her voice had a lilt and a burr to it.

King Eiric spoke. "Iseabail, we thank you for your wise counsel. Speak, Ivar Ivarsson."

"Me Lord, me wife and me 'ave luvly twin daughters; they've only seen seven summers. They're all we 'ave. Three days ago, while playin' outside our 'ouse, they vanished. No-one saw or 'eard anythin'."

The telling was too much for Ivar; he broke down and began sobbing. He fell to his knees again. Annie reached forward and placed her hand on his shoulder, her touch calming him. He took a deep breath and continued. "I'm 'ere to ask for your 'elp to find our children and to punish whoever did this."

King Eiric spoke. "We have had no reports of raiding parties in or near Jorvik. This is the first I have heard of this appalling deed." He waved over the emissary who had led Ivar's party to him. "Do you know of these events, Hamr?"

"I have heard nothing, my Lord."

"Is this sorcery then, that no one has 'eard or seen anythin'? They just disappeared into thin air." Ivar stood and in his agitation, flung his arms wide. The guards stepped forward, followed by Meg.

"My Lord, as I said previously, I am a völva of the highest order. I practice both *seiðr* and *spà*—"

"—So say you, woman. You speak of *seiðr* and spà. Therefore, you are saying you have knowledge of prophecy, of spirit journeys, of magic healing and even shapeshifting. What proof do we have of this—or are you a practitioner of idle boasts?"

Queen Gunnhild's voice taunted Meg across the space between them. A cloak pin could have dropped in the mead hall and sounded like a crack of thunder.

Meg smiled and slowly lowered her covered basket to the ground. Lifting her staff, she tapped the basket.

"By the power invested in me by the Goddess Freyja, she who represents both love and war and is the most powerful völva of all; I invite her to enter our world and share her knowledge."

A large and ferocious-looking black cat flew out of the basket and landed at the feet of Margarette of Wessex. Everyone close by gasped and reared back, including the royal party. Before the guards could move in, Meg swiftly opened the pouch hanging from her belt and, thrusting her hand inside, withdrew a handful of seeds, and released them into the air. The seeds exploded into puffs of red smoke, which surrounded the royal party, then drifted back into the main area before gently flowing upwards. No guards moved.

"Cat of Freyja, what story do you have for us. Speak."

Cat of Freyja (otherwise known as Bea) opened her mouth and spoke. "I tell you this truth—two children, as sweet and innocent as lambs born on an early spring day, have been taken from us by someone inside this mead hall. Only a person with power and influence has the means to remove these children from their loving home and spirit them away—and may have already done so. The motive is avarice. This person is corrupt and cruel. This is my story."

No one stirred. All appeared as if turned to stone; all except Gunnhild, who rose from her chair and moved toward the cat, her arms reaching out as though to seize her. Annie stepped forward tapping her staff against the covered basket. Out shot another large, black, fierce looking cat. This cat hissed loudly and reared onto her back legs, claws unsheathed, shapeshifting into a lithe black panther. The queen stepped back and held her hands in front of her in defence as she attempted to scramble behind her chair. Meg raised her staff and beat the floor three times. In a blink, the cats returned to their baskets, covers on.

The gathering released its breath as one.

King Eiric stood. "What did we just witness, völva? Did you create this madness or did the goddess speak truth to us?"

"It was trickery!" Gunnhild's voice rasped, lifting her chin in an attempt to regain her dignity and return to her chair.

"Gunnhild, allow this woman to speak if you will," Eiric ordered. "I ask again, did you create madness or truth?"

"As the Goddess will witness; you heard the truth, my Lord. She spoke to you through the cats. It is well-known cats are sacred to Freyja. I know not who the perpetrator is of this crime but it makes sense he or she must be powerful. It also makes sense they have been taken from Jorvik already as no-one has had sightings of them."

Meg spoke quietly but firmly. She acknowledged none but the king, looking him fully in the face. Annie's heart filled with pride, vowing that one day she too would command such respect.

The fair-haired queen again spoke quietly into the silence. "What would you have us do, powerful völva? How can we help?"

"*Fruvor:* noble lady, if you have no knowledge of this crime, is it possible you can make enquiries?

"I am from Suderland; you know my country as Scotland, and I am familiar with *spae-wives*. They have the gift of seeing into the future. Can you do this and find the children using the gift of prophecy?"

"Alas, my Lady, if I can I will, but naught comes to me as yet."

"What of us, weak and false völva; can you prophesy our future?" Again, the dark queen challenged Meg.

"I can and will if you so desire—after the children are returned my mind will be clearer and better able to do so."

The king spoke again. He still looked shaken after the Goddess Freyja's visit. "If I find out more, Ivar Ivarsson, I will send for you. If you need my help in your search, send word to me."

Ivar, who had remained quiet throughout all of the drama, now spoke. "Me Lord, we beg to leave. We 'ave much work to do. Thanks to thee for listenin.'"

As the emissary, Hamr, escorted them through mead-benches and out to the still-gathered neighbours, jarls drew back, whether with respect or fear it was hard to tell.

Ivar shook his head in response to the neighbours' babble of questions. "Well, a suppose that were better than nowt. King Eiric listened. At least we know it weren't a raid and t'king did say 'e'd 'elp if we asked."

Meg took Ivar to one side. "Do not speak anymore of this until we are home. Annie, I want you to seek out the young redheaded man who stared at us earlier. I'm sure he has information we need."

7

Gytha and her parents looked pale and anxious when they arrived home. Gytha rushed forward. "Did they 'ave news? Dus the King know what 'appened? Are the children—?"

"—I just require a moment to send your husband and Annie on a mission. Meanwhile, I will tell you all of the happenings: a good story if I say so myself."

Meg hugged Gytha and her mother. She turned to Ivar and Annie. "Find the young boy, almost a man, with the reddish hair, who stood outside the house earlier. Ivar, do you know who I mean?"

"I think tha's talking about young Lars Larsson. 'E works down at t'docks, loading t'ships. If 'e in't there, 'e lives just down t'street, four 'ouses away. Mistress, a just want t'say 'ow great tha were up at palace—and thee, Mistress Annie. Am reight proud of ye both."

Meg spoke again, "Before you go I want to place a protective spell on all of us. I do not trust Queen Gunnhild; I suspect she knows of this wickedness. Her hostility toward us is without reason."

Meg arranged them all in a circle, including the cats, meowing thanks for their release from their baskets. She pulled a dark green stone shot with streaks of red out of her pouch. "This is a bloodstone, Annie," she explained. "Listen carefully to all I do and say." She raised her arms as if to enfold them all, the bloodstone held in her left hand. "Goddess Hecate, I call to you: help us. Surround us with your protection."

Slowly, a warm pink glow flowed out of the bloodstone, filling the dark room with a rosy light. Gytha and her mother looked alarmed but Meg quickly reassured them.

"All I do here is for the greater good. I ask this light surrounding us to keep us safe from evil. Hecate, Goddess of magic, witchcraft, the night and the moon; create a barrier no malevolent spirit can penetrate. My friends, wrap this protection around you, be safe and sheltered inside and outside of yourselves. If you feel threatened, recall this light."

Annie and Ivar went on their mission and left Meg to relate to Gytha and her mother the events that had occurred at the palace. Annie was reluctant to leave, wanting to know how Meg had created the illusion at the palace. Ivar decided they would go to the docks first as daylight still lingered and the boy should be back at work.

Streets and docks remained busy. They soon spotted Ivar's neighbour, young Lars Larsson, on the wooden wharf, loading baskets into the central hold of a large trading ship. Positioning themselves where he would eventually see them, the two settled down to wait.

Jorvik and the River Ouse provided a gateway to the world. Ships came in, seeking the safety of the port as darkness became imminent; men rowing with sails furled as no wind blew to fill them; ships being loaded and unloaded with thralls carrying the heavy loads off the wharf into the town.

Eventually, young Lars straightened his back and walked passed them, still gangly, still growing, not offering a glance; only a slight movement of his head signalled he had seen them. Ivar allowed a couple of beats to pass before following. The young man stopped at a stall advertising eel soup, already eating his flatbread and drinking his soup as Ivar and Annie arrived. The crude sign, a wriggling eel, turned Annie's stomach. Ivar ordered soup for himself and Annie and they moved off to the side of the stall. Annie resolved to drink the eel soup without pulling a face and, to her surprise, found it quite palatable. Lars wandered over and stood next to them.

"*Kveðja:* greetings, Master Ivarsson." He nodded his head politely and went back to dipping his bread.

Annie spoke quietly while holding the soup bowl in front of her mouth. "My name is Mistress Thornton. I am a friend of the Ivarsson family, here to comfort them in their time of need. You have news for us, Lars Larsson."

"A do, Mistress, but a beg tha dusn't tell anybody a telled thee.

Two days ago a saw a couple o'men load two large baskets onto a skute. Locals: 'ave seen 'em around but a can't place where—not around docks anyway. A remember it being same day them twins went missin' and just getting' dark—a strange time to go out t'sea. We'd all just finished work. These men kept their 'eads down; sailors usually chat but not these two. That's another reason why it struck me as odd. A skute is a small fast boat and they loaded a small cargo, just two decent-sized baskets that looked 'eavy, a couple of small baskets of food and a wooden barrel. T'crew were a woman, a girl really, a thrall—a could see 'er iron collar—and them two men, both scruffy lookin' buggers. A skute dunt need many oars as it relies on its sail more, so they'd be able to manage it well enough."

"You think the baskets contained the twins?"

"Aye, am guessin' it could be so. Am off now, a don't want t'be seen speakin' to thee."

"Why is that?"

"Well, we dunt know who's be'ind it, do we. Best be careful."

Ivar spoke, his voice strained. "Does thy 'ave any idea whereabouts t'swine 'ave gone?"

"Aye, a checked. They told t'arbour master they were goin' to t'Baltic: a place called Birka. It's a regular run frum 'ere, as tha knows."

8

Ivar and Annie hurried back to Ivar's home. Meg lay on the fur-lined bench, resting after her arduous session at the palace. Gytha was weaving at the loom and her mother spun yarn.

"We have news," Annie called as soon as she and Ivar entered the house, relieved to see Gytha working again. The three women quickly came to them.

Ivar told them they had found Lars at the docks and shared his information about him seeing strange men loading a skute late in the evening. Gytha burst into tears again and began rocking backward and forward. Her mother clasped her tightly and rocked with her.

"Be calm," Meg comforted them. "This new information tells us what is happening, and shows our next move. Dry your eyes, Gytha and help us to plan. Heat some water, Lioba. Annie will make an infusion of rosemary to help us think more clearly."

They sat facing one another on the benches and sipped their hot drinks as the sweet scent of rosemary filled the room, mingling with the slight curl of smoke drifting upward from the hearth-fire. Rosamund and Bea began their campaign to be part of the proceedings by winding themselves around everyone's feet. Ivar knew the Baltic Sea well, having sailed in and around there many times. He had also visited Birka on the island of Björkö.

"It's a busy tradin' centre. Traders cum there from all over t'world, even frum Frisia, Germany, t'Baltic countries, Constantinople and t'Far East, and frum 'ere, o' course. We must get to 'em before they leave or we'll nivver know where they go frum there."

Panic entered his voice and he half stood. Annie lay a hand on his shoulder.

"We will, Ivar, we will." She had no way of knowing if they would but had total faith in her aunt.

Meg spoke. "I believe we need reinforcements for this search. I propose we invite Lars to join us, as a young man's strength is always useful. Ivar, you, of course, will be with us, provided Gytha and Lioba can manage while you are away."

"Of course, we'll manage," Gytha nodded her head firmly. "We've got good neighbours; they'll 'elp us wi' 'eavier tasks."

Rosamund and Bea meowed loudly.

"Without question," Meg reached out and rubbed their ears. "We couldn't manage without you."

Their planning meeting continued for a long time. Lioba left them to prepare the *nàttmàl*, another fish stew.

As dusk descended, Ivar went to look for Lars as he made his way home from the docks. Ivar wanted to include Lars' family when asking him to join them, although he knew Lars was just about old enough to take off on his own, in the Viking way. He would be aware, like all the young men in Jorvik, that the king would spend his summer refitting his ships and preparing for his autumn raiding sorties around Scotland and Ireland, seeking booty and slaves.

Ivar and Lars joined the women for some stew: his family had readily given their blessing for their son to go with Ivar. Lars kept staring at Annie with big, puppy-dog eyes, making her feel uncomfortable. A love-struck adolescent might create complications.

Planning began in earnest, deciding what supplies they needed, including food, clothing and weapons. They would use Ivar's fishing boat; a tight fit for four people but the men could make it ready to sail without attracting attention.

As they listed their supplies, an officious knock came at the door. Gytha paled. Ivar answered the door and found Hamr standing there, the emissary from the palace who had escorted them to the king.

"Ivar Ivarsson, I am requested to escort you and your wife to the palace. Queen Iseabail has asked to see you both."

"'Ave tha 'ad news, then?" Ivar's voice faltered.

"No. I believe, from what she said, she wishes to be of help to you."

A flurry of activity commenced as the women made Gytha ready to go before her queen. Lioba dug down into the seemingly bottomless clothes basket to find finer clothes. Although born English, Gytha robed as a mature Viking woman and wore her softest kirtle with an overdress: its straps secured with broaches, loops of colourful glass beads hanging between them. Her mother combed and braided her long fair hair. A white linen coif completed the picture. Meanwhile, Ivar paced impatiently at the door.

When they left, accompanied by Hamr, Meg turned to Lars.

"There is something you must know, Lars," she said. "I am a völva: a sorcerer."

Lars' eyes opened wide and he took a step backwards.

"I am here to find those precious children, as is Annie, who is also a völva."

Lars' eyes opened even wider. He looked like a hare caught in a beam of light. Annie could sense him wondering if he had made a rash choice.

"I only tell you this because you may see happenings which make you question your own mind. We will only do worthy deeds unless others force us to defend ourselves. You are one of us now and come under our protection."

Meg turned to Annie. "I know you wished to know more of the events at the palace, I will also share them with Lars. Lioba has heard the story once, but it is a good tale, worth a repeat."

9

"*Hyoscyamus niger,* commonly known as henbane, is a powerful and potent herb. It is known to have dreamlike powers—" Meg turned to Annie and Lars "—as it creates images in the mind. I had to show the royal party, and particularly Queen Gunnhild, how powerful I am. I threw the seeds into the air and turned them into smoke so people would breathe in the vapours. As a result, they saw what I wanted them to see: the cats' transformation. Bea spoke in the Goddess Freyja's voice and Rosamund," scratching under Rosamund's chin, "became a panther. Well done, Annie, for following my lead."

"A wish ad bin there," said Lars. His eyes had reduced to their normal size and he looked a little more comfortable with his new companions.

"We will have times when we shall use our powers. I ask you, Lars, not to be afraid when this happens and to trust us."

Lioba listened to all this with her gnarled hands, knuckles swollen, clasped in front of her heart. "A now know tha *will* bring our babbies back to us. Thanks be t'God and to his blessed son, the Christ." She made the sign of the cross and knelt down with her head bowed.

Annie marvelled at the two belief systems harmoniously living side by side: Paganism and Christianity could be compatible after all.

The four sat in an easy silence as they waited for the return of Ivar and Gytha. Lioba went back to spinning her yarn and giving Annie a lesson, much to the amusement of the other two as Annie's fingers grew into large thumbs.

The door opened and Ivar and Gytha came in from the darkness.

"I'll make a draught of chamomile for you," Annie rose, thankful to escape from the distaff and spindle.

When they had settled with bowls of the calming herb, Gytha began her tale. She spoke first of the mead hall and the men. "T'day being so drawn in, t'jarls and their men 'ad supped well, lots of shoutin' and singin'. We 'ad to pass by all t'mead-benches to get to a separate room at far side of mead 'all. Nobody took no notice of us. We saw t'king—all dressed up 'e were—but no wimmin. T'man who took us left us inside another big, fancy room. It 'ad woven 'angin's on t'walls an' furs everywhere. An' a great big bed sat in t'corner wi' more furs on—"

Ivar jumped in, impatient to get on with the story. "T'queen were sat there in a big chair. It were blond 'aired un. She told us—"

"—Nay, she asked us," Gytha butted in. She was the most animated Annie had seen since arriving in Jorvik.

"Alreight, she asked us to sit down and tell 'er what 'ad 'appened. So we did, an' she listened to every word."

Gytha and Ivar's audience sat, riveted.

Gytha picked up the tale. "An' then she said how sorry she felt about it an' 'ow awful it must be for us. An' then she said as 'ow she wanted to 'elp us."

Ivar looked excited. "She gave us this." He held out his hand; a small leather box rested in his large palm.

"She called it a phy . . . lact . . . ery." Ivar spelled out the difficult name slowly, as he had memorized it. "A phylactery—by Thor—a've remembered its name!"

Gytha jumped back into the conversation. "Open it, Ivar; open it!"

Ivar lifted the lid off the small, exquisitely tooled black leather box. Everyone craned forward to look inside. Three tiny objects lay inside nestled on a bed of pale blue linen.

Gytha pointed to a black iron hammer with runes across the top. "The runes say 'this is an 'ammer'. It's Thor's 'ammer, o'course."

A crucifix lay next to it, consisting of five amber-coloured teardrops bound together with silver.

"T'stones is made of Baltic amber," Ivar explained.

"Interesting." Meg raised her eyebrows.

"What is this?" Annie pointed to a shrivelled piece of bone.

"That piece is t'best of all," Gytha looked up, eyes shining. "It's a saint's relic. It's actual finger of Saint Andrew of Scotland. Queen's uncle gave it to 'er. 'E's a Christian saint, an' 'e's still livin' an' he 'ad visited t'palace last year. He's called Caddroe an' he were frum same place as 'er, up north."

Ivar spoke again, his voice pitched high and his words running together. "She said this box will protect us from 'arm." He sobered. "She also said we should be careful. She knew of another powerful völva who might 'ave summat to do wi' all this."

Meg carefully lifted the tiny jewel. "Well, the clue is in the Baltic cross. The Scottish queen suspects something and wants us to know. It is generous of her to give the phylactery to us—"

"—Am jumpin' in again," said Gytha. "She'd like to 'ave t'finger back but we can keep t'uther jewels."

"I know of phylacteries," continued Meg. "They're common in many religions as amulets: their purpose is to protect from danger or evil. It is just what we need right now."

"She gave us this too," Ivar held up a leather pouch, shaking it. "It's full of silver coins wi' King Eiric's face stamped on every one. They'll cum in real 'andy."

He yawned and his jaw cracked loudly. "Well, I'm for sleep. We 'ave t'be up before daybreak tomorra, Lars, A'll walk thee 'ome, just to be safe. Tha might 'ave tha pink light, Mistress, but I've got me sea ax." He pulled out a wicked looking knife with a long narrow blade. "I can use this for guttin' fish or for guttin' bellies."

10

As the sun rose over the horizon, turning the waters of the Ouse blood red, a small fishing boat left the already bustling Jorvik harbour. Both crew and passengers turned their faces to the warming rays and to whatever lay ahead of them.

Ivar and Lars handled the oars as they moved down river. Rosamund and Bea lay quietly in their baskets, out of sight until Jorvik was far behind them. Meg and Annie, wool hats covering their hair and dressed in men's tunics and loose pants with rope belts holding everything together, chanted an invocation to the Goddess Hecate, asking for success in their mission.

Obstruction to their undertaking had arrived earlier. As they opened the door to leave Ivar and Gytha's home, both Meg and Annie sensed the energy of a malicious spirit rapidly approaching. Meg quickly reached for the bloodstone in her pouch and held it aloft. "I call on the Goddess to protect us," she cried. The same soft pink light from the previous evening filled the dark room.

"Cover us with this light; allow no chinks to escape. Keep this sacred light around Gytha and Lioba while we are away. Send this evil fiend back to the one who spawned it."

The sun had climbed only a short way into the sky when the flow of the river changed. It became tidal and the tide was with them. Ivar raised the sail, "…it's woven frum wool and coated with fat frum an 'orse's neck t'mek it waterproof," he explained to Annie.

"Thanks, Ivar; that was way too much information."

Ivar settled Lars at the *hjalm*: the rudder, then sat down with Meg. "A need t'talk to thee about time. Like, we're runnin' out of it. Four days 'ave passed since our babbies got teken. It's three days sailin' to Birka. They could be gone anywhere in t'world."

"I thought about that too, Ivar. I think we must harness the wind to help us once we break into the open sea."

"An' 'ow do we 'arness t'wind? Is tha talking about t'sail 'cos we're already usin' that?"

"Of course," Meg smiled. "You do your job and leave the rest to Annie and me. You and Lars will need all of your strength. We'll be in Baltic waters by tomorrow."

11

Annie had never experienced such exhilaration. She watched the London Olympic sailing events on television in 2012, but this sailing would have won all of the gold medals! They simply flew over the sea. Filled with magical power, the sail took on a life of its own. It strutted, it swaggered, it pranced and it sent them across the sea to the Baltic in the blink of an eye—or in about twelve hours.

Rosamund and Bea, however, were not so exhilarated. They stayed down in the hold, safe in their individual baskets, heads just raised over the rims. They were pleased to accept the occasional dried fish offered to them, and the strong stink of fish permeating the hold didn't seem to bother them at all.

Lars had never experienced anything like this in his young life. "If this be magic," he shouted, "'am all for it."

He and Ivar were hanging on to the *hjalm,* trying to control the direction of the enchanted vessel. Ivar had plotted their course while they sailed down the River Ouse. To Annie's delight, he showed her his navigation device: a sunstone. The sunstone was a block of crystal he looked through to find the sun, useful on the many cloudy days around these islands.

Eventually, the fishing boat left the ocean behind and entered a narrower stretch of much calmer water. Meg removed the wind-harnessing spell and the little craft responded by moving more sedately, its glorious wildness now just a memory. The rocky coastline required Ivar's full attention as he sailed around what appeared to be a long peninsula into narrower waters.

"We're in Baltic waters now." Ivar handed Lars the rudder and took out his sunstone. "This is t'Mälar Sea, lots of islands and rocks in 'ere. We 'ave to go slower, but this is where t'pirates 'ang out. Keep thy eyes skinned."

On hearing this news, Meg and Annie began rotating their necks. Had they had the ability to turn their heads one hundred and eighty degrees like an owl they would have done so.

As though on cue, within minutes of being amongst the thickly treed islands, a Viking longboat emerged silently from behind one of the small islands and moved to block them. If Annie had not been so scared she might have admired the sleek lines, the colourful sail, and the oars moving in symmetry. All she could see was darkness and danger; the way the ship had hidden in the inlet reminded her of old movies she had seen of World War 2 and the Battle of the Atlantic.

"Time for action," muttered Meg. Again digging into her pouch of many hidden wonders, she threw a few henbane seeds into the air. As before, at the mead hall, the seeds burst into a cloud of red powder and settled over the pirate ship.

Three events happened simultaneously: the oars of the pirate ship stopped, and in some confusion, clattering against one another. The sail lowered abruptly and the ship came to a halt, swinging wildly in a circle as Ivar's little boat came to a more dignified stop, drawing alongside the longboat once it became motionless.

"Who sails this ship and what do you want with us," Ivar called in a robust, authoritative voice.

A large man climbed onto the prow of the longboat, dressed in similar fashion to many of the warriors Annie had seen in the Jorvik mead hall. He also wore armour comprised of strips of leather, bound tightly together and covering his chest. He looked like someone out of a nightmare, yet no weapons showed.

"I am called Thor Finne Skull-Splitter. I am here to offer you safe passage, Lord, along with your mighty dragon-ship and your many fierce warriors. We will lead the way to protect you. What is your destination, Lord?"

Ivar blinked. "We travel to Birka on an urgent mission. Thanks to Thor for your protection. These waters are full of men going a Viking. It is good that there are also good men like you around. We are in great haste. Use your speed to the full."

The pirate ship swung around, the sail raised and the oars moving in a smooth rhythm. Once Ivar manoeuvrered astern of the long boat, like a puppy following its master, he looked at Meg in wonderment.

"I've 'eard of this bugger. 'E's Norwegian. 'E'd as soon kill thee as spit. Mistress, why are we not dead or bound as slaves?"

"They saw what I wanted them to see, Ivar. Thor Finne Skull-Splitter knows he is no match for a huge dragon-ship with thirty-six oars and a hundred men and a giant of a man standing in the prow, looking and sounding like a mighty chief. You played your part well."

"What 'appens when magic wears off an' they see us for what we are?"

"We'll be on land and safe in the protective arms of Birka."

Meg and Annie made an effort to enjoy the beautiful landscape. Small tree-covered islands dotted the waters. Although the cool air ensured they wrapped wool cloaks around themselves, the blue sky and serene atmosphere calmed them, despite the circumstances, as they made their way north. Eventually, after carefully winding around many small islands and large jagged rocks, a much larger rock loomed into view with a building perched on it. The longship ahead of them slowed and Thor Finne Skull-Splitter called back to them.

"We must be on our way. Ahead lies the island of Björkö where Birka sits, guarded by the fortress. You are safe from pirates now. Just follow the coast north."

The Viking longboat turned with military precision and manoeuvred around them, the pirates demonstrating their ability as seamen, and they sailed away, no doubt to find more bounty on a sea filled with traders full of valuable cargo.

"Am reight glad t'see back of 'im. 'E's off in an 'urry 'cos 'e know 'ow well Birka's defended. A've seen many a longship leave t'arbour with lightnin' speed when a pirate ship's spotted. It's reight important that Birka stays safe for visitin' traders. Its business depends on it. T'King of Sweden meks sure traders know they're safe 'ere."

The little boat with its cargo of desperate seekers sailed north following the western side of the island and pulled into a small manmade harbour. Ships lined the jetty, many built of a different style than Viking ships. Ivar pointed out two-masted dromons from Constantinople; cogs from Fresia and quite a few knärrs: the workhorse of traders. A smaller ship lay aside and partly concealed by a knärr.

"That's it! That's t'ship I saw leavin' Jorvik that night," cried Lars, so excited he jumped up and down, making the small boat rock alarmingly.

"'Ow dus tha know?" Ivar barked.

"A recognise that carvin' of a serpent on its side. That boat were in an' out of docks all the time."

The foursome gazed at the skute as though willing it to give up its secrets.

"It means the men are still here," Meg reached for her niece's hand.

"Ay, but it dun't mean me babbies are still 'ere," Ivar cautioned.

"Well, it's a lead," detective Annie declared. "It tells us we're on the right path."

12

Lars leaped onto the jetty as only an agile young man can and secured the craft fore and aft. He helped the women off the boat, their limbs stiff from being in a cramped space. Annie and Meg held the cat baskets and attempted to regain their land legs. Ivar deftly secured the sail, the oars, the hold, then joined them.

Looking around at her first view of Birka, Annie found the fortifications reassuring. A foreshore leading up to the town sloped gently and appeared heavily built up save for a space between the waterfront and the surrounding rampart. A high wooden palisade sat on top of the earthen embankment. Wooden towers spaced at intervals looked out to sea and an oval-shaped fort sat on their right.

Ivar pointed north of the town. "There's a bloody large garrison of warriors barracked up there. Their only job is t'keep law and order on the island and they dunt mess around."

Annie sensed the vibrant energy radiating from the town, especially after the tranquillity they had experienced on the last leg of their sail to Björkö, apart from pirates. A smell of roasting meat and exotic spices drifted over to her. As Ivar had explained to them, Birka was the hub of major trading routes across the known world.

Ivar rubbed his hands together. "First job is to ask around. See if anybody 'as seen the twins; they're easy enough to spot as bonny as they are. There'll be lots of folk in t'central marketplace." He looked hard at Meg and Annie. "Tha might see sum sights tha wish thy 'andn't, and there's nowt tha can do about it, so both keep tha mouths shut." Having issued his orders he marched up the slope toward the crowded houses, his crew following meekly behind.

The winding, narrow streets of Birka immediately enfolded them within an international community. Streets bustled with men of different nationalities and shade of skin, wearing trousers with long tunics or coats weighted by heavy fur collars. Some men wore embroidered silk and flowing robes. All looked purposeful and intent on their various objectives.

Warriors from the garrison, dressed in their helmets, leather leg bindings and chest armour comprised of leather strips, stood out. Carrying colourful shields, swords and axes, their peacekeeping mission was clear.

Women also showed their presence, either accompanied by men, or not, and demonstrating pride in their appearance. Annie recognized women of Viking stock in their overdresses, secured with elaborate metal broaches and draped with many colourful beads. Other women offered a strikingly exotic appearance, walking behind their men, wearing heavily embroidered swirling gowns and eyes made large with kohl, above silken veils: easterners, a long way from home.

Annie's head whirled with sights, smells and sounds. The hubbub of noise and the combined aroma of spices and roasting meat grew stronger. Ivar maintained a purposeful pace, seeming to know the route. He turned a corner and stopped abruptly, causing Meg and Annie to stumble into his broad back. They had entered the market. On a platform directly in their path, a large man had pinned down a young woman onto the planks while a crowd looked on. The woman was screaming and waving her bared legs in the air but the big man held her arms firmly to the floor as he focused on his business. A large crowd offered advice and lewd comments; no matter that the calls created a babble of different languages, the meaning was clear.

Ivar immediately turned his group around. He spoke quickly and quietly. "These people are Rus. It's their custom to 'ave er... relations with a slave girl before she's sold. It's expected."

"Who are Rus?" asked Meg, remaining calmer than her niece who was being held back by Lars.

"They cum frum east of 'ere, frum Volga River. A've 'eard Kiev mentioned: a city there. They're fierce traders an' travel miles an' miles to sell their furs and slaves. They even go to Baghdad in t'east to trade for silver."

"We have to save her. That young woman— a girl really—is being raped. And people are watching and cheering, it's awful." Annie began to cry.

"Annie, Annie, you have to remember this is the ninth century. Values are different, even from my time in the fifteenth century." Meg put her arms around her niece. "We're here to save the twins; we can't save everyone."

"I will save her," Annie shook her head, rejecting her aunt's advice. "I'll buy her and set her free."

"What will you use for money?" said Ivar impatiently. "This isn't what we cum 'ere for. This 'appens all time. We need to keep goin'."

Annie fingered the gold locket around her neck, hidden by her clothes.

"I'll sell this, or barter it. Lars, please take this locket and offer it to that abominable and disgusting animal as soon as he's..." she paused, struggling to find a word, "...available."

Removing the heart-shaped locket from her neck, she handed it over. The same locket had saved her from dying at the stake last year in fifteenth-century Hallamby. This time though, she would not be getting it back.

Ivar turned away in frustration. "We 'aven't got time for this. We 'ave t'find a *hús*, an 'ouse to stay in for the night. There's a man 'ere I know who looks after that business."

He led them up into the town, leaving Lars behind. Small houses, crowded together, looked similar to the wattle and daub houses in Jorvik; an occasional one being log-built and caulked with clay, no doubt the homes of the wealthier traders. Ivar stopped by one of the log-built houses and went inside, leaving the two women outside. He returned shortly, taking them further up into the maze of narrow passages and unlocked the door to their new lodgings.

They crowded inside a room, as dark and small as Gytha and Ivar's home in Jorvik. Ivar fumbled around and found a small oil lamp which he lit using his fire-steel and flint. A tiny spark created a flame in the stone bowl, and though casting shadows against the daubed wattle walls, it provided enough light for Meg to look around with interest at their temporary home. Annie remained agitated and un-interested in her surroundings. Rosamund and Bea, finally released from their baskets, proceeded to walk around the walls, sniffing every object before they asked to go outside.

Just as in the Jorvik home, wooden benches lined the walls. Grubby sheepskins lay on top of them. A hearthstone covered with grey ash and surrounded by iron cooking pots provided a central focus. A small collection of pots, pitchers and drinking vessels lay scattered on a wooden table.

"This'll do," pronounced Ivar. "We won't be 'ere long."

Annie turned back to the door. "I'll go fetch Lars back here and find out what happened."

With that pronouncement, she disappeared into the street.

13

Lars waited until the Rus stood and adjusted his clothes. He felt no discomfort with what he had witnessed. Lars was born and bred a Viking and knew the Rus originated from Sweden. Like the men from Norway and his Danish family, raiding, pillaging and raping were part of their warring tradition prior to becoming settlers and traders. Interestingly, violence against a free woman in her own community was forbidden and severely punished. Right now, he had important business for his lovely Annie, daft though it seemed to him.

He shouldered his way through the group of men surrounding the platform. "I'll tek 'er," he called. "I'll buy 'er wi' this." He held up the golden locket swinging from its fine chain.

"She's mine," a rough voice shouted. "I bid for 'er first." A burly man, with a full red beard and a matching red face filled with annoyance, moved to stand next to Lars.

The Rus looked down at the two men and smiled, his eyes narrowing. Lars could see he liked the idea of haggling. *Hevete!* Up would go the price. He only had the one jewel.

"She reminds me of me sister," he said hastily.

The crowd laughed. Lars blushed when he realized what they were thinking. "I 'ave a jewel beyond compare," he said, suddenly inspired, "just like me sister." He quickly handed the locket to the Rus who examined it closely.

"Where did you obtain this?" asked the big man. "I have not seen the like before."

"Raiding in Ireland," Lars answered, fabricating as quickly as he could. "It belonged to a chieftain's woman."

"She is yours; take her."

The other man called out indignantly.

"I have more where that one came from," said the Rus. A grin quickly removed the anger from the man's face.

Lars leaped onto the platform and lifted the young woman from the wooden slats. Her matted hair and dirt-encrusted skin hid her features. She smelled terrible. Vikings were clean people and bathed regularly; he would be handing her over to the women as soon as possible.

He stood in the market square, supporting the thrall and wondering what to do next when he felt a light tap on his arm. Annie stood there, still in her fishing disguise. She threw her arms around him and thanked him, her tears falling again.

"Follow me, Lars Larsson; you are my knight in shining armour."

Lars had no idea what she was talking about but it sounded like she was pleased with him. He followed, still holding up the pitiful young woman.

When Lars and Annie, along with the rescued slave, arrived at their temporary lodgings, Meg had taken charge. She found the well out back and sent Ivar to the ship to bring back the basket containing food. The *máleðr*, meal-fire, crackled away and a large cooking pot, hooked onto the iron trivet, heated water.

When Meg saw the condition of the girl, she sent Lars down to the ship to bring back their clothing basket; then gave him firm instructions to stay outside with Ivar and not come in until called. Both cats also sat outside the door, keeping guard.

Eventually, Meg allowed them back in. Ivar had done nothing but stamp his feet and curse. Lars' stomach growled so much, its noise drowned out the cursing.

The former slave girl sat on a bench dressed in a pale grey woolen dress. Her cropped hair, still damp from its scrubbing, was fair and her complexion, though pale, showed freckles. A raised callous circled her slender neck showing where the slave collar had rubbed. Meg applied a balm of yarrow to sooth the skin. The girl's eyes, however, were downcast, and she jumped nervously when the two men entered the room.

Annie placed a gentle hand on the girl's arm. "They are friends," she said and touched her heart with her other hand then pointed to the men.

Ivar continued to glower at them all.

"You won't be looking like that when we tell you what we've found out," said Meg.

Lars stared at the girl in wonder. "I know 'er," he blurted. "She's the one; she's the one with t'men."

"What's tha babbling on about?" Ivar looked as though he had chewed on some tainted fish. "What men?"

"He means those men who took the twins. The men Lars saw get in the boat with big baskets and a thrall that evening. The men we've followed to Birka." Meg sat back and smiled at Ivar. "She's the thrall: our new guide."

Ivar fell to his knees before the now freshly alarmed girl and began firing questions at her.

Annie wrapped her arm around the girl's shoulder. "Ivar, she doesn't speak our language. It sounds Gaelic—maybe Irish—to me. Her name is Breck Ní Mhaolagáin or something like that. I think I just made a mess of her family name. She pointed to her freckles when she said it, so I think it means 'freckled one.'"

"By the 'ammer of Thor, I don't give a rat's arse about 'er freckles. We need t'know where they went."

Meg spoke. "We *need* to eat and rest before we do anything else. Ivar, you *must* rest. No one has slept since we left Jorvik or during that crazy voyage. It will be daylight for a long while yet. I will prepare the *ðágmál*. Just a short rest, Ivar, and then we'll find some answers."

14

With bellies now full of flatbread, fried perch from home, pickled cabbage, and apples for dessert, no one had to be persuaded to sleep. Each found their own small space on the benches lining the walls. Annie wrapped herself around the girl, whether for protection or warmth she couldn't say; her action felt instinctive.

Ivar awoke first. He called the others to wake up. He was impatient to get information from the slave. The others sat up, blurry eyed and drowsy.

"We 'ave t'move on, time's not waitin'. Ask the *hora*, whore, where are my girls? What 'append after you got 'ere?"

Annie tried to ignore Ivar's language; she could empathize with his anger. She indicated to Breck, using mime, they needed to know where the twin girls had gone and when.

Breck appeared baffled by the gesturing and shook her head. Ivar's temper mounted: he looked close to shaking the information out of the girl.

Annie saw Meg's lips move, no doubt reciting an incantation for the girl to release the truth.

Breck spoke. "Constantinople," she said in a tiny voice, then louder, firmer, "Constantinople."

When Ivar heard this, he let out a howl and sank to his knees, his face in his hands.

"We'll never get 'em back. Me babbies: me little girls. What shall I tell me wife. It'll kill 'er."

Meg lay a hand on the back of his head. "I tell you again, Ivar Ivarsson, we *will* get your children back. Annie and I shall use all of our skills to do so. Do not forget we are powerful völvas."

Ivar leaped up. "Them men must still be 'ere; their ship were down at t'wharf. Am off to find 'em an' wring truth out of their scrawny necks."

He reached into his tunic and pulled out the pouch of coins and the phylactery: the gifts given to him by Queen Iseabail. "Tek care o' these 'til 'am back." He threw the objects onto the small table, checked his long knife was in his belt, and left the house.

Annie took a deep breath. Ivar had sucked all of the oxygen from the room with his departure.

Meg spoke. "Lars, you must follow him. He is not responsible for his actions."

After Lars left, the two women looked at each other. Breck continued to stare at the floor.

"Annie, I believe we must use this time to look into the future. We need help from the Goddess."

Meg infused some chamomile leaves and offered a bowl of the steaming liquid to Breck. She then took Breck's hand, led her back to a bench, and indicated that she should lie down again. A quietly chanted incantation ensured the chamomile would be doubly effective.

Once Meg had ascertained that Breck was in a deep sleep, she arranged herself, Annie and the two cats in a circle on the hard-packed earth floor, cats alternating with women. Bowing her head, Meg began the proceedings. Rosamund and Bea began purring. Meg and Annie added to the soothing sound by humming. Annie was so comfortable with this method of preparation for invocation she immediately moved into a meditative state—unlike her reactions to the Norse magic she had so far witnessed, which scared her.

As the sound deepened, energy quickened in the room. A small flame from the oil lamp brightened and sent darts of light spinning around the walls. The darts spun faster and faster, finally fusing, forming a funnel. A female shape flowed from the top of the funnel, shining with light. Her robe billowing around her created a gentle wind, ruffling the women's hair.

"You asked for my help?" The voice was light, silvery and soothing.

"Goddess, we did," answered Meg. "You are aware of our mission. We ask you to show us what barriers are in our path and what we must do to make our way smooth."

The Goddess Hecate hesitated, her eyes gentle and full of compassion. "Your path is fraught with many dangers. A powerful force is attempting, even now, to prevent your success. Beware of circumstances that are not as they appear as falseness surrounds you. Your strength has diminished. Seek help from those you tru—"

A loud hammering at the door startled them. Goddess Hecate vanished abruptly, the rest of her message left unsaid. Darkness returned. The door flew open. Lars stood there, his face ashen; behind him stood a giant of a man. Annie recognized the Rus from the marketplace and her startled brain tried to absorb the fact that he held a man in his huge arms, as easily as if he were a baby. As though in slow motion she saw Meg move toward the man, and Breck, suddenly awake, attempting to hide under the small table.

"Itwerethemtwo men, t'buggars frumJorvik." Lars was gabbling, the words spilling into each other. "They werein t'marketplace, boldas yer like–"

"Later Lars, later." Somehow, Meg managed to lay a gentle hand on Lars' arm even as she brought the man with his burden into the room. Annie stirred herself and straightened sheepskins on the bench so the inert body—she recognized Ivar with a gasp of dismay—could be laid onto the bench.

The Rus spoke. Annie and Meg looked at him in consternation. His speech was incomprehensible to them. Meg quickly turned her attention to Ivar. Annie, now spurred into action and professional mode, moved to her side with a bowl of water and a linen shift grabbed from the clothes basket. At least Ivar was breathing evenly though he was unconscious. Once they had removed the copious amounts of blood, some crusty, some fresh, from his face and scalp, they could see a large, cleanly sliced wound at his hairline. Meg opened her herbal medicine pouch, never far from her side, and pulled out a small linen packet labeled yarrow.

"It's dried," she showed the package to Annie, "but better than nothing; it should stop the bleeding." She pressed the dried leaves into the wound and asked Annie to apply pressure. "Lars, go back to the market and bring me honey and sour wine."

Meg cut open Ivar's bloodied tunic, searching for more wounds. Finding none, she ran her hands down the rest of Ivar's unconscious body. "His lower arm is at a strange angle," she said to Annie. "No bone sticking out though; the Goddess be thanked."

Annie was impressed with her aunt's clinical assessment of Ivar, given she lived in the fifteenth century: breath, bleeding and bones. She couldn't have done better herself and she was trained in trauma care.

Meg spoke again. "Bring that huge man over here; we'll get him to hold Ivar still while we straighten this arm."

Annie looked at her aunt in horror. "I'm not going near that pig,"

"You will and you'll do it now," Meg turned from her patient and looked steadily at her niece. "Ivar is unconscious; we can set this bone before he awakes."

The scalp wound was just oozing blood now, so Annie waved to the Rus to come to her, not giving him eye contact. She demonstrated for him to hold Ivar down using his big, hefty arms on Ivar's chest and legs He appeared to understand, no doubt having seen many battle injuries.

Meg asked Annie to help her re-align the lower bone in Ivar's forearm; Ivar moaned and squirmed in his unconscious state but the weight of the Rus kept him steady. While Annie kept a firm grip on the forearm, Meg rooted around in the pile of firewood for a straight stick, tore a strip off another linen shift, formed a splint on Ivar's lower arm, and bound the wood to the arm. Ivar continued to moan quietly but remained unconscious.

Lars burst through the door carrying his precious purchases.

"Thank you, Lars," Meg said. "We'll cleanse the wound with the wine and use the honey to keep it clean, nothing better."

Annie spoke up. "Aunt, if I had a needle and thread I could sew this scalp wound closed. It will heal much more quickly."

Her aunt looked at her niece in surprise.

"Of course, I have needle and thread, here in my basket." She handed Annie both, the needle made of bone and the thread of linen. Annie used the wine to cleanse the needle and thread and stitched the edges of the gash together, Lars and Finne, holding Ivar down just in case he moved as Meg, at her side, watched in fascination.

Meg then cleansed the neatly stitched wound with the sour wine and smoothed on the sticky honey. She left Annie to wrap more torn up linen strips around Ivar's head. "Now we just watch and pray there's no further damage to his skull," she said. "I am not sure why he is still unconscious. What a disaster."

Lars, still pale but with two bright spots of red on each cheek, held up his hand. "Can a speak now, mistress?"

Meg nodded.

"A saw Ivar go into t'marketplace and start askin' folk questions. 'E looked an' sounded upset, wavin' 'is 'ands about an' shoutin'. Sumbody pointed to two men. Ivar went over to 'em an' yelled at 'em. One of t'men drew 'is knife an' slashed at Ivar. Ivar threw 'is arm inter air to defend 'imself an' t'uther man 'it 'is arm with a stick 'e were carryin'. Ivar fell t'ground. 'E were bleedin' all over place. Then this Rus cum chargin' up." Lars' voice grew louder as he became more excited, reliving the scene. "T'Rus took 'em both down wi' a big swipe of 'is 'and. They're both in t'lock up reight now."

The Rus began speaking. Again, his words were unintelligible to the women. Lars broke in. "I can tell thee what 'e says."

He translated the Norse words. The Rus had been in the marketplace seeking Lars. He was fascinated with Annie's locket and wanted to know how the people got in there. Who had trapped their spirits inside?

Annie realized she had not removed the pictures of her parents in her agitation to save the girl. She was dismayed. How could she have left this…animal, this…pig…with her parent's photos? The Rus was holding the golden locket in front of him by the chain. She snatched it out of his hand.

"*Hva poker driver du med?*" The Rus shouted, his face darkening.

"He says, 'what the hell are you doing?'" Lars translated, looking anxious.

Annie was fumbling with the catch on the locket with the intention of removing the photos when a big hand enfolded her hands. She looked up and saw the Rus shaking his head slowly. He spoke again.

Lars spoke quickly. "He says the locket belongs to him and so do the people inside it. He says to give it back now."

15

JORVIK

The sun had not yet risen when a harsh thud rattled the door of Gytha and Ivar's home in Jorvik. Whoever caused it was impatient as the thud came again. Aeldred put down his bowl of porridge, looked into the startled faces of his wife and daughter, and went to the door.

"Are you the one they call Aeldred?"

Aeldred looked at a tall, wide man with a full red beard and mustache. His helmet concealed his hair and most of his face. A woolen cloak around his shoulders was pinned back to show a long knife secured at his waist. A large, meaty hand held a heavy wooden staff, apparently the source of the thumping on the door. His aggressive stance had the desired effect on the old man whose knees began to shake and he felt an urgent need to visit the privy out back. Aeldred nodded weakly.

"Come with me. The queen wishes to see you."

Aeldred looked back at his wife and daughter. His wife wrapped his cloak around his thin, bowed shoulders, her hands trembling. "T'queen were good to us, remember. She would never harm thee. Go with God."

"NOW! Let us be gone. The queen is waiting."

How Aeldred found the strength to make it to the palace, he did not know. His guide—or guard—maintained a brisk pace. They passed through the huge door of the mead hall without a challenge from the guards posted there. Aeldred, remembering the story Mis-

tress Meg had told him, had braced himself to be surrounded by boisterous Vikings but the hall was empty except for a few hounds root-
ing through the rushes on the floor for scraps—but not quite empty,
he soon realized. He found himself thrust before a raised dais with
three thrones. The central throne; a huge wooden chair with carvings
of dragons writhing up the massive legs had one occupant. Aeldred
knew of Queen Gunnhild and of the stories swirling around her, as
did all the inhabitants of Jorvik. And there she sat, not the fair queen
described by his daughter from her visit, but a dark queen, her black,
elaborately braided hair contrasting with her white skin and blood
red lips. Her dark eyes, made larger by black paint of some kind,
gazed with kindness on Aeldred.

"Welcome, old man. Gösta, bring a bench for this poor man; you
have worked him too hard. Then bring him mead so he may reclaim
his strength."

Aeldred sat down gratefully and sipped at the sweet honeyed
drink. He felt its warmth as it slid down his throat.

"Better, old man?" Queen Gunnhild's mouth curved sweetly at
him but her dark eyes looked hard and cold. "I invited you here as I
have something of importance to ask you. Gösta, please stand behind
our guest to support him, if needed."

Aeldred watched the guard until he moved out of his sight. He
could sense his presence behind him; it was not a comfortable feeling.

"Aeldred, where are your son-in-law and your guests, the so-called
völva and her helper? I have been told they are not to be seen in
Jorvik." Her smile remained warm and inviting.

Aeldred stared at her, his mind spinning. 'Adn't Mistress Meg said
summat about not trustin' this queen? Best say nowt.

"Come now; where are they." Her voice sounded harder this time,
the smile no longer there, her eyes like black pebbles.

Thwack! The mead vessel flew from his hand and rolled across
the flat stones on the floor, the sound echoing in the empty hall. Dogs
raced over to lick the sweet, sticky liquid.

"A want t'speak to King Eiric," Aeldred's voice quavered, to his
frustration.

"Unfortunately, the king and his jarls are at the wharf, messing about with their ships, as is their wont. As you can see, only we three remain here in the palace. No one can hear us. I will ask you for the last time; where are Ivar Ivarsson and his companions."

"E's gone fishin' an' they've gone 'ome." He flinched as he felt the rush of air on the back of his head, but not the blow.

"*Helvete!*" This expletive burst from Gösta. "Something stopped my hand." Again, Aeldred felt the wind caress his head, but no blow landed.

"This is sorcery," hissed the queen in disgust. "The völva braggart has somehow managed to cast a protection spell."

"She won't stop this one," snarled Gösta. Aeldred flinched again, anticipating the next blow but the guard's long knife, his *seax,* clattered to the floor, making the dogs scatter, tails curled under.

The black queen stood. "Enough of this childish nonsense. I will work to end the spell, although I suspect they have gone to Birka. It seems the logical course. Someone must have seen the ship leaving and checked its destination. Meanwhile, lock up this sad English wretch; a lack of food and water will soon loosen his tongue. I have safeguards in place, Gösta. They will not thwart me."

16

Annie continued to outstare the Rus even though her neck ached from looking up at him. He held the chain and she the locket, both in a death grip yet afraid of snapping the fragile necklace.

Meg lost her patience, a rare event. She flicked her fingers toward the pair. "Burn!" They both yelped in pain and the locket dropped to the floor.

"It's amazing how quickly gold can heat up," Meg smiled as they blew on their reddened palms. "Lars, please pass me the locket. Use a piece of cloth to do so."

Lars did as Meg asked, warily watching the Rus.

"Now, ask this man his name."

The man answered in English, "I Finne, from Holmgård. I Rus trader."

Lars continued to translate as Finne talked in his Norse language. The big Rus turned toward Meg. "You are sorcerer? You must be to heat the jewel. I honour you and all your kind." He bowed his head then flung his arm out toward Annie. "What does this girl have against me? I have done her no wrong. I am peaceful trader. I bring furs and slaves to the Birka market every year. I travel with other traders from Kiev. My wife, Yaroslava, is with me, also my boy, Biørn, and little girl, Militsa, still at her mother's breast."

Annie scowled. "You raped this girl," pointing to Breck, still crouched under the table.

Finne looked at Annie in amazement. "She thrall. Is nothing. Is what we do.'" He shrugged his massive shoulders.

Meg interceded. "Lars, please explain to Finne these pictures are of Annie's mother and father. It is important to her heart and mind that she has them back, otherwise, harm may come to them back home as they are no longer protected by the magic of the locket."

Finne's eyes widened at these words. He gingerly took the locket from Meg, checking its temperature first, and then offered it to Annie bowing. "You Ani, take *faðir*, *móðir*."

A loud moan interrupted the drama as Ivar tried to sit up. A string of Nordic curses followed the moan, judging by the sudden grins on the faces of Lars and Finne. It took a while to explain to Ivar what had taken place and about his injuries. Once Ivar grasped the circumstances, he began to rant again. Blood seeped from his linen binding. Meg tried soothing him. Finne sat with him, occupying the rest of the bench. Rosamund and Bea, now feeling neglected, jumped onto the bench and sat on Ivar's belly, purring. Even Ivar had to smile at them and calmed down.

Annie rescued Breck from under the table and sat as far away as possible from the large Rus. She had difficulty using his given name even though he had shown understanding about retrieving her parents' pictures.

Lars shared with Ivar the news that the two men he had approached in the market place had now been jailed for disturbing the peace by starting a fight.

"They can add stealing children to their crimes." Ivar's face reflected his anguish.

Finne asked what Ivar meant, so Lars told him the sad story of the twins' disappearance. Annie could not believe what she saw. Finne's eyes filled with tears! He raped women—girls—with impunity, captured slaves for profit, but was mush when it came to family.

"What will happen to the men?" Meg asked. Lars translated.

"They and Ivar will go before the *Thing*, the Assembly, where the dispute will be settled by local free men."

Ivar became agitated again. "A need to find me girls, not piss around wi' all this," he yelled. Both cats leaped off his belly, alarmed by the sudden loud voice.

"Do you know where your children are now?" asked Finne, Lars still translating.

"The slave girl told us they are on their way to Constantinople," Meg picked up Bea. "She came here with the men who brought the twins from Jorvik. But you must have bought the girl from them?"

"No, I found her alone, begging in the marketplace. I could see she was a thrall with no owner, so I claimed her for myself."

On hearing these words via Lars, Annie put her arm around Breck and glared again at the Rus.

"You talk of Constantinople. I go Constantinople." Finne smiled and held out both arms, presenting the solution to their problem.

The words dropped into the room like sharp stones thrown onto a frozen pond, crack and crack! Everyone stared at Finne, and then started firing questions at him, except Annie and, of course, Breck.

Eventually, Finne explained that he and his family and fellow warrior-traders from Rus would set sail to Constantinople within a few days, once they had completed their trading in Birka and loaded up their ships with slaves, jewellery and furs.

"We are named Varangians by the Greeks of Byzantium, rulers of that great city," he said with pride. "'Var' means 'to pledge' and we have sworn an oath to protect each other; both Scandinavian and Rus and travel together to keep the pirates and hostile tribes at bay."

Meg looked puzzled. "I have heard of Constantinople, but what of Byzantium?"

Finne shrugged. "They are both the same city. The great Roman Emperor, Constantine, built his new capital at old Byzantium after the fall of Rome and named it Constantinople. The city is at the heart of the Byzantine Empire and is like nothing you have ever seen. Constantinople is a centre of learning, art, and, importantly for us, commerce. We Rus are welcomed there to trade and the city is rich in trade goods."

Annie listened to Lars' translation of Finne's lengthy and glowing description of Constantinople. Better not tell them it was now called Istanbul. That would really confuse everyone.

17

Everyone slept well. So much had happened since setting sail from Jorvik. After finishing the *ðágmál*, Lars headed into town with orders for fresh meat and vegetables. Ivar slept on and snored mightily, following another spoonful of poppy seeds boiled and made into a syrup with honey.

Finally, Annie and Meg had the opportunity to talk, as Breck appeared to be deep in contemplation while tucked in a corner of the dark room.

"Thank the Goddess, as you would say, Aunt Meg; we have a quiet moment. I have never experienced such a hectic time in my life."

The two women sat by the open door sipping a mint infusion, both needing a stimulant after the energy draining events. Annie explained her anxiety not having contacted Adam, her boyfriend, nor Mary, her best friend, back in the twenty-first century. "Three days since I came here and they don't know where I am."

"We can speak to your friend just as we did last year using light and vibration as a method of communication between alternate times. I use the method quite often in my travels. You called it scoping." Meg inhaled, savouring the scent and warmth of her drink.

Annie frowned. "'Skyping,' Aunt Meg. We named it 'magical skyping' to be precise, just so Mary could understand what was happening to her in the twenty-first century."

"We can do it now. Bea and Rosamund are here. Mary is used to our ways. She can tell Adam you are away on family matters, and anyone else you need to inform." Meg paused, "there is something else I must discuss with you. We haven't had a moment to talk about what the Goddess said to us; about falseness being around us, and our strength being diminished…" she looked back at Breck and lowered her voice. "…I can only think of Breck concerning falseness. She came with those men and must have connections back in Jorvik."

"I don't believe that for a second. The poor girl has been abused from the word 'go'. We need to nourish her, not distrust her."

"Well, we must also remain vigilant. The Goddess is correct about our diminished strength. I want to bring Will here to help us until Ivar regains his health."

Annie stared at her aunt in amazement. "Will," her voice sounding strangled. "Why Will?"

"We travel to Constantinople. We must protect ourselves, and not just with sorcery. Will Boucher is a trained soldier, a longbowman with King Henry. He fought at Agincourt—"

"—I can't believe you have forgotten already that Will and I fell in love when you dragged me to medieval Yorkshire last year. It's taken me months to get over him and now you're putting us back together; besides, he's much too busy running his inn."

"Annie, what we are attempting is not about you. Remember our two beautiful, lost twin girls. I don't know why you act so strangely." Meg put down her cup and took Annie's hands into her own. "Where is my sweet and generous niece? You seem more focused on protecting Breck than finding the twins. Somehow, you have lost your way."

Annie pulled her hands away. "I know how I feel. I don't want Will to come here. I love Adam. We need to get on with the skyping, A.S.A.P."

Meg looked at her niece, puzzlement written across her face.

"As Soon As Possible," snapped Annie, jumping up from her seat and walking out of the door.

Annie had walked all the way down to the jetty before she became aware of her location. She sat on a rock and looked out onto the Mälar Sea. Dark, green, frothing waves looked angry, lashing against the large rocks forming the harbour. She was one with the waves: churned up, tossed around and filled with darkness. Spray stung her face. Salt burned her lips.

Acknowledging her ill temper, Annie wondered where her pleasant disposition had gone. Right now, her skin crawled with irritation as though she had biting ants running amok beneath her clothes. Trying to analyze her feelings created more confusion. The Rus trader had upset her so much, she'd, as Aunt Meg said, lost her way. Well, she would find her path again.

Counting the huge waves as they rolled into shore, Annie remembered being a child and doing the same. The seventh wave was always the biggest.

As her mind relaxed, her resolve grew.

Priority 1: protect Breck, especially as everyone else hated the poor, former slave.

Priority 2: prevent her aunt and the others from joining that disgusting man to go to Istanbul/Constantinople/Byzantium. How ridiculous for a city to have so many names. Annie did not have time for that nonsense. She had visited Istanbul on a week's holiday to Turkey previously. So, been there, done that!

Priority 3: no way did she want Will in her life again. Will been offered his chance. He could have come back to live with her in the twenty-first century last year, but chickened out. Well, too bad. Her aunt must be senile, thinking of such a plan. Clearly, her role was to ensure Breck returned safely to Jorvik. They must waste no more time on this silly and useless search for twins who were out of reach.

There! Her path was now clear.

Something warm and furry brushed her hand. She leaped up in alarm. Rosamund!

"You followed me all this way," Annie crooned, bending down to pick up her familiar. She stopped half way. "I didn't ask you to come. Am I not allowed to be by myself for five minutes? Leave me alone." She stalked up the path toward town, leaving behind a smart but mystified cat.

18

JORVIK

King Eiric, surrounded by jarls, made his way through Jorvik town toward his palace, anticipating an evening of feasting. He and his men had spent the day repairing any damage done to his dragon-ship during their spring raids. The warriors reminisced about their battles and their celebrations; they told jokes, the more ribald the better; boasted of individual feats, stories growing wilder by the telling; all told, a perfect day with no women in sight.

Initially chattering amongst themselves as they traversed the streets, the men slowly grew silent. Eiric was perplexed to see deserted streets, normally so crowded. As the men came closer to the palace he caught the sound of raised voices, becoming louder and louder. His jarls moved closer to their king and unsheathed their long knives.

The returning warriors looked in amazement at the scene outside the palace door. The sentries had formed a miniscule shield wall against a rabble consisting of men, women, and children; no weapons in view, just raised fists and angry shouting.

"*Helvete!* What's happening here?"

The rabble turned to look at the new development. Many appeared to recognize King Eiric but most, being English, could not understand what he said. Eiric ran an old-fashioned Scandinavian court with no English influence or language. A jarl stepped forward. "What is the problem creating such public mischief?"

A young woman stepped out of the crowd, which became silent.

She appeared exhausted, displaying black rings beneath her eyes, her shoulders bowed, yet she spoke determinedly.

"Am called Gytha, wife of Ivar Ivarsson. Tha saw him a few days back, 'ere, at t'palace, because of our twins havin' been stolen."

Eiric nodded his head after the translation by his jarl.

"A man cum to our 'ome yesterday and took me old father away. 'E said t'queen wanted to see 'im. We 'aven't seen him since."

A rumble, like distant thunder, arose from the people.

King Eiric knew intuitively Gunnhild must be responsible for the deed and he would have to confront her. He would rather go to war. The king ordered his jarl to bring the woman and he marched into the mead hall.

"Find Gösta," he barked to his man, Hamr. "He must escort his mistress to me at the throne dais."

A defiant-looking Gösta appeared alone, infuriating the king even more.

"The Queen Gunnhild has gone away for a few days, Lord," he said with a bow.

"Gone away? Where? How?"

"I know not, Lord."

"Do you know anything of the detention of an old man?"

"The old man exhibited discourtesy when questioned by Queen Gunnhild so has been locked up overnight. I am to release him today."

What had Gunnhild been questioning the old man about? He viewed Gösta's account with skepticism but felt relieved he didn't have to confront his sharp-tongued wife.

"Release the man to his daughter," he instructed and stomped off to find his favourite wife, Iseabail, and to prepare for the feasting to come.

19

When Annie walked back into the house, her jaw dropped. A dazed-looking Will Boucher sat on a bench. He had not changed since she saw him last year in Hallamby, Yorkshire in the year 1415. His hair was as blonde as she remembered; his eyes as green and his shoulders as broad. Her heart turned over. An urge to throw herself into his slowly opening arms overwhelmed her. No! She recalled her intent. Her objective was to prevent an expedition to Constantinople, ensure Breck returned safely to Jorvic and then go home to Adam. The twins were long gone, too late to save them.

Meg jumped up. "I visited Will in Hallamby during your absence and brought him back. His assistant will take care of the inn. He is prepared for an adventure, and," she paused, "he wanted to see you."

Annie stared at her aunt. *Visited Will and brought him back.* Unbelievable! Her aunt had taken time travel to new heights. Annie wagered she didn't drop him into a midden. Well, Annie Thornton would soon put a stop to this nonsense.

"I don't want to see Will and I am not going on a foolish journey to Istanbul."

"Istanbul? Who said anything about Istanbul? I know nothing of this Istanbul. Will is here now and we are all grateful to him for coming to help us. I have told him of our search and the possibility of a voyage to Constantinople."

Will stood and walked over to Annie, a smile on his lips and his arms still held wide. Annie swung around on her heels and headed for the door. She tripped over Rosamund sitting behind her and landed in an ignominious heap on the floor.

"God damn it, get out of my way, you stupid cat!"

Meg looked at Will and raised her shoulders. "I am so sorry, Will. I have no idea what has become of the Annie we both hold so dear."

The already meagre amount of light inside the room dimmed. A large warrior appeared at the open door, helmet, shield and sword in evidence, blocking the daylight.

"I demand to see Ivar Ivarsson."

Lars walked to the door. "He is injured, officer. He lies over there."

"I care not what state he is in. Bring him to me."

Lars and Will lifted a still woozy Ivar from his bed and walked him to the officer.

"Ivar Ivarsson, you are commanded by King Olaf to appear at the Thing, today, before the lawspeaker, when the sun has reached its height. Bring your witnesses. Failure to appear will result in imprisonment." He turned and marched away.

Shock filled the room.

An anxious and puzzled Meg asked Lars what the man meant about a 'thing' but Ivar intervened.

"It's an assembly. It's where Vikings sort out rights and wrongs: disputes an' such. A can't understand why I 'ave to go. It's clear as t'nose on yer face a were in t'right."

Annie, arising from the floor, looked across at her new friend Breck and saw a small smile on her face.

The expanded group of searchers prepared to attend the Thing, having persuaded Ivar it might be an opportunity to discover information about who had taken the twins. As part of the strategy, Meg and Annie would again become völva and attendant. Lars and Breck would accompany Ivar to affirm the ruth of the events leading up to the fight in the market place. Will was responsible for Ivar, still unsteady from his poppy seed medicine, his broken arm secured in a makeshift linen sling which Meg had made. The cats would travel in their baskets, in case Meg needed them.

Annie went along willingly with the group plan, realizing that Breck appeared happy with the way events were proceeding. She donned her Jorvik robes as a völva's attendant, studiously ignoring Will, who was beginning to look as puzzled as Rosamund and Annie's aunt. Behaving like the old Annie for a few minutes, she shared with

Meg a remembered news item back home about the discovery of a Viking Thing site in Sherwood Forest, Nottingham, reputed home of Robin Hood.

"Who's Robin Hood?" asked Meg, looking relieved that she had her Annie back.

"Hallamby will hear about him in a few years, lots of stories and ballads," Annie shook her head impatiently. "The point I'm trying to make is how fascinating it will be to attend a real Thing."

People in Birka marketplace were happy to give directions to the location of the Thing. "Just follow us. We are all going,"

"Why is everyone dressed so beautifully and looking so cheerful?" Meg asked as they joined the throng. "Isn't this Thing a serious business?"

Lars explained the Thing *was* an important gathering, yet provided an opportunity for families to socialize and to show off marriageable sons and daughters. "It's party time as well—for some."

As the northern sun rose higher in the sky, Meg's group made their way to a field strewn with boulders on the eastern edge of town. Many people had gathered, forming a large circle within a natural amphitheatre, creating a medley of colours. A low buzz of conversation filled the air; children chased each other at the outer edges, intent on getting their fine clothes sweaty and dirty as soon as possible. The adults waved at new arrivals and clearly enjoyed the festive atmosphere. Warriors from the garrison stood at attention, unyielding in their battle gear.

A circle marked with hazel poles linked by ropes formed the epicentre and inside this circle sat the council. These important-looking men were resplendent in heavily embroidered tunics of red and green, blue and brown. Soft wool cloaks fastened with elaborate clasps adorned their shoulders, while wool hats with tassels or braid trim sat upon their heads. Beards demonstrated every manner of style, including jewels woven into facial hair. The most influential members of Birka, heads of clans and wealthy merchant families, comprised this august body. One man stood apart from the rest. Ivar pointed him out as the lawspeaker.

"Birka 'as its own laws 'cos it's so unusual. Three jurisdictions meet 'ere and they 'ave to protect both t'citizens and t'visitors, by royal order. King Olaf meks a lot of money from Birka an' he wants to keep it cummin.'"

A large man arrived at the field, drawing attention from the crowd, accompanied by a woman and two children. He outshone the council members. Meg laughed. Annie frowned and pulled Breck closer to her.

Finne.

He had dressed with purpose. His bright green tunic, his fiery red loose and flowing pants: the matched braiding on his tunic and the tassels on his cap harmonizing with both, signified an affluent man of fashion. He wore many armlets in silver and bronze and a Hammer of Thor amulet hung around his neck.

As soon as Finne saw his new friends, he came over and introduced them to his wife. Yaroslava was also beautifully dressed, but differently from Viking women. Pleated rolls of fine linen covered her hair, secured by a beautifully embroidered band. Silver rings and chains adorned the band, hanging gracefully at each temple to frame her face. Her dress was made of a fine wool, dyed blue, and multi-coloured glass beads formed a necklace. As an acknowledgment to her Viking husband, she also wore the typical Viking matron's chain containing her scissors, earwax spoon, and tweezers. Yaroslova's high cheekbones and Slavic name indicated her heritage. She carried a baby in her arms and a young female thrall held a small boy by the hand.

Annie tried to hide her conflicting emotions: sadness as she noticed her gold locket was dangling from a pin on Yaroslova's dress, yet comforted having the friendship of Breck as a replacement.

Once the group settled themselves on a cluster of rocks Annie became aware of curious glances directed at them by people in the crowd. She thought at first it must be Finne's flamboyant outfit but realized her aunt provided the focus of interest: the crowd recognized her as a völva.

As the lawspeaker talked to the crowd, Lars translated. The lawspeaker explained the law as it applied to two men standing before him. The dispute was about the location of their stalls in the market. One man had moved his stall into the other man's spot. A fight had developed. Blood spilled before the other stallholders could separate them. The lawspeaker levied a fine against the culprit: one-third of the total to go to the King, one-third to the council and one-third to the victim.

An official called a name and a woman stood, tall and proud before the people. Another woman stood beside her. The woman said her husband had slapped her in public for the third time; this woman by her side was her witness. She asked for a divorce and for all of the rights to which she was due. After the council discussed the details, they granted a divorce with the discussion of finances postponed.

Again, the lawspeaker called out a name. "Ivar Ivarsson, present yourself to the council. This case concerns non-residents of Birka so different laws may apply."

The lawspeaker described Ivar's offences in detail. How a well-built man answering to his description had approached two smaller men in the marketplace and shouted insults at them, for no reason that spectators could see. How he had then raised his fists and tried to punch one of the men; and how a passing Rus separated the three before the well-built man could do more damage.

A warrior marched two men into the circle. They were both small of stature, in need of a good bath, their clothing soiled and nondescript. One man had a cast in his eye and the other a misshapen mouth.

Annie stared at them. She could only imagine what a nightmare they must have presented to the two little girls. How fortunate Breck had been there for them.

The lawspeaker continued. "These two men are named Boric and Carnac. Ivar Ivarsson, you are charged with attacking these men in a public place without cause."

20

Ivar's group looked dumbfounded. When did Ivar become the guilty one? Finne grasped Ivar's good arm and silenced him with a glance as Ivar's mouth opened to protest. He beckoned to Lars and led Ivar to the centre of the circle. Lars followed, holding Breck by her arm.

Meg's mind whirled. First, Annie's bizarre behaviour since Breck came into their lives, and now this. An outside influence *must* be at play.

To add to the drama, a ragged black cloud appeared in the previously cloudless sky and blocked the sun. It spawned a cool breeze, dropping the temperature and ruffling peoples' hair and head coverings.

A raven landed on top of a birch tree overhanging the north side of the circle. Large, black and glossy, the bird looked around with bright, black eyes. Its raucous cawing drowned out the lawspeaker. People reacted. Murmurings like bees working a flower patch rose upward.

Meg knew Vikings held ravens in high regard. Two ravens, Huginn and Muninn, were the eyes and ears of the powerful God Odin. She observed the two Jorvik men and Breck staring fearfully at the raven.

Questioning of Ivar commenced. What had been his purpose in approaching the men? Why did he strike the first blow? Ivar attempted to answer but the bird continued to drown out his words.

Finne began to speak, but his words also died under the raven's clamour. So it continued. When the chained men described their version of events, their words rang clear; when Lars spoke, the raven answered louder. People began to enjoy the action, rewarding the raven by clapping. The raven increased its repertoire, adding hopping from leg to leg on the branch to emphasise a point. Events were spiralling out of control.

"Enough!" Meg's voice rang out through the gathering. She strode into the centre while firmly holding her niece's hand, after ensuring Annie still clutched the cat basket in her other hand. "This is not law: this is sorcery."

As before, at King Eiric's court at Jorvik, Meg appeared taller, her black hood of animal fur, wooden staff, blue gown, pouch at her waist, all denoting a powerful völva.

The raven cawed all the louder, attempting to make the völva's words vanish. A council member stepped forward and led Meg and her assistant to the highest flat rock, bowing to her, showing his respect.

Meg tired of the raven's noise. Standing tall on the rock, she raised her staff. "Be silent, raven!"

The bird quieted, but its sharp eyes watched closely.

Meg turned to the lawspeaker. "The truth shall be heard. I repeat, the truth shall be heard; I ensure it. Ask your questions again."

The questioner, another council member, stepped forward and addressed Boric and Carnac.

"How did you both come to be in Birka? What is your business here?"

This time, the two men answered differently and the raven remained silent. Meg's power held sway. The man with the cast in his eye spoke first.

"We're frum a long way south of Jorvik, south o'River Ouse, south even o'Lincoln. Vikings cum ashore last autumn. Them buggers cum ashore so fast, we couldn't get away. We were workin' in t'fields. Us two were captured along wi' sum wimmin. It were King Eiric's ships. We were put to carrying night soil from privies to middens since then in Jorvik." Just for a second he looked up defiantly at the questioner. "You'd 'ave dun same if sumbody offered you your freedom."

The other man took over their story. His speech was difficult to understand due to his misshapen mouth. "All we 'ad t'do were grab them kids and stuff 'em out of sight. It were easy 'cos we 'ad a cart wi' big buckets. People see us all t'time in streets, scraping out privies. We just threw sacks over their 'eads and put 'em in t'buckets. Then we were on our way 'ere t'meet yon Arab."

Ivar lurched forward and almost had his hands around the man's throat before the guards pulled him away. In his rage, he had forgotten about his broken arm and he clutched the offending limb, rocking backward and forward in pain.

"I have questions," Meg looked at the lawspeaker, who nodded his head. She addressed both men.

"Who offered you your freedom if you carried out your instructions and what role did the slave girl, Breck, play in the undertaking?"

"She were in service t—"

A disturbance broke out in the crowd. Men and women leapt to their feet and shouted, shaking their fists at the sky, screaming angrily, seemingly for no reason. The noise covered the words spoken by the man. Meg looked up at the raven. Their eyes met. *You want a battle; I will give you a battle—Gunnhild.* Meg sent the silent message to the raven, letting the queen know she had seen through the shapeshifting disguise.

Meg stamped her staff on the rock. Silence descended again. She turned to the crowd and addressed them in a loud, ringing voice.

"This bird is not a bird but a fiend out of hell. This monster, who has taken on the shape of a raven, plotted the theft of two innocent children from a quiet street, in a peaceful town: not the work of raiders, but of a powerful person consumed by greed. Ivar Ivarsson is the loving father, as you are loving fathers. His wife, Gytha, is in Jorvik, crying for her lost children, as you mothers would cry."

The single cloud above multiplied into rolling, boiling, black clouds careening violently across a darkening sky. Large hailstones, the size of pebbles, crashed down on the people, who called their children to them, covering their heads and shouting in alarm.

"Enough foolery," Meg pointed her staff at the raven. A lightning bolt sped toward the bird who hopped away. The hailstones ceased. The sky lightened. The clouds melted away and the sun shone.

Meg turned her gaze to Breck. Breck remained a mystery, lurking in the shadows but, somehow, manipulating Annie: Gunnhild's sorcery, surely. Meg did not believe Breck had the skills of a völva.

"Breck, describe your relationship to Queen Gunnhild of Jorvik and I want the truth?"

Breck raised her eyes to Meg and tilted her head toward the raven.

She knows Gunnhild is the raven, Meg realized. What would she do now?

Breck did nothing, said nothing and hung her head.

Crooning softly, the raven left its perch and flew in circles high above the Thing. With each circuit, its body grew larger, casting a giant shadow, eventually blocking out the newly emerged sun. Day became night. On the raven flew. People struggled to breathe in the oppressive, dark and throbbing air, sensing an approaching calamity.

Meg's staff slammed against the rock. "Break the spell," she cried. "I call on the Goddess Freyja to break Raven's spell."

Rosamund and Bea leapt out of their baskets, welcoming Freyja.

A sound like glass shattering made the people cringe, but no shards were visible. Air became lighter and breathing easier as the throbbing sound ceased. A communal sigh floated upward. The raven perched in the same tree as before. Rosamund and Bea meowed gently.

"Enough game playing, Raven. It is time for answers."

Meg delved into her pouch. Retrieving a small object, she held it aloft.

"This is a *hnefi,* king piece belonging to the board game hnefatafl, which I obtained from the mead hall of Eiric, King of Northumberland and husband of Queen Gunnhild. King Eiric knew of the stolen children and offered to help. I call him to us. Now!"

King Eiric materialized before them. Raven fluttered into the air and landed again, black feathers ruffled.

Eiric looked as he should—regal. He wore a purple wool tunic, trimmed with gold stitching. Loose, black pants flowed gracefully into soft, leather boots. A heavy, blue, wool cloak draped one shoulder, held back from the other shoulder with a golden, double headed dragon pin offering a view of his large sword, the blade so burnished it flashed in the sunlight. A gold crown circled his head with a golden dragon resting in the centre of his forehead. His red beard flaunted two braids, tied with golden thread.

"I offer tribute to King Olaf and recognize I am on his lands," Eiric cried in a loud voice. "I send greetings from my consorts, Queen Gunnhild and Queen Iseabail—' Raven fluttered into the air again, feathers even more ruffled "—and I come to help my former raider-in-arms, Ivar Ivarsson.'

Meg nodded grimly at Raven; checkmate Gunnhild, she thought, her power making the king appear flesh and blood.

"My Lord," Meg bowed to the king, "I wish to ask a question to the girl, Breck." The king nodded. "Breck, I ask again, what is your relationship to Queen Gunnhild?"

To the surprise of Meg's group, Breck spoke in English—all of their previous attempts at miming unnecessary—"I am the queen's thrall. She owned me, yet she offered me my freedom on condition I complete this task. My father is, was an Irish chieftain. I led a life of privilege until captured by King Eiric." She bowed to the king. "Still a child, but now a slave, he gave me to the queen. No one wept for me. No one searched for me."

Raven became agitated, making small hops on the branch.

Breck continued. "My duties were to care for the twins on the journey to Birka and feed them an elixir to aid unawareness. They are too valuable for any harm to come to them. Once these men handed the twins to the Arab, I had to watch for followers to prevent their progress. I stayed in the marketplace guessing anyone searching for the twins would arrive there first. I met the Rus," she offered a sly smile to Finne, "and he led me to her." Breck pointed to Annie, "I used her to stop the search. Her simple mind became my toy."

Annie made a small distressed sound and reached blindly for Rosamund. Meg turned to Annie and, at the precise moment of her distraction, the king vanished. A bolt of intense light came hurtling from Raven toward Ivar, bouncing off his chest and hitting Breck, who crumpled to the ground.

Pandemonium broke out amongst the crowd. Warriors raced to guard the council. Meg was devastated. She had lost control and, as a result, Gunnhild won. Raven soared into the air, and cawing triumphantly, flew away.

21

Will gathered Breck's limp body into his arms, head lolling back, exposing her long, white neck and its circle of scar tissue. He looked at Meg and shook his head.

The lawspeaker and the questioner helped Meg down from the high rock. Breck's lifeless form showed no sign of trauma; she appeared asleep, yet no breath escaped her lips and no light shone from her eyes.

'We have a graveyard for non-residents,' offered the lawspeaker, sounding efficient rather than empathetic. "A warrior will assist you." He stood and faced the quieted crowd.

"The verdict on the dispute involving Ivar Ivarsson is as follows: Ivar Ivarsson is absolved of blame in the fight in the marketplace. We banish the two men, Boric and Carnac, from Birka, never to return. We cannot comment on the prior crime of stealing children. That issue is outside of our jurisdiction. The Thing is over. Return to your homes."

The people drifted away, but not before trying to catch a glimpse of the dead girl, jostling one another for a better view. Warriors stepped in to provide order. Meg collected Annie from the rock, where she had remained, as still as a marble statue, and brought her, rigid and shocked, to join the others.

Lars turned to Ivar. "Is thy alreight, Ivar? That were a real thump tha took."

Ivar, cheerful for once, said, "T'bolt 'it that box, tha knows, t'one our fair queen gave us. A tucked it in me tunic 'fore we cum out. A've got a bruise, a think, but that's all."

He opened his tunic and his audience admired the large bruise blossoming on his chest. He brought out the leather box. The top showed a dent, scorched at the edges and smelling of singed leather. "That bloody raven. Were it a magic un, Meg?"

"Yes, and created by a powerful sorceress, who turned out to be stronger than me."

Will shook his head and spoke for the first time. "I saw everything, Mistress Wistowe, and I witnessed that your love for Annie came first. You reached out to her when you saw her distress."

"Thank you for saying that, Will. We need to get her home. Lars, ask Finne if he will accompany you and this warrior to the graveyard and bury Breck respectfully. Will shall walk with Ivar, Annie and myself. The raven aimed that bolt at Ivar, not Breck. The phylactery did its job well, thanks be to the Goddess."

Will carried Annie most of the way home. Her movements were jerky and uncoordinated, as though she was a puppet with jumbled strings. When they arrived at the house, Meg wrapped her in sheepskins. Will put his arms around Annie and began to rock her. Rosamund jumped up onto the bench and began licking her face. Annie fell to her knees and began to wail. The sound was heart wrenching. Rosamund and Bea wailed in harmony. Meg and Will looked at each other in dismay, and then Meg, nodding her head, said, "Let her be, let her be."

By the time Lars returned from the burial, still accompanied by Finne and his family, Annie had sobbed herself dry and empty. She clung to Will as a drowning swimmer cleaves to her rescuer.

Lars looked scared when he saw Annie, hardly daring to report back, but Meg asked him to go ahead.

"We looked after 'er proper. That warrior who came with us 'elped to dig t'grave. Then we laid poor lass on 'er side—like she were sleepin'. Mistress Yaro…" Lars blushed and looked over at Finne's wife; he couldn't pronounce her name. "She took off sum of 'er beads and put 'em in t'grave—for lass's journey in t'afterlife. That were another thing Mistress Finne did. She took off her little scissors and put 'em on t'-girl's chest; that were to stop 'er cummin' back as a *draugr*."

Seeing the blank look on Meg's face, Lars explained how Vikings believed people could come back into their bodies after death and haunt living people. They were concerned Breck might do this as she had the ability to control Annie while she was alive. Open metal scissors, placed on a dead person's chest, prevented a return from the dead.

After filling the grave, Lars reported, the mourners had said a prayer to Freyja asking that Breck's spirit go back to Ireland. Lars looked a little bashful when he recounted this part, but he added that they felt sorry for her short life of slavery.

Meg watched with compassion as Annie slowly released her grip on Will and walked over to Lars, kissing him on his forehead. The tips of his ears flared a bright red. She hugged Yaroslova. Finally, turning to Finne, she held out her hand.

"Thank you. I have not been myself, you may have noticed. Lars, please translate for Finne and his family. I've really struggled with certain aspects of this culture; however, I now realize people are not all good or bad, just human. I also acknowledge my impulsive nature gets me into trouble. By bringing Breck into our lives, I could have derailed our search. Ivar, I am sorry I distracted us from our mission."

Ivar cleared his throat and shuffled his feet. Meg hugged Annie.

"Time to move on. Finne," she said. "Constantinople…?"

22

"The Rus traders will leave Birka in two days," Finne explained. "We will have completed all of our trading deals by then. Once the ships' holds fill up with goods bartered in Birka, Hedeby and Gotland, we, and our Scandinavian fellow traders will sail and row our ships on seas, lakes, and rivers to reach Constantinople. Where there is no water, only land, we will portage the ships on rollers. Nothing will prevent us from arriving at the rich and legendary capital of the Byzantine Empire. Our name for Constantinople is *Miklagarðr*, the Great City. We Rus make the journey every year in spring; returning before the beginning of winter and coming home loaded with silver, wine, spices, jewelery, glass, expensive fabrics, icons and books, for trading the following spring in the Baltic." The Rus held out his arms in an expansive gesture. "I invite you all to join us."

Annie thanked Finne and his wife again, her voice wobbling.

Finne and his family left to return to their tent village. Ivar drank his poppy seed syrup and settled for a nap. Meg sent Lars back into the market with instructions to buy fresh meat and vegetables.

Annie looked around the almost empty room. "What do you think, Aunt Meg, This might be a good time to contact Mary? I really must let her know where I am so she can inform people. Will, you can stay or leave, it's up to you."

Will gulped. Then he nodded. "When I agreed to meet Annie again, I suppose I accepted the fact that you are w-witches." He took a deep breath. "I love you, Annie. So, yes, I will stay."

Annie had no tears left to cry but offered him a misty smile. "Right then, let's begin."

Meg organized them into a circle, Annie, Rosamund, Will, Bea and herself. Each held the other's hand, keeping contact with the cats to complete the circle. For a few seconds, only Ivar's gentle snores filled the room, the sound curiously soothing. Both cats started purring. Annie and Meg joined in by humming and Meg nodded to Will to join them, his deeper baritone adding a richness to the hypnotic sound.

The flickering flame from the oil lamp lengthened. Walls vibrated; air shimmered and a column of light formed in the centre of the circle. Within the column, slender filaments of brighter light formed.

Annie watched Will's face as his initial reaction showed fear, but he remained seated; the last time he had witnessed this phenomenon he bolted in fear. The fine filaments of light floated apart, then joined and finally fused to form the features of Mary, Annie's friend, living in the twenty-first century.

"There you are, Annie! I might have guessed you are up to your old tricks. I wondered why I hadn't seen you around. I guess Aunt Meg whisked you off again. Oh, my Goodness! There's Will. Hello, Will, remember me? I made the movie you didn't like."

Annie explained to a voluble and excited Mary that she was in the tenth century and would stay a while. Could she please let her parents and her workmates know she was out of town on business. In addition, tell Adam that family matters had taken her away. She risked a glance at Will when she said this but his eyes remained focused on Mary.

Mary's excitement bubbled over. "Tell me what Vikings are like in real life: are they as fierce as in the history books? Do they wear helmets with horns like in the pictures? Are you safe being with them? Do they really go around raping and pillaging?"

Silence met this question and Meg tactfully moved the conversation onto safer subjects such as Viking fashion and Viking ships. Mary declared herself gobsmacked when Annie told her they planned to travel to Constantinople.

"Jonathon and I went to Turkey last year and spent a wonderful time in Istanbul. Make sure you visit the Hagia Sophia."

Finally, Mary said her goodbyes. Her parting words; "I'm sure there is a book in it for me. My story of your last medieval adventures is due for publication soon."

The fine strands of light forming her face became looser and more fragmented until she faded away.

Annie had just started to explain to the others that Constantinople is now called Istanbul in her century when Lars burst through the door in his usual fashion.

"A know who bought t'twins," he cried.

Ivar rose up into a sitting position, his eyes wide open.

"A man cum up to me in t'market," Lars said. 'He attended the Thing. He said he felt sorry for us, losing t'girl like that, an' he'd enjoyed t'show wi' völva an' raven. He'd seen twins change 'ands in t'-market place, 'aving left it 'til last to pack up 'is stall. It were almost dark when 'e saw 'em: same two men and t'girl. She were 'oldin' twins by their 'ands. 'E said little 'uns looked sleepy but their bonny faces stood out. 'E said he thought he were seeing double for a minute and rubbed his eyes."

Ivar was hanging on to every word as a man deprived of water sees a spring bubbling from the ground. "The man—the man—who took me babbies, who was 'e?" he spluttered.

"'Is name is Abdul Azim. 'E's well known 'ere. 'E's an Arab trader frum Constantinople."

"By Odin an' Thor, he's sellin' 'em t'slave market," groaned Ivar, his face growing deathly pale.

"NO!" Lars cried.

Everyone looked startled. Lars stood taller, commanding the stage; his audience stared at him, not breathing.

"Abdul Azim collects treasures for a rich Greek in Constantinople. 'Is name is Gennadios of Mytilene." He stumbled over the foreign sounding names.

"Treasures?" asked Meg.

"That's what this man told me. The Greek is a goldsmith. 'E meks stuff for t'Emperor and t'Church. 'E's so rich 'e lives in a 'uge palace an' collects stuff that's different—unique—that's t'word me new friend used."

"We have similar people in my century," Annie shook her head. "Rich people. They don't know what to do with all the money they have, so they collect things; paintings, sculptures, cars, animals. But people?"

"When?" demanded Ivar. "When did t'exchange 'appen? When did they set sail? 'Ow far ahead of us are they?"

"'E didn't know when t'Arab sailed but they left before we arrived, so three or four days by now, mebbe a bit more. We might even overtek 'em on t'journey."

"At least your new friend told you the twins looked well," said Annie. "And if the rich man wants them, the Arab will keep them safe from harm. So, Ivar, we just have to be patient and prepare to go to Constantinople."

23

Standing on another of Birka's wharves, the Jorvic group gazed at the frenzied activity. This wooden wharf lined a natural harbour north of the town, named *Kugghamn* after Frisian ships called cogs. Rus traders had anchored eight clinker-built ships, each with a large hold for their goods.

Finne enjoyed showing off the ships as he enjoyed showing off everything Varangian. Aunt Meg had been right when she said—how long ago it seemed—*Vikings appreciate a first-rate boaster.*

"These ships are constructed especially for voyages to Constantinople," he said. The strips of wood are thinner and the draft is shallower than normal. When we haul the ships over land, we want them to be as light as possible."

Many Scandinavian trading ships had already arrived in the harbour, having completed their business, and now awaited the start of the convoy to Byzantium. Traders watched with hawk-like eyes as thralls loaded numerous chests onto each Rus ship. Thralls had carried the goods from town in a long procession escorted by town folk making the annual departure of Rus and Baltic traders into an occasion, dressing in their best clothes and carrying baskets of food and flagons of ale; they planned to settle by the wharf and party as they watched the ships being loaded. As each hold filled and stacked higher than the height of a man, chests were secured with hemp rope and covered with skin tarpaulins.

"As you can see," Finne explained, "there is little room. Our families, along with slaves, will sit on the decks during the voyage, sheltered from the sun and rain by canopies. If Njord does not send the wind, we row. We use our sea chests from the hold to sit on and brace our legs on the chest in front in order to manoeuvre the heavy oars. Hard work, but we can do it." He thumped his chest, grinning. "Even more ships will be joining us in Kiev."

Annie watched Will who obviously enjoyed all the activity. Ivar; however, paced up and down in his impatience to follow the trail of the Arab, Abdul Azim, oblivious to all.

The last two days had proved hectic for Annie and her friends as they gathered supplies of food, clothing, tents and more weapons. King Eiric's coinage proved useful. Annie and Meg relished shopping for clothes in the market and haggling over prices. Annie had vivid memories of accompanying her granny to the market as a small child and feeling embarrassed by her gran's aggressive bartering skills but she must have absorbed something as she held her own against the cheerful but tenacious stallholders. Linen under-dresses and light wool overdresses; soft linen coifs and warm shawls found their way into their baskets along with turtle brooches and glass beads, arm bracelets and soft leather ankle boots. Meg bartered long and hard for a bar of chestnut soap and, in the end, cared less whether she had secured a bargain or not. The fishermen's gear, worn by the women on the journey from Jorvik, was washed and packed away.

Finne had invited them to sail with him and his family and share in the daily routines.

"Our crew is made up of about ten men, all traders. They share both the space and the labour equally. Some have their wives and children with them, like me. As I told you, space is tight on the ship. We try to anchor each night and sleep on land but if not, you might have to sleep sitting up."

Lars accompanied Annie to Breck's grave where she sat for a long while, marshalling her conflicting thoughts about her brief and perplexing alliance with the Irish slave girl.

Eventually, they boarded Finne's ship. The men raised the sails and manned the oars. One by one, the ships moved into the Mälar Sea, accompanied by cheers from the watching crowd.

Finne brought a hand-drawn map over to Ivar and squatted down to show them the first part of the journey.

"I will show you our route. The Greeks of Byzantium call it 'The Trade Route of the Varangians to the Greeks'. I told you before that the Greeks gave us the name of Varangians because they know we band together for safety on this dangerous journey and we swear an oath, a '*Vary*,' of brotherhood. "We are here," he pointed a thick, stubby finger at the island of Björkö. "We will pass through the Baltic Sea into the Gulf of Finland and then on to the Neva River. The Neva flows out from Lake Ladoga. This whole area we call *Garðariki:* it means Realm of Towns, as there are forts along the Volkhov River. We have a trading centre at Ladoga and small settlements from then on. When we reach Lake Ladoga, we turn south toward *Miklagarð*, the Great City, and our name for Byzantium: that which you call Constantinople. We stop each evening and make camp ashore. The women prepare the *náttmal*, and in the morning, the *dagmál*. The slaves dig latrines. You must perform your hygiene routine ashore as we have no means on board ship. We set guards as darkness falls. Lars and Will can help—" Ivar interrupted to protest. "—you too, Ivar, once your arm is healed. There are many fish to catch and lots of wood to collect for fires. We will have a good time, yes?"

As before, when the searchers had sailed in the Baltic Sea toward Birka, the scenery was pleasant. Islands with stands of birch trees created a mellow backdrop. Njord, god of wind and sea, sent wind to fill the sails and a gentle murmur of conversation rose from the decks of the ships. People played board games or shared stories and poems. Mothers breastfed their babies and chatted to each other and older children sat in circles playing what looked like complicated hand games.

Will stood with Annie at the stern of their ship, watching the wake made by the ship's passage and the bow on the ship behind them cutting through the wake. The view became mesmerizing after a while. Will reached out and gently held Annie's hand. "It's good to be together for another adventure," he said. "Do you agree?"

Annie smiled up at him. "I'm looking forward to it. I'm especially going to enjoy this part of the journey. It seems as though it might be restful and we need that right now. What a crazy time we have experienced for the last few days. Now I can get to know you again." Squeezing Will's hand, she returned to watching the water.

As the sun began to slide toward the horizon, the lead ship entered the much narrower waters of the Gulf of Finland. The trees changed to spruce and pine, birch, willow, and rowan; the banks offered a green and sloping vista. Lengthening shadows cast by the trees signaled time to find a landing place. Like puppies lining up to find their mother's teats the ships pulled into the bank and anchored side by side.

A well-rehearsed routine unfolded as the men unloaded chests just as Finne had described. A small number of men stood at the outer edge of the encampment guarding the perimeter with a variety of weapons to hand. As a village of tents arose; hearth fires in the kitchen areas began sending out smoke and enticing smells; latrines were dug and children ran around, letting off steam after finishing their chores. Everyone had a job, from putting up shelters, to collecting firewood, to preparing food. As the sun set all the people gathered around campfires enjoying a hearty stew and drinking ale. Another light guard was set—Lars was about to experience his first shift—and the people settled for the night. Meg and Annie snuggled together with the cats, leaving the other tent for Ivar, Will, and Lars. The women prepared to arise early to make the *dagmál*.

The sun had not yet risen when Meg and Annie sleepily stirred large caldrons of oat gruel, other women baked barley flatbread, cut blocks of cheese and watered down ale. As soon as all had eaten, the gear was back on the ships, just as efficiently as the evening before. Thralls feverishly filled in latrines, extinguished fires, and left the site looking as though no one had visited. The ships moved on before the sun was over the treetops. Hugging the northern coast, the convoy moved steadily forward, taking advantage of a constant wind. Many small bays with abundant sand dunes offered inviting anchorage in an emergency.

"Today we will throw lines out for fish," Finne shouted across the backs of the rowers. "We will see what we can catch for *náttmál*. There are lots of good eating fish and eels in the Gulf, even salmon, if we are lucky. Will, are you a fisherman?"

"I've done some fishing at home, in rivers," said Will, after a sleepy Lars had translated. "I'll give it a go. Annie can bait the hook for me."

He laughed when he saw Annie's face.

The sun soon disappeared behind gathering clouds which made being on deck more pleasant. A freshening wind allowed the ships to make good time down the Gulf. Before Annie became assistant fisherwoman to Will, she checked Ivar's scalp wound. It was healing well.

"I'll wash all that honey out of your hair when we are ashore," she promised Ivar. His red hair was pointing upward to the sky, and, with his arm in a sling, he resembled a one winged, scarlet-crested parrot.

Finne handed Will the fishing gear—an antler bone hook and a hemp twine line. The other Rus on the ship sorted out their favourite equipment, including nets made of hemp. One man was weaving a fish weir from fine willow branches he had collected on shore.

"I'll set it up tonight and collect the eels in the morning," he explained to the interested Will and Lars, who were familiar with fish weirs from their own regions. "It's an easy way to catch dinner: the eels will be guided by these hurdles and swim right into the basket."

It soon became obvious that the fishing had turned into a competition. The Rus turned everything into a game, each striving to beat the others. Bait was in plentiful supply as the children had been digging up worms for bait as the sun rose and the camp was dismantled. Time passed quickly with a variety of fish hauled into the ships. The air rang with insults from one fisherman to the next, usually comparing the size of a particular fish to male organs.

"Mark my words, and don't forget I can prophesy," a relaxed Meg confided to Annie, 'We'll be busy salting fish for the next few days."

24

Routines remained unvaried and travel through the Gulf proceeded smoothly. Meg had been correct in her prophesy. Men fished every day and women layered whatever remained after each evening's meal in salt. Empty barrels, brought on board at Birka filled up rapidly. Hands became red and roughened from constant contact with the salt and Meg made up some yarrow balm to share with the other women. When the women learned of Meg and Annie's knowledge of herbs and women's health, both wives and thralls developed a habit of stopping by their tent after completing their chores. One of the Varangians spoke Slavic as well as his own language so, with the help of Lars, they translated any advice Meg and Annie gave to the women. Both men did so with red faces and eyes firmly fixed on the ground.

"They've increased their knowledge of women's bodies and minds tenfold. Must make them better husbands," Annie giggled later.

Annie's removal of the sutures in Ivar's scalp using a borrowed pair of miniature scissors, offered interesting theatre for the crew. Her audience applauded, much to her embarrassment. Ivar could now take his arm out of his sling for short periods and exercise his hand. Will and Lars took their turns standing watch and catching up on sleep during the day. Annie and Will spent a little time together, sharing stories of their lives in the different centuries. Life was good: the spring weather pleasant with warm days and cool nights.

One morning after they were all back on board, Finne came to speak with them.

"Today we will leave the Gulf of Finland and enter the River Neva.

It is not a long river but its banks are steep and the river has rapids we must negotiate. Steep banks make it too difficult to berth so we will keep going until we reach Lake Ladoga." He looked at his guests and smiled. "The holiday is over; now we work."

Thinking back, Annie thought that might have been the longest and scariest day of her life—so far. Amazingly all the ships had now safely anchored on the River Volkhov, at Staraja Ladoga, a surprisingly busy trading emporium.

The River Neva had many twists and turns and, at its narrowest point—Annie felt as though she had to pull in her shoulders—the ships found rapids. The experience replicated a modern-day scary ride at a fair; however, the shallow-bottomed ships managed to descend the fast moving waters with a certain amount of control. The children certainly screamed like children do on a twenty-first-century rollercoaster. Annie and Meg clung to Ivar and clamped the cat baskets between their thighs, in a less than dignified manner, as they also braced their feet against the towering hold to stop them sliding down the deck. The ships traversed the rapids one at a time to prevent collision, with loud cheering erupting as each ship successfully arrived at the lower level.

"We're fine, just fine; we enjoyed ourselves," Annie told the others but she saw the scepticism on their faces.

Will and Lars each took their turn at sharing an oar during the descent and looked flushed with exhilaration at the exertion required. As the ships moved into the calmer waters of Lake Lagoda, rowing became easier and the voices of the rowers swelled with songs of war and victory. Finne took time to visit his guests and ensure they had recovered from the day's adventure.

"We come to civilization soon," he assured them, having commented on Annie and Meg's pale faces. "We curve around the south edge of this lake and enter the River Volkhov. Staraja Ladoga is our destination. It is a busy town, you will see."

25

JORVIK

Queen Gunnhild smiled. Those searchers of the twins believed they had left trouble behind on their journey to Constantinople. How foolish of them, particularly the one calling herself völva: the woman she triumphed over when she, Gunnhild, became Raven.

Gunnhild had worked hard to close the deal on the beautiful twins. The first time she saw them playing in the streets, she knew her friend Gennadios would covet them; indeed she discerned he would desire them with all his might, and, more importantly, with all his money. Plans to get them safely to Constantinople required much time and these little people—these nothings—would not thwart her. She and Abdul Azim had worked together a number of times in the past: the Arab trader offered efficiency and discretion. He had contributed many coins toward her security plan. Who knew how long Eiric would live, leading a life of violence. She had many sons to care for, to bring to greatness, and determined not to be reliant on the king for protection. If or when Eiric lost his life, she desired to return to Scandinavia and work towards creating kingships for her sons. Her strategy required money and lots of it. Feeble milksop, Iseabail, could scurry back to Scotland and be damned.

Gunnhild had created a cloak of invisibility to protect the ship of Abdul Azim carrying the twins so pirates and hostile tribes did not present a threat. The dhow would sail alone to the Bosporus and its precious cargo delivered into the welcoming arms of Gennadios of Mytilene, now of Constantinople. Eiric had spoiled her fun with the old man: grandfather of the twins, so she would have fun with the hapless seekers, and she would curb the powers of the self-proclaimed völva.

She clapped her hands and her man, Gösta, entered her private room. "A goblet of mead, Gösta, and stand guard outside. I plan to enter my otherness and plot more mischief for Master Ivarsson and his foolish companions."

26

A remarkable display of sights and sounds and smells lay before the travellers. Annie, Meg and Will leaned on the rails, waiting impatiently for permission to leave the confines of the trading ship. The town of Staraja Ladoga boasted so many buildings, all made of wood. One after another, they lined the streets that led to the wharf, almost like the spokes of a giant half-wheel. Clearly, the wharf had created the town. Even though the day had drawn in, the area bustled with hectic activity: thralls to-ing and fro-ing with heavy loads, vendors calling out their wares in a medley of languages, families in groups waving to the people on the newly docked ships. The spring evening still held some daylight and the air felt cool and fresh. The tantalizing smell of roasting meats and fried onions drifted toward the hungry travellers, making their stomachs rumble.

The word finally came to leave the ships. Everyone eagerly disembarked, tripping over each other to reach the ladder first. Ivar and Lars caught up with Annie, Meg and Will on the wharf.

"Finne says to stay together," Ivar cautioned. "This is a rough town wi' lots of different nationalities 'ere: Finnes, Slavs and Norsemen. Town's only job is to keep t'ships moving so it's all about mendin' t'-ships an' loadin' 'em with supplies. What shall we eat? Owt but fish, a think."

Annie intended to keep a close eye on Lars. His behaviour had made her feel uncomfortable recently. Those big puppy-dog eyes whenever he looked at her were disconcerting He hadn't looked at her like that since the beginning of the journey. He also seemed dejected, so unlike his usual cheerful demeanour.

The tavern was noisy and crowded but all agreed it felt so good to be on dry, unmoving land. Annie even managed to enjoy the roast squirrel and avoided looking around at the outlandish gathering of individuals around her. She decided they all looked like they would— as her granny used to say—cut your throat for sixpence.

Will must have sensed Lars' mood because he chatted away about the wars in France and re-told Lar's favourite story of about Vikings being given land they called Normandy—land of the Northmen—as a bribe to leave the French alone. Will had told Annie previously that Lars usually begged him to share these stories when they were on watch together but tonight Lars focused on his food, drank lots of ale and refused eye contact with his friend.

Back at the Staraja Ladoga lodgings, just a short walk from the wharf, the new arrivals explored their surroundings. A long, narrow building, the main room held rows of straw-stuffed mattresses and had privies out back, luxury after being on the small ship. There were separate areas for both men and women, and a water pump—an outright indulgence, thought Annie.

"Would you like to go outside and watch the moon come up," Will asked Annie once beds had been determined.

"Not going to 'appen," Lars muttered as he inserted himself between the two. "It's too dangerous in t'dark."

"It's alright, Lars, we'll just be outside the door." Annie reached out and touched Lars gently on the shoulder.

"A said no. A'm only following Finne's orders. Will should never 'ave asked thee. E's riskin' tekin' thee into danger."

"I am not. I am quite capable of taking care of Annie." Will wrapped his arm around Annie's waist.

"And I'm quite capable of taking care of myself," Annie removed Will's arm.

"*I* think it would be a good idea if we all took advantage of having a mattress to sleep on for a change," Meg interjected, looking perplexed at the sudden bickering. "You men are down at the other end. Sleep well," she added firmly.

27

Their stay in Staraja Ladoga had promised to be a treat; instead, Annie and Meg became weary of Lars and Will constantly bickering. Ivar had no tolerance for the behaviour of the two men and expressed his impatience frequently. He also expressed his impatience with the slow healing of his arm as well as his impatience of such a lengthy delay. Annie and Meg wearied of his complaints.

The women avoided all three men and spent their time at the wharf watching the activity as workers overhauled the ships and re-supplied them; however, Lars was required as a translator occasionally and now stood beside Annie and Meg looking like a sulky ten year old. Meg asked Finne if she could forage for herbs, her supply dwindling. Finne told her, quite strongly, she must not venture outside of the fortifications.

"Wild tribes live outside our boundaries; they thirst for fresh kills. By the way, I did ask around Ladoga if an Arab ship had passed through. One of the workers told me a strange story. He said a small, lightweight dhow, typically Arab with its triangular sail, appeared at the wharf about three days ago. The ship disappeared after taking on supplies, his words exactly—'it disappeared.' Just to add to that, the men on the wharf pulled a sailor out of the water yesterday, half drowned, speaking some sort of gibberish—he could be an Arab, the way he's dressed."

"That's a coincidence," Annie turned to Meg. "I wonder if he is connected in some way to the Arab who took the twins, what was his name...?"

"Abdul Azim," said Meg. "I also find it interesting that the ship 'disappeared'. Sounds like an invisibility spell to me. No wonder there have been no sightings 'til now."

"Finne," Annie asked in her most persuasive voice, "do you think you might use your remarkable influence to arrange for Meg and me to see this half-drowned sailor before we leave. He just might have some information on the twins. Maybe he fell off the Arab ship."

"No arranging to do. He's recovering in the local lock-up until they sort him out. Let's go now."

Annie, Meg and sulky Lars followed Finne to the local lock-up, a single log-built room at the edge of the wharf. There was no security. Finne just unbarred the door and walked in.

A small, brown-skinned man squatted in a corner on the hard-packed dirt floor, a tin mug and plate beside him. A wooden bucket sat in another corner, offering a pungent smell.

Finne loomed over the lake victim. "I Finne, you...?"

The man looked up at the large trader with frightened eyes and shook his head.

Frustrated, Annie shook her head. "He doesn't understand you, Finne. Is there someone in Ladoga who speaks Arabic?"

"I find. You two outside. I return. Lars, stay." He barred the door and left them standing on the wharf.

Finne returned within minutes, another small, brown-skinned man at his side and a triumphant grin visible above his beard.

Finne pointed to his 'find'. "Abdi. Work on wharf. Come from Baghdad long time ago. Speaks some Danish."

A complicated dance of languages began with Annie asking questions in English, Lars translating into Danish, Abdi converting into Arabic, then back to stumbling Danish, which Lars reported in his Nordic English. Meanwhile, Meg muttered her 'the truth shall be heard' spell, her eyes boring into the man on the floor.

The process reminded Annie of the party game she had played as a child—sitting in a circle and whispering a sentence into the ear of the next person who whispered it to the next person and so on. When the sentence came back to the starter, it bore no resemblance. She prayed fervently this was not going to have the same result.

The sailor's story emerged, excruciatingly slowly. His name was Kamil. He had signed up with Captain Abdul Azim in Constantinople.

Their dhow had been to Birka and was now bound back to Constantinople.

When asked how he had finished up in Lake Ladoga, Kamil became agitated and a torrent of words burst from his mouth. Abdi, struggling to understand, waved his arms in the air.

Lars translated the resulting, slower explanation. "'E sez t'Captain threw him overboard—for nuthin'! Only by clingin' to a tree branch was Allah able to save 'im. 'E 'ad dun no wrong. T'main cargo was of two girlchilds and an old slave woman who cared for 'em, all brought on board at Birka. 'E, Kamil, 'ad only whispered to another sailor that the girlchilds would bring lots of gold to whoever sold 'em. 'E sez 'e was innocent of such bad thoughts, but thinks the Captain believed 'im up to no good."

"Ask him if the girlchilds were well," Annie asked, apprehensive about the answer.

"T'old slave took good care of 'em. They played on deck if sea were calm."

"Finne, what will happen to this man now?"

"Annie, you so caring of people. Why you worry for such a rat? He hangs around the wharf, picks up work until he finds berth on ship."

Annie begged Finne to give the man a few coins. Clearly, this Kamil had been planning something and Abdul Aziz had caught wind of the plot. At least now they were reassured the twins were safe: good news to share with Ivar.

As Annie, Meg and Lars walked back along the wharf, Annie brought her attention back to Lars. He looked as downcast as before.

"You don't appear cheered up by such great news, Lars. I would have thought you would be delighted to know the twins are safe and we are on the right track?"

"'Ave uther things on me mind."

"What other things?"

"Will, 'E's mean to me."

Meg raised her eyebrows in surprise. "Will, like you, Lars, is a good man. What has happened to cause such bitterness between you?"

"Nowt for you to know; no offence meant, Mistress Wistowe."

Annie put her arm around Lar's shoulders. "I'll speak to Will, Lars. He'll listen to me. Now, let's go share this good news about the twins with Ivar."

28

Eventually, the head of the convoy called for boarding and soon the line of ships slowly moved south on the Volkhov River. Men rowed in rotating shifts. Finne put Will and Lars on different crews as the enmity between them grew more obvious. Annie could see the Rus traders kept a wary eye on them.

When Will was relieved of rowing detail, Annie approached him.

"I am so distressed to see you and Lars behaving like adversaries. What is the cause? How can Meg and I help?"

"Nothing to do with you or Meg."

"Will, you are a grown man; Lars is still an adolescent. You need to have more patience with him."

"Ado-what? You use such strange words. I do not understand you. Stay out of men's business." Will turned his back.

Close to tears, Annie was sharing this inexplicable conversation with her aunt when Finne approached.

"Ivar, I need you," he waved Ivar over. "What's wrong with Lars? I asked him for help translating and he turned his back. He shrugged me off. Me, Finne!"

Ivar tried his best to interpret.

"Neither he nor Will are feeling well," explained Meg.

"Well, I hope it's not something we'll all catch. Whatever is causing the problem has to be resolved. I will not tolerate this behaviour; long journey, small ship.

"We are making good time," Finne continued more cheerfully. "Our next destination is Novgorod. We Rus call the town Holmgård, my birthplace. Holmgård is the capitol of Garðariki: also the seat of

Sviatoslav, Prince of Kiev. He is still a boy so his mother, Princess Olga, rules us. Warring tribes killed his father, Prince Igor. Prince Igor was famous for attacking Constantino—*Helvete!* What has happened?"

A fistfight had broken out at the other side of the ship. Voices shouted encouragement. Finne took off.

"It's Will and Lars, they're fighting." Annie looked at her aunt. "What is happening?"

By the time they made their way around to the scene, Finne had Will and Lars by the scruff of their necks and shaking them as a terrier shakes a rat. "You my guests. Not do this. Take oars. Work. Everyone, back to work." He approached Ivar and spoke fiercely in their language before striding away.

Annie touched Ivar's arm "What did he say, Ivar?".

"He said I should have better control over them; they are an embarrassment." Ivar looked both angry and shamefaced at the same time.

No further incidents occurred involving Ivar's group as Ivar, Meg and Annie used all of their ingenuity keeping Will and Lars apart; not an easy task on a small ship.

The convoy made good time, the men rowing, their boisterous singing providing the rhythm for the oars. Soon the buildings of Novgorod came into view and shortly thereafter, the ships pulled in and anchored at the substantial wharf. Most of the town's inhabitants had come to greet them as cheering people crowded the narrow quay.

Novgorod offered an impressive sight. The travellers marvelled at the wood-lined streets and the solid wood buildings: the most impressive being the royal palace, sitting at the end of a large square and bearing a resemblance to King Eiric's mead hall in Jorvik. Its high wooden walls curved inwards. The thatched roof looked thick and substantial and a pair of carved dragons reached up into the sky from the peak of the roof.

Annie and Meg stood in the square with some of the women from their ship. Annie carried the cats' baskets. Rosamund and Bea needed some unrestricted playtime before returning to the confines of the ship although there would be more space on board once they returned. Apparently, the traders' wives and children were leaving the convoy in Novgorod and returning home for the summer.

Annie looked with sadness at her locket, still dangling from Yaroslova's broach. Finne explained the only women staying with the ships would be the thralls. He did not explain why the wives were leaving except a terse, "is custom."

As Annie and Meg stood in the square comparing the diverse facial features of the inhabitants of Novgorod, Finne came over, pulling Ivar along with him to translate.

"I have told Ivar he must watch those *dungas:* useless fellows. It is important we have no trouble here. Princess Olga always extends an invitation to us. She enjoys talking about trade with Byzantium and has a list, always a long one and profitable for our traders. You will wait out here until we complete our business."

He left them and joined a troop of traders heading through the heavy wooden doors, dressed for the occasion in brightly coloured tunics and loose pants secured at the knees. Elaborately woven strips of wool encased their lower legs, braids adorned hair and beards, and woven tasselled hats completed their ensemble.

Annie watched the admiring glances from the women in the crowd enjoying the flamboyant display. Knives, axes and swords piled up at the door, watched over by hard-faced, helmeted guards bristling with their own weapons and shields.

Spectators lifted their faces to the warmth of the sun. A buzz of conversation rose and fell. Children ran around freed from the confines of the ships. Rosamund and Bea had disappeared on their own hunting trip.

Abruptly, the peace and harmony were shattered. A disturbance had broken out at the other side of the square; Shouts of alarm arose.

"Oh, no," groaned Annie. "Please don't let it be our two idiots." She and Meg attempted crossing the square but stopped when they saw guards dragging Will and Lars through a door at the side of the palace.

"A tried to stop 'em," a distraught Ivar called, coming over to them, sporting a bloodied nose. "They were arguing over you, Annie; it's all been about you, like dogs with a bloody bone. Then t'silly buggers started throwing punches. When a tried to separate 'em, they started on me."

Meg shook her head. "I am thinking our Queen Gunnhild is behind this mischief once again. Interestingly, I have no sense of her manifestation and have no desire to intercede. She must have woven a powerful spell to make me feel so ineffective against her antics. Annie, it is now you who has the power."

Annie stared at her aunt. "I have no power, Aunt Meg, I am just learning. Please do not rely on me to get us out of this mess."

They stood with the rest of the people, Meg and Annie gripping each other's hands, Ivar muttering to himself. The sun grew stronger; heat bore down on the silent crowd.

A guard emerged from the large front doors of the palace. He waited until the buzz he had caused by his appearance died down then called out to the crowd.

"He wants us," Ivar translated. "He wants the companions of the fighters. We must go."

29

A guard ushered the anxious group through heavy doors, bumping into one another as they stopped abruptly, their eyes adjusting to dimness after bright sunshine, and then staring in wonder at the spectacle displayed before them. Although the outside of the building may have resembled King Eiric's mead hall, the inside did not.

Silk fabric hung from the walls, exhibiting every colour of the rainbow. Silk swayed and rippled as the guard-led group walked by, creating the unnerving effect of moving walls. A collector's paradise surrounded them. Marble pedestals of various shapes and sizes displayed bronze statues, glass vases, silver figurines, ivory carvings, and colourfully illustrated manuscripts and books. Sacred icons hung on fine chains from the roof beams: images of saints, Christ, and the Madonna looked down on them. The effect dazzled; colours jarring. Confused, still clinging to her aunt, Annie stared at another spectacle ahead, its contrast startling.

A raised dais, draped in white silk, supported two bejewelled thrones. All was white except for the soft glow of colour from gemstones embedded in the elaborately carved seats. A young boy sat on the smaller throne. He wore a white tunic, white loose pants and white bindings around his little legs. Blond hair hung to his shoulders. A woman sitting on the larger throne wore a white robe under a long white cloak, her hair covered under a white coif. The trio walked slowly toward Prince Sviatoslav: ruler of the States of Kievan Rus' and Princess Olga: regent ruler of the States of Kievan Rus'. A courtier announced their titles as they came toward this extraordinary tableau.

The warrior-traders of the Varangian expedition clustered on the right of the dais, stern faced and unsympathetic. Ominously, Finne refused eye contact with them, his eyes lowered to a carpeted floor of intricate design.

Annie had the strangest sensation of being on the inside of a kaleidoscope, remembering as a child looking and marveling at the interplay of colours and shapes, except that then she could control what happened with a twist of her fingers. Now she had no control. Colours whirled around her, changing shape rapidly, yet the centre was white. Light-headed, she reached out for Ivar's arm too. What would the next few seconds bring?

A man dressed in fine courtly clothes stepped out from behind the throne of Prince Svietoslav.

"I am called Asmud, tutor to Prince Svietoslav. Her Highness, Princess Olga, has requested I speak with you as I have spent time in your northern lands and know your speech. The penalty for fighting in sight of the royal palace is death. The Princess has decreed that, as your friends enjoy fighting so much, they will fight each other until only one remains. The guards will then kill whichever man survives. This will take place in the square now as a lesson to our people. Go with the guard."

Ivar translated from Norse in a low monotone, faltering as the message became clear. How they staggered back outside, Annie never knew. Her numb legs had separated from her brain. Ivar and Meg looked ghastly, even their lips were bloodless; only the prodding of the guard kept them moving.

The bright sunshine dazzled them as they joined the large circle formed by people. Guards cleared an approach to the front. Annie's shock intensified. In the centre of the circle stood Lars and Will, both stripped to loincloths and lacking the protection of shields. Each held a Viking *seax*, the long blades of the fighting knives glinting wickedly in the sun's rays. More guards struggled to hold them back from each other. Annie hardly recognized her dear friends—red-rimmed eyes and mouths forming a rictus of hate. A further disturbance caught the attention of the crowd as guards brought two heavily ornate chairs to the front of the circle and courtiers seated Princess Olga and the young prince with a good view of the proceedings. Tutor

Asmud stood behind.

Prince Svietoslav raised his white-clad arm and dropped it—a signal to begin the fight. The guards released their rabid captives who immediately moved into a crouched position and began circling, holding their weapons at eye level. Annie remained rooted to the spot, her tongue sticking to the roof of her mouth. Meg squeezed her arm—hard. "Do something."

Shaking herself like a dog emerging from the water, Annie stepped forward. An electrifying energy she had never experienced before surged through her body, and she was acutely aware of the rhythmic pumping of her heart and the pulsing of blood through her arteries. A dog scratching its fleas across the square grated on her eardrums. Approaching a man standing nearby, Annie reached out and gently took his staff from his hand. In one fluid movement, she slammed the staff onto the ground and cried "*STODVA*, STOP!"

Both fighters froze into crouching statues. Rosamund and Bea reappeared, shapeshifted into lithe, black panthers and patrolled the edge of the circle. No one moved. No one could move. The silence intensified.

Annie strode into the centre of the square and stood beside the rigid combatants. Her small, slender figure might have been diminished next to a tableau of large, rigid men if it were not for an aura of flickering multi-coloured light radiating from her. It was as though she had absorbed the kaleidoscope of colours from the great hall of Princess Olga.

Annie spoke in Old Norse, the words coming easily.

"I am *fjölkunnigr-kona*: knowledgeable woman. These two men you see before you, Will Boucher and Lars Larsson, are as brothers and share the love found between brothers. A sorcerer who practices black magic has created the anger you witnessed between these men. The sorcerer is preventing them from rescuing children stolen from their parents. A bewitching spell caused the enmity. In the name of the Goddess Freyja I now remove the spell."

As she slammed the staff into the ground again, a guttural croaking came from high above. Without looking up, Annie pointed the staff at the sound and released a bolt of fire. The croaking turned into a high-pitched shriek. A pungent smell of singed feathers drifted down over the crowd.

The two panthers dematerialized and Rosamund and Bea meekly climbed back into their baskets. Will and Lars reverted to their human state and slowly brought movement back into their limbs. They stared at one another and their seaxs fell softly to the hard-packed earth. A chant arose from the crowd, "*fjölkunnigr-kona, fjölkunnigr-kona*: knowledgeable woman, knowledgeable woman."

Princess Olga raised her hand. The chanting stopped. "Powerful völva, speaker of truth, come forward."

Annie handed the bewildered owner his staff, turned to her Aunt Meg and crumpled to the ground in a dead faint.

30

When Annie opened her eyes she was lying on a couch with five anxious faces looking down at her—Aunt Meg, Ivar, Will, and Lars. Young Prince Sviatoslav had positioned himself at the forefront. He prodded her. "You are alive, witch. This is good. I like you. I enjoyed your show."

Annie blinked at him. *She understood his language!*

"Aunt Meg, I want us to be alone. I...I...really need to talk to you."

Meg quickly ushered the men out of the small anteroom and politely requested of the tutor Asmud that Prince Sviatoslav leave too.

"I told them it was 'women's' business, Annie. They left quickly."

Annie sat up and gripped Meg's arm. "What happened in the square? I can speak and understand their language. Where did my power come from? Are our men okay? Do you think I killed Queen Gunnhild?" Annie collapsed back onto the couch, exhausted.

Meg smiled and took her hand.

"What happened in the square is that Annie Thornton came into her own as a powerful völva. I am so proud of you. I knew you had the potential but I think you were used to relying on me. This time I could do nothing and you stepped in. I have also heard of the gift of languages coming instantly to exceptional witches so now you may consider yourself an exceptional witch. I am not sure what okay means. Lars and Will feel drained, but realize their good fortune in surviving such a terrible curse. Queen Gunnhild has much to answer for. Did you kill her? No, I believe you singed her pride as well as something else. I'll be surprised if she had any hair left on her head when she shapeshifted back from her raven form."

Annie looked at her aunt as her eyes filled with tears. "Am I still the same person? Can Will love me: an exceptional witch?"

"Of course. You've just increased your skill level in one of your occupations and that's a good thing." Meg hugged her niece. "Your concern about Will intrigues me after all your talk about Adam. I am going to infuse some chamomile, and then you will sleep. Princess Olga has asked to see you once you feel refreshed. By the way, I'm told the convoy leaves in the morning."

An hour's sleep found Annie rested and escorted back into the hall of many colours and Byzantine treasures. Princess Olga and her son welcomed her graciously.

"I trust you are recovered from your exertions?" the princess inquired. "I have a request to make. You have demonstrated your power as a völva so I wish you to prophesy on behalf of my son and myself."

Annie's mouth dropped open in an un-völva-like manner, and then she turned and told her aunt what the Princess had proposed.

Meg quickly interceded.

"Translate for me, Annie. Your Highness, whilst you witnessed the amazing power of this young woman, I am the one who carries the gift of prophecy. I feel honoured to look into your future. I will perform *Verðandi*; 'that which is becoming.'"

Lars went back to their ship to fetch Meg's 'völva bundle' and staff. While waiting, Meg retreated to meditate while Annie told Princess Olga of their travels in search of the special twins. Princess Olga expressed interest in the involvement of Abdul Azim.

"I know him," she said, nodding her regal head. "He has done work for me: honest work only," she added hastily. "I am also on excellent terms with Emperor Constantine; we have a strong trading relationship."

Lars returned with Meg's accoutrements and the staff prepared the great hall for *Verðandi*. A high chair was set at the side of the dais. Everyone departed from the hall except for the princess and prince, his tutor, Asmud, and Annie and the cats. Two guards posted at the far end of the hall watched the proceedings intently: out of sound but not out of sight.

Meg walked into the hall from the anteroom, her face radiating tranquillity and wearing the blue robe with its black fur lined hood demonstrating her high status as a völva.

The tutor, Asmud, guided the völva to the tall chair onto which she climbed using a step. Seated on a cushion of feathers, Meg signalled for Annie to bring Bea, the cat settling quickly on her lap. The room was silent. Meg's eyes closed. A soft chanting filled the air as she commenced singing *Varðlokur,* a mesmerizing sound which channelled Meg's energy as she entered her trance. Meg tapped the staff framed by Aeldred back in Jorvik on the ground in harmony with her chanting. Goosebumps rose on Annie's arms, not having seen this aspect of *seiðr,* or Norse magic, before. When *Varðlokur* ended, Meg asked Goddess Freyja to show this humble völva the truth by shining a light through the darkness revealing what was yet to come.

Nothing happened for a long while, yet no one spoke or moved. Bea, sitting motionless on Meg's lap, looked like a regal, black statue. In a voice unlike her own, low and monotonal, Meg began speaking.

"Princess, I tell you this: I see a wooden cross, symbol of the Christ King. I see many buildings rising, each with a dome and a cross reaching skyward. You are the Mother of Kievan Rus' with your grandsons around you." Meg paused, and then smiled. "Emperors will court you but will not succeed. You will live after death as a saint in your country." Meg's voice sobered. "Your son, Prince Sviatoslav, is a fighter, not a ruler. He lives to have a sword in his hand, not a throne beneath him. He stays with his old gods, the gods of the Slavs; however, his progeny will carry the Cross of Christ for Mother Russia. This is what I see; *'that which is becoming'.*"

Princess Olga remained silent for a long while after Meg stopped talking, then summoned an attendant, requesting mead and sweet refreshments for the small group.

When they had eaten and drunk the Princess spoke. "Thank you. You have done me a service of great magnitude. I have struggled with my desire to become a Christian and to bring Christ to our people. Your prophecy shows me the way forward. Now, I will do something for you. Prince Sviatoslav will spend the summer working on his fighting technique with his arms teacher; it appears he needs the practice more than he needs statecraft and Greek. Asmud, the prince's tutor, shall accompany you to Constantinople. He will carry a message from me to the Emperor Constantine. I will ask the Emperor to assist you in reclaiming the twins and ensuring they return home safely. Asmud is a Varangian and will enjoy being with his companions. Is this sufficient to thank you for your prophecy?"

Annie and Meg stared at their new benefactor, both speechless. Annie could not believe their good fortune. This powerful woman was about to pave their way to Constantinople—to the Emperor, no less. They could not wait to tell Ivar.

31

Arm in arm, the two völvas walked toward their companions waiting at the end of a now deserted square.

"You were amazing, Aunt Meg. How did you know what to prophesy?"

Meg laughed. "I found the prophesying easier than you might think. When I meditated before we began, I called to Hecate, Goddess of Darkness, Mystery, and Bringer of Light, and asked for her help. She told me all I needed to know; however, I did not share everything she had told me. She said Prince Sviatoslav would die violently when he was only thirty: not information for sharing. When I asked for Goddess Freyja's help it provided an extra piece of drama; after all, she is a Norse god."

Will and Lars came to meet them. Annie warmed to see their polite manners. Each waited for the other to come forward first, a reversal of their recent conduct. Then, to her consternation, she detected a reserve in them: a sense of awe.

Do not do this. Do not treat me as someone different. I just want to be Annie, she thought.

"How can we show our thanks and gratitude to you?" said Will.

He hesitated before he reached for her hand as though he should ask permission to touch her. Lars spoke shyly, without his usual cheekiness and teenage bravado.

"Mistress, you saved our lives. You *are* a powerful völva."

To Annie's further dismay, Lars fell to his knees and kissed the hem of her gown.

"Stop it, both of you," she cried, lifting Lars back to his feet. "I am still me, Annie. I'm thankful I was able to help you both to be released from that terrible spell, but don't do this. Don't treat me as someone different—I'm Annie—still Annie." She shook her head in frustration.

Will and Lars looked shocked at the result of their actions—the opposite of what they had intended. For a few seconds, they remained silent then Will looked at Lars, looked back at Annie, put his hands around her waist and swung her into the air. Lars followed his lead, took the now squealing young woman from his friend, and swung her in a big circle. Annie was both laughing and crying when Lars set her down.

"Back to normal," Meg was laughing too. "Annie, I have one more task for you before we return to the ship. Examine me for signs of a bewitching spell possibly bestowed by Queen Gunnhild. She prevented me from becoming aware of her mischief and from doing something about it, so it is an ingenious spell. What can you see?"

Annie now sobered from laughing and crying, took a deep breath and looked at her aunt through almost closed eyes. Once again, tingling flowed through her body. Will and Lars backed away.

"Grey scales cover you, almost like a fish." She reached out and tentatively touched the grey matter. "Oh! They are soft, like cotton wool. They must be acting like a buffer, numbing your witch senses."

Annie took Meg's staff from her. Pointing it at the western horizon, she proclaimed in a loud, ringing voice:

Witch of the Darkness
Know you are found.
Scales that hide truth
Are cast to the ground.

"Well done, Annie. That takes care of that. She *is* an accomplished sorcerer. We must remain vigilant. By the way; what is cotton wool?"

Early the following morning, men rowing and singing, the ships moved out of safe shelter in Holmgård and continued south on the Volkhov River, on route to crossing Lake Ilmen. Asmud, true to the promise of Princess Olga, had joined them on Finne's ship the previous evening. Finne's usual swagger increased and his chest puffed with pride at the added status bestowed upon him by the addition of Prince Sviatoslav's tutor. In addition, because of Annie's actions in the square, and news spreading of Meg's prophesying for Princess Olga, the rest of the fleet now viewed his guests as 'super' völvas.

Even with increased space on deck due to wives and children leaving, the passengers and rowers were in close proximity, non-rowers forming tight clusters to avoid the painful possibility of an oar poking them in the ribs. Morning progressed quickly as Asmud shared anecdotes of his life at court with his eager listeners. As he spoke both English and Norse he acted as his own translator and to Annie's continued enjoyment, she could understand both versions. Asmud, the Varangian tutor proved to be a pleasant addition to the searchers. He was a Viking: big in body and striking in looks but more polished, as though sharp edges had rubbed away.

Ivar looked relaxed for the first time since Annie met him. The news of the princess's involvement offered him real hope of finding his babies and bringing them home. He whispered to both Meg and Annie he wished for a way to let his wife know of their progress. Could they use their magic to send a message?

Meg had pondered this lack of communication with Jorvik for a while, knowing how her friend Gytha and her parents must be suffering. "We will think on it, my friend and will find a way."

As they entered the wider waters of the lake, the crew raised the sails, which filled with spring winds. Rowers thankfully laid down their oars and were soon lounging on the deck with the others. *Hnefatafl* board games emerged and talking quietened as players focused on capturing each other's king. Anticipation was high as the watchers waited for the first outburst of cursing from players.

Finne took advantage of the easier conditions and sat down with his esteemed guests.

"I trust you are all well," he said with an ingratiating smile, quite unlike his usual style. Annie hoped he would soon revert to the Finne she knew and (almost) loved. Now she translated for both Will and Meg.

He pulled out his map from his leather purse and unrolled it.

"We are here. We will soon enter the River Lovat and make our way to the mighty Dnieper River and on to Kiev. We will experience a couple of portages before we get to the big city as the river becomes too narrow. It is not bad. The local tribes help us pull the ships along the land on rollers. They also bring food. Be aware they do not come as friends but know that if they do not help us, bad things may happen." Finne bared his teeth.

Annie shivered. He looked feral, capable of anything.

"We do not stay long in Kiev. More ships will join us there on route to *Miklagarðr*. Like us, the Rus' of Kiev lead a hard life, spending winter visiting Slavs who pay them tribute, either in furs, slaves or even coins. In spring, men return to Kiev with their bounty and prepare boats for the journey south. They are content to watch waters rise from the spring melt and wait for our return from the Baltic."

Finne paused in his monologue. He ran his fingers through his long, immaculately combed hair, and then cracked his knuckles, slowly and deliberately, one at a time. He cleared his throat. His audience shuffled uneasily. Something bad was coming.

"As Asmud knows," he nodded his head at the tutor, "the next part of the journey after Kiev can be," he paused again, "difficult."

Asmud acknowledged Finne's hesitant approach to the subject. "Yes. I have made this trip a number of times. What Finne is referring to are the nine rapids on the river. The rapids begin where the river turns south and descends down a cliff."

Will frowned. "I'm confused. How do we get the ships down a series of waterfalls? That is what you are talking about, isn't it?"

Finne shook his head. "We can't; we have to go around some of them. There's another little challenge." He offered a lopsided grin. "The local tribe isn't interested in being amenable to—"

"—Still?" asked Asmud, eyebrows raised.

"Still. Therefore, we have to mount a strong guard as well as manage the portages. Once we've done that we are free and clear and sail on to the Black Sea."

He sat back, relieved that he had completed his task—unlike his audience who looked apprehensive.

"How many times have you made this trip, and clearly survived?" asked Meg, ever practical.

"Oh, a dozen times."

"Then our chances are good," Meg paused. "Now I see why your wives' and children's journey ended at Novgorod." She turned to Annie. "I do believe it is time to change back into our fishermen gear."

32

Having absorbed such hair-raising information from Finne and Asmud, Meg took Annie to one side—an achievement on the crowded deck—and suggested they discuss how to contact Gytha.

"What did you say in Birka, Annie: we need to do this ASAP?"

Annie offered her aunt a thin smile, remembering how obnoxiously she had behaved at the time.

They looked at the choices before them, sending a message via a creature, be it a bird, seal, human, cloud formation...

"I know we all read things in cloud shapes but really!" They both burst out laughing.

"I suppose we can't use our magical skyping, Annie. Gytha would have to be involved in Jorvik. We could ask the Goddess to visit but that is disrespectful; she is not a messenger."

Aunt Meg, I believe you have to go—in whatever guise you can. You have the power to shapeshift, so use it."

"True, but I'd rather stay here during this dangerous part of the voyage. Let me think... I've got it!"

Meg delved into her pouch and pulled out the little *hnefi*, the game piece representing the king she had acquired in King Eiric's mead hall.

"This precious piece came in handy in Birka when I summoned the king. I'll use him again."

"You are not sending King Eiric as a messenger? That's about as rude as sending the Goddess." Annie was confused.

"I'm going to send King Eiric a message through a dream, using this powerful little man, and the king can bring a messenger to Gytha."

33

JORVIK

King Eiric rolled over in bed, threw off heavy furs, and awoke his favourite wife, Iseabail, acting on one of his many principles—if he is awake then everyone else should be awake. "Isy, I have had the most interesting dream." He shook her again ensuring she had awakened. "You remember the missing *tvinnr*: twins? The father begged for my help. He came to the mead hall with the völva. She used the cats to—"

"—Yes, *mo chridhe*, my heart. I remember them well."

The Queen sat up in bed and gave her husband her full attention, neglecting to mention she had sent for the parents and helped them begin their search.

"The völva visited me during the night—in my dream—not in real life—I think. It is the second time she has done so—visited me in a dream—I mean. I didn't tell you about the first time. Then, it seemed that I visited her. I stood on a rock surrounded by many people. I looked quite magnificent in my purple tunic and I carried my Ulfberht sword, *Leggbir:* Leg-biter. I also wore my best gold crown, the one with the dragon on the front. I can't remember the rest of the dream."

"What about *this* dream?" asked patient Queen Iseabail.

"The völva told me the *tvinnr* have travelled to Constantinople having been sold to a rich man. She and their father are following them, along with strong and brave companions, much like me." He patted himself on his bare and hairy chest.

"They are all safe and hope to have the children back soon. A rich man in Constantinople desires the children as companions. He must have paid someone to commit this deed. Powerful people like us... a princess as well as a queen are helping them to return the children. Margarette of Wessex—that is her name, I think—also advised me not to tell 'the dark queen' of this. I knew Gunnhild has had something to do with this mess all along. Do you remember she wore something wrapped around her head on returning from Odin knows where the other day? That woman *never* wears a head covering. I swear Gunnhild spends more time messing with her hair than anyone. I don't know what happened to her hair, but it seems to be missing."

Iseabail listened to this monologue with rapt attention. "What will you do with this amazing information, *mo leannan*, my sweetheart?"

"Our völva asked that I tell the mother of the *tvinnr*, in order to relieve her anxiety. I'll send my man, Hamr."

Iseabail smiled inwardly at 'our völva'. Eiric was claiming her. "He is such a busy man, *mo chridhe*, tending to your needs. Ask him to bring the family to me. I will save him the chore of speaking at length with them."

Her soft lilting brogue always soothed Eiric.

"A perfect solution, my precious." He rolled back into bed. "But first..."

Queen Iseabail received Gytha and her parents privately. Goblets of mead, a platter of prunes stuffed with honeyed cheese and a bowl of hazelnuts sat on a small table. When her guests arrived, the Queen's heart ached witnessing anxiety written in deep lines on their faces.

Iseabail's life at King Eiric's court meant she could never do what she desired. Rather than riding a spirited horse on the Scottish moors, she did needlework; rather than singing robust Scottish songs she recited prayers, and rather than speaking her mind to her husband King and to her sister Queen, she held her peace. This act; however, would fulfill her desire to help people and ease their pain.

"Please sit," the Queen gestured to the seats.

Gytha, Aeldred, and Lioba stood rigidly, not seeming to breathe.

"Do sit and enjoy some mead. All will be well."

Iseabail's serving woman fussed around the three, almost forcing them onto the padded benches and pushing cups of sweet mead into their cold and resisting hands, only leaving the room after a signal from her mistress.

Silence deepened.

"You are aware that the woman who came to see our king with your husband is a völva: her name, Margarette of Wessex, I believe."

Gytha stared at the queen blankly. The name obviously meant nothing to her. "T'woman who went with me 'usband t'see t'king were called Meg; she's me good friend."

"You do know she is a völva: a sorcerer of great skill?"

Gytha gave a tentative nod of her head.

"And she and your husband seek your children?"

Again, a slight nod of the head but the tears began their familiar slide down Gytha's cheeks.

"Now we come to the crux of the matter. The völva Margarette—your friend Meg—visited King Eiric in a dream last night requesting he send a message to you. Völva Margarette and your husband have news of your children."

All three of her listeners stood, as one, their mead cups falling unheeded to the ground.

"The twins are on their way to Constantinople to be companions of a rich man. He enjoys collecting precious objects and special people around him; this is good news as he will value your twins and keep them safe."

"Constanti—what's that?" Gytha stumbled over the unfamiliar word.

Iseabail paused. "Constantinople is a beautiful city, so I have heard, east of Jorvik, across the sea, ruled by an Emperor. People there are learned and rich, dining on gold plate and wearing cloth of gold and many jewels. They are Christian and worship our Lord God, the Blessed Jesus, and his mother, Mary." Iseabail genuflected. She felt on firmer ground now. "The message said a powerful princess is helping the searchers too. Your husband will be bringing them home as soon as he can."

When Iseabail saw the reaction to her news, a deeper ache entered her heart and she, too, released tears. Gytha and her mother knelt on the ground, sobbing, and the old father still stood but had his arms around both of them with tears streaming down his wrinkled and worn face.

"Come, come," the queen chided. "Let us kneel together and offer thanks before partaking of these treats. My woman will clean up the mead and bring more."

And so they sat, sipped and rejoiced, unaware of the many tribulations lying in store for their valiant searchers.

34

Annie marvelled at the scene. As anticipated, the Lovat River had narrowed with water levels so low the shallow-bottomed ships were in danger of becoming mud-bound. Volunteers stripped and, naked as newborns, climbed overboard. Their task was to test the depth of water with wooden poles. At a point where they could not risk passing further, a signal travelled back to hold fast.

A local Slavic tribe, familiar with the river, were waiting. In a dramatic moment, men and women emerged from the surrounding forest like actors appearing silently on stage. Carrying no weapons, people raised their arms in greeting to the convoy.

The first annual portage had begun.

Annie swore she witnessed the impossible—it could not be done—but it was done.

Thralls and locals emptied heavier cargo from holds and carried them on litters or their backs. One by one men, both crew and tribesmen, dragged the ships from shallow water onto wooden logs laid along a path following the river. Men hauled each ship, in turn, over rollers, one after the other… after the other.

Annie, Meg, and Ivar played their part, carrying what they could, along with Rosamund and Bea secure in their baskets. Will and Lars hauled with the others. High, marshy banks hemmed what was left of the river; a muddy path caused rollers to sink in places. Abundant flies and humid air produced an unpleasant and irritating environment, yet, amongst the grunts and ripe oaths, men joked and shouted encouragement to each other.

As dark appeared imminent the Lovat relented, opening wider its banks, allowing ships to slide back into their natural element. On land, women soon had kitchen fires burning and hungry warriors breathed an aroma of roasted salt beef and oatcakes. Ale flowed freely and memories of the day's hard labour melted away. Annie and Meg diligently applied soothing calendula balm to blistered hands and inflamed fly bites. Tired warriors circled the area watching throughout the night for unfriendly visitors.

Once again on the following day, the river almost disappeared and a second portage ensued, assisted by the same tribe. After ships slipped back in the river and the holds refilled with cargo, the tribes people presented food before vanishing back into the birch forest, having paid tribute and fulfilled their contract with the Varangians to provide assistance so that the tribe would not to be attacked or slaves taken. The fleet sailed on without further incident and entered the Dnieper River.

"A mighty river," Finne told them. "It will take us to Kiev and on to the Black Sea."

An outline of the buildings of Kiev was visible from a distance before the ships came into the large harbour. Early Slavic founders built the city on a series of buffs along the steeply sloping west bank of the Dnieper River. Buildings sprawled sideways and upward into the hills from a central core. Kiev looked like a city on the move. Sounds of hammers hammering echoed above a babble of voices at dockside and piercing cries of seagulls cut through all.

Kiev harbour held a variety of ships, mostly small knärrs like the ones from the Baltic. Asmud, their new travel guide, pointed out here, a merchant ship from the east and there, a Byzantine dromon, next to it a Mediterranean galley from the west.

"Kiev," he said with pride, "is the hub for traders from all of directions: north, south, east and west."

Asmud spoke eloquently. His eyes sparked. Annie could see his love for this country. Although primarily a Viking, he was also Rus. His commentary interpreted the scene before them; however, Annie noticed something odd, with so much to see around her, Aunt Meg looked only at Asmud. Asmud went on to describe Kiev's history and how it had grown to become so central to both western and eastern trade.

"Kiev's growth and success are due to Varangians. Over a hundred years ago the local Slav population invited Vikings here to rule. They constantly fought amongst themselves with weak or no leadership and decided we, men of Scandinavia, had ability and strength to rule, so they invited us here, thus uniting the region. Princes of Kiev have been in power ever since. That is why our heir to the Princedom traditionally has a Varangian tutor, in order to teach our future ruler the traditions of our fathers; hence me." He offered a smile. "You may have noticed Prince Sviatoslav has a Slavic name. Our heritage weakens as more generations of our men marry Slavic women." He shrugged his massive shoulders. "Such is life. Over many years, Kiev princes have developed a strong trading practice with Constantinople and have grown rich. Kievian ships will join our convoy here."

The little tour group broke up and Annie watched Rosamund and Bea chase each other around a temporarily empty deck. When she looked back a long while later Asmud and Aunt Meg still looked absorbed in each other's conversation.

35

Reflecting on the brief time they spent in Kiev, Annie remembered only two things: the growing interest shown by her aunt in tutor Asmud and her own total naivety regarding the next part of their journey. She recalled what Finne had told them of rapids and hostile tribes but decided he must be exaggerating—his usual style. What he had described was not humanly possible.

The first part of the journey south was enjoyable. The wide Dnieper and a helping current allowed the rowers a break and the riverbanks showed off a spring display of newly budded trees and spring flowers. Meg fretted because the forest floor flourished with plants she coveted for her herb chest.

Annie and Will took advantage of the relaxed pace and, when Will had no other duties, they took their usual position at the stern. Their relationship was a constant topic of conversation—where it might go—but always faltered on the rocky reality of time differences. In frustrated moments, Annie thought the relationship required a 'boot up the backside' to move beyond talk. Realistically, no privacy existed—anywhere—at any time.

One serene evening, at the close of day, the convoy pulled in and set camp as usual, but this time heavily armed guards patrolled the boundary. Annie ignored the implication of increased security and occupied herself cooking and catching up on personal hygiene and washing clothes, although she and Meg kept the cats close by, ignoring complaints about their freedom being restricted.

Dawn found the convoy back on route after an uneventful night but the feeling of relaxation had vanished. Conversation ceased during this edgy part of the voyage. Annie and Meg watched compassionately as men, exhausted after standing guard overnight and now having to watch the river with evermore vigilance, found a backrest during their break, leaned against the boxes piled in the central hold of the ship and fell instantly asleep.

They had been heading in a southwesterly direction for many miles when the movement of the vessel and the angle of the sun showed Annie and Meg that the convoy had turned south. Both women sensed the growing tension on deck as men no longer slept and if not needed for rowing detail, leaned over the side, observing and listening.

Rowers raised their oars from the water as the vessels gained speed; trees on the banks moved away from them more rapidly. Annie pointed out the visible increase in height of the bow spray of the following ship.

Scenery on the banks had changed; the pleasant view of birch trees vanished. Grey granite walls now towered over them, prematurely turning the late morning into a gloomy dusk.

A dull roar alerted everyone, the sound galvanizing crews into action. On Annie's ship, they took up station at the prow, amidships and stern, holding thick staffs. Two brave men stripped off their clothes and, tying thick ropes attached to the gunwale around their waists, leaped into the fast flowing water, feeling the rocks below with their feet and using a staff to probe through the water. Men on the other ships followed suit. The first rapid was almost upon them.

Annie would never forget the next few hours. The sequence of events blurred as fear took over. She and Meg had no activity to distract them other than to secure Rosamund and Bea in their baskets and hold on tightly to ropes lashed around the hold contents. Will, Jack, and Ivar fought alongside the warrior-merchants to keep their ship safe from the jagged rocks and rushing waters.

At times ships found a passage around the main rocky turbulence using slightly calmer channels running alongside, but three or four times these stalwart men hauled ships out of the river, unloaded cargo for slaves to carry, and portaged around the worst of the rapids.

Annie gritted her teeth as she and Meg helped as much as they physically could. Annie's heavily soaked trousers flapped around her cold, wet legs and her feet squelched in leather boots, hindered her movements, but, like Meg, she carried and pulled. This time, as no friendly locals helped, and as some of the men were strictly on guard duty, fewer hands were available to haul on ropes. Even the men hauling on the ropes over the granite surface had their shields slung on their backs and axes in their belts.

All the rapids had been given names and as the next one came up the men would shout its name in unison: *Supa* (the Drinker); *Ei sofi* (Sleep not), and *Edfors* (Impassible). As Annie could now understand their language, she could anticipate the level of difficulty ahead, not necessarily of benefit to her peace of mind.

As their ship was hauled out of the water yet again—at *Edfors*— Annie became aware for the first time of their position; Finne's ship lay at the tail end of the fleet—only five or six ships followed them. At least now, the slope went downhill as she and her aunt followed their ship, arms full of cat baskets and anything else they could carry.

"I hope this one is the worst we'll experience," she shouted to Meg over the roar of the rapid.

They had a good view of the raging water as it tumbled over the granite boulders. The fierce movement of the water sent spray splashing over them, stinging in its coldness.

Meg shouted back at her, "Annie, the back of my neck is prickling and it's not from spray. I am sure someone is watching us."

As the words blew away, Rosamund and Bea leaped out of their baskets and took off toward the forest bordering the granite pathway. Annie cried in alarm. Dropping everything, she ran after them, closely followed by Meg, both ignoring shouts from the toiling men.

It was darker in the forest and trees grew close together, allowing little room as the two women weaved and dodged around them. Branches whipped their faces and fallen timber invited a stumble. Calls from the men faded away. They almost ran into the cats concealed in long grass. Rosamund and Bea sat, still as statues, just their heads showing above the greenery.

"Oh, thank God, you naught—Oh my God!" Annie screamed. "Run, aunt, run!"

Annie had glimpsed figures standing silently and unmoving under tree cover, bows in their hands. Scooping up the cats, they turned and ran. Immediately, the men followed but the thick tree growth prevented them from firing their arrows. Again, after struggling to find a clear path out of the maze, Annie and Meg finally broke through onto the cliff top yelling, "*Háski! Háski!* Danger! Danger!"

The line of ships had almost moved beyond them before their screams penetrated. Instantly, the last few ships came to a halt and the closest men swung around forming a shield wall as a warning horn sounded. Someone shouted "Pechenegs!"

Warriors ran back to support the shield wall. Annie and Meg slipped behind the barrier as the first Pecheneg arrows bounced off the shields of the Varangians.

The second line of the wall held their shields over their heads. Meg and Annie held each other with Rosamund and Bea between them. The next few minutes lasted a lifetime: the deafening noise made by yelling Pechenegs, arrows swishing through the air and clattering onto shields, a grunt from a Varangian when an arrow found its mark; the smell of sweat and testosterone; Annie had never experienced such terror.

Meg shouted, "ENOUGH!"

Thrusting Bea into Annie's arms, she opened the purse hanging from her belt, pulled out a handful of Henbane seeds, ducked under the shields and threw seeds at the attackers. Annie screamed at her aunt to come back, joined by the wailing of Rosamund and Bea. Meg dashed back behind the shields. Silence descended—powerful in contrast to the previous clamour.

The two women peered around the thick bodies of warriors. Pechenegs stood motionless, their bows hanging by their sides as they stared above the heads of their foes, mouths hanging wide open. Then, as though practised in a military strategy, they wheeled around and retreated into the forest at a run.

No one moved for a few minutes. Once the Varangians had decided their attackers were not returning, they stood down and looked at each other in puzzlement. In the babble that followed, Annie heard their confusion at the abrupt cessation of fighting.

"What happened?" questioned one warrior.

"We must have looked unbeatable," answered another.

"Nay, your ugly face scared them off, Gunnr."

Laughter and more insults followed as the adrenaline still flowed.

"What did you cause them to see, Aunt Meg?"

"Giants! They saw huge giants towering over them, arms and legs as thick as tree trunks, their swords and axes the length of a man. The giants gnashed their huge teeth, ready to suck the marrow from the bones of the Pechenegs. Varangian giants are what they saw. They'll have quite a story to tell their children if they live long enough."

Both women collapsed into each other's arms again, crushing the protesting cats, who made it clear for the rest of the portage that they were the heroes for discovering the attackers.

36

"We have great *gœfa*!" exclaimed Finne as they checked for injuries. "We have the power of luck with us."

Two men were victims of arrows: one to his left shoulder, the shaft still piercing his body, and one, blood soaking into leather strips surrounding his chest, had lost an earlobe. Finne ordered them placed on his ship until they could receive attention in a safer place. Meg insisted on staying with the men in order to care for them.

The portage continued.

Finally, exhausted Varangians came to the last rapid. Annie thrilled to hear its name called out, '*Hlæjandi*' (Laughing).

"That's the sound it makes, mistress. No problem for us, easy from now on." This welcome news came from one of the traders.

As the river widened again, granite-darkened day gave back its light and eventually, the exhausted fleet rowed to a small island. Only steep and rocky cliffs were visible at the northern end so they continued south where a beach allowed easier access. One by one, weary men hauled ships up onto sand and made them secure. Despite exhaustion, a camp grew quickly by the water, helped by the longer spring daylight but dusk soon closed in.

Meg and Annie carried oil lamps to find the injured men and ward off the encroaching gloom. Annie's bones ached. She could see a comparable tiredness mirrored on her aunt's face. Tired or not, it was time to apply their healing skills. As soon as Finne spotted them, he came over.

"I will help."

An injured warrior leaned against a rock, a cloth held to his ear—or what was left of it.

After Finne had harangued him for not wearing his helmet, (he said it rolled away as he joined the shield wall), Annie inspected the damage. An arrow had taken half his ear in its flight.

"He's lucky that arrow didn't pierce his eye or his brain," Finne fumed, "not that he has one."

Anne cleansed the chastised man's ear with boiled, salted river water. She wrapped linen tightly around his head, packed with yarrow as Meg made up a poppy seed infusion.

More effort was required for the warrior with an arrow embedded in his shoulder. Finne efficiently cut off most of the arrow shaft leaving enough to grasp. He pulled out the arrowhead as two others held the warrior down; mercifully, he screamed once and fainted. Annie allowed blood to flow freely then quickly washed out the wound with salted water. She gingerly removed any cloth driven into the flesh by the arrow barb, using the miniature tweezers on her apron broach. She was about to pack the ragged hole with Meg's remaining stock of yarrow when Finne handed her a small container.

"*Hvönn*. We use it for wounds like this." He saw the doubt on Annie's face. "We grow it for this reason."

Meg smelled the powdery substance. Her face lit up. "Angelica; I know this. Yes, fill the wound. I will make a double strength poppy seed drink."

After the poppy juice took effect, Annie and Meg returned to their campsite. At last they peeled off their heavy, wet fishing gear, putting on crumpled but dry woolen shifts.

How wonderful to be on level ground again. Annie watched with compassion as tired guards took up stations, but the occasional laugh and conversations meant tensions were evaporating.

Kitchen fires were soon ready and the smell of flat barley bread cooking on the grills tormented appetites, followed by an unbelievable aroma of onions mixed with dried fish. Ale flowed as the celebration of still being alive began.

Annie and Meg reunited with Ivar, Will, Asmud, and Lars, whom they had hardly seen recently. Their men looked grey with weariness but were able to lift bowls of ale with no effort and soon regained some ruddiness.

Annie and her friends savoured their flatbread piled high with fish and onions. They sprawled around a blazing campfire feeling full and relaxed as Finne came over to speak to them.

"We have decided to make camp here for two days. Our stay will allow us to recover and check ships and stores." He turned to Meg. "Forage for your herbs if you wish but take someone with you to stand guard. I have never seen anyone else on this island but we must remain vigilant."

37

As the sun began its climb across a clear sky, no one watched its path. Kitchen fires from last night smoked lazily. Sentries slept at their posts. Fatigue from the energy expended at the rapids, combined with last evening's celebration, had taken its toll.

Annie poked her head out of the tent; both cats sat purring behind her. Aunt Meg slept on. She looked around at a remarkable sight— no humans moved over the landscape. Annie made a decision. She gathered both clean and dirty clothes and a precious nub of chestnut soap, bought in Birka and shared with her aunt, and a scrap of linen for a towel. She was ready for the bathtub, the bathtub being the River Dnieper.

As she walked down to the river, Annie worked on building enough courage to step into the cold spring runoff. Using a ship as a screen from the camp, she removed her shift and entered the cold water slowly, inch by torturous inch. Once her body had recovered from shock, Annie began to enjoy herself, washing her hair and scrubbing her body, being careful to stay in shallow water; a childhood fear of immersion underwater remained with her. Raising a lather proved impossible but the chestnut soap tried valiantly. Deciding she could do no more, Annie stepped back onto the sandy beach, shivering vigorously. After a quick towel dry and a clean shift pulled over her head, she prepared to scrub her dirty clothes. Rosamund and Bea had patiently sat and watched these strange goings-on with curiosity but suddenly jumped up and left to hunt for something other than fish.

"That looked like fun," a male voice broke into Annie's peaceful world.

She spun around in alarm. Will stood, smiling.

"How dare you spy on me?"

"I didn't. I was awake and heard you leave your tent; I thought I would stand guard. I had my back to you, watching for intruders. I have seen nothing. I must say, you look wonderful. You're actually glowing."

Annie calmed down. "Why don't you copy me? I'll lend you my soap, but maybe you're chicken?"

"I'm not a chicken. Why would I want to be a chicken? But I'll take you up on your offer."

Without another word, Will began to strip off his grungy clothes. Annie gasped and bent over her washing, scrubbing pants so vigorously she was in danger of making more holes. She heard a splash from behind. When she looked back Will's head popped up from the waves he had made. Utterly discombobulated and suddenly shy, Annie threw the nugget of soap at him and turned away.

"I can't swim," he called after a while. "Will you rescue me if I sink?"

"Maybe, maybe not, and do not lose the soap."

To Annie's horror, Will disappeared before her eyes. Forgetting her fear, she bound into the river, calling his name, soaking her clean shift. Will rose up in front of her, laughing and, wrapping his arms around her, pulled her to him and gave her a long kiss.

Annie pulled away and drew breath. "That's a cheap trick I've seen done so many times in movies."

"What's a movies? You do talk strangely at times, but I love you for it." He kissed her again and, scooping her up into his arms, he walked onto the beach.

Afterward, Annie recalled in awe their ability to make passionate love while freezing, although they did warm up quickly.

Annie had started an epidemic. Soon the entire camp had immersed itself in water with warriors at one end and female thralls at the other. Meg joined the women and thoroughly enjoyed herself. Once they scrubbed their bodies, they scrubbed their clothes. Meg left when both groups combined. She made her way back to camp but only

Annie and Will were there, sat close together, and huddled over the fire.

Meg studied their faces. They both looked like cats after lapping up cream. She wondered…

"Where are Ivar and Lars?" she asked

"I believe they are bathing," replied Will.

Meg and Annie began preparing oatmeal gruel and set Will to making bread cakes. Meg kept offering her niece sideway glances but Annie gave nothing away.

Meg smiled. Mmmm, two can play that game.

Soon Lars and Ivar came back to camp. Lars bounced up and down, his eyes shining and his face flushed, but choosing not to share the reason for his exuberance. Ivar, as least appeared cleaner and more relaxed. Annie looked around at 'her men' seeing them with new eyes. Darling Will still looked the same: blond hair and beard, amazing green eyes. Lars sported a fuller beard now, and he had filled out, his broad shoulders and muscular arms showing results from his rowing and hauling. Ivar and Asmud had long beards and mustaches, now washed and groomed. At one time Ivar had told her Vikings ridiculed a poor, unfortunate man who could not grow a beard: a sign of lacking machismo, she surmised.

One by one, men and women drifted back, all looking scrubbed and relaxed. Within minutes, wet clothes draped on tree branches, over bushes and laid on grass, looked like a gigantic patchwork quilt.

Meg left her friends to finish cooking the *dagmál* and went to see her wounded warriors. Birger One-ear, newly named, was recovering well. She quickly changed his dressing. The other unfortunate was doing poorly. He was feverish and red streaks radiated from the centre of his wound. Meg knew she needed some powerful cleansing herbs.

Annie and her companions sat around the fire eating oatmeal gruel laced with dried berries—a treat to celebrate such a special day. Bread cakes filled with dried apples sizzled on the iron griddle watched over with pride by Will. Even Ivar looked content to do nothing for a while.

Meg stood abruptly, thrusting her bowl at Annie. "I'm going to look for herbs."

"I'll go with you, Aunt," said Annie, standing and handing her bowl to Lars.

"Maybe next time; I feel like being by myself." As Meg said this, a blush slowly rose from her neck to her hair, still wet from bathing.

"I will accompany her," said Asmud, coming forward from his tent. "Finne has insisted that she must not go alone."

They walked away, Asmud looking incongruous: dressed in a mismatch of clothing, his helmet in place, his axe in his belt, his shield in one hand with his cloak draped over his arm and a basket, tiny in comparison, clutched in his other. Meg gazed firmly ahead, her wet hair hanging down her back making her seem younger somehow. They left behind a group of flabbergasted individuals who were in danger of catching spring flies in their open mouths. The bread cakes began to burn.

38

Once Annie had recovered from the shock of her aunt absconding with Asmud, she finished her scorched bread cake and chose not to make eye contact with the others.

Aunt Meg, prior to her surprising departure, had mentioned their patient's infected arrow wound. Annie decided to check on him and she was pleasantly surprised to see Finne sitting with the fevered man.

"I've said a prayer to Eir; she's our Goddess who looks after sick people and I've inscribed some runes on a rock: most powerful medicine. See, I've placed the rock by his shoulder. If this does not work and Mistress Meg cannot find any herbs that are powerful enough we will have to cleanse the wound with fire."

"I'm not sure when she will be back."

"Oh, yes, she has gone with Asmud to search for herbs. Perhaps she too will find some magic, just as you did this morning." Finne looked at Annie, a sly smile on his face.

Annie blushed and almost fired back a sharp retort but reconsidered as she remembered privacy did not exist in Viking country. She chose to ignore his remarks. "In the meantime, what shall we do for this poor ma—what is his name, by the way?"

"This is Sigurd. He is from the same town as me. We have travelled together many times. I hope we can save him but if he dies, he will go to Valhalla. He will drink and eat with the Gods. We wish for nothing more than to die with a sword in our hands."

They decided to wait for Meg and her supply of fresh herbs. Finne brought two young female thralls to watch over Sigurd, adding instructions to bathe his body frequently with cool cloths.

Annie went back to their camp. Ivar's snores reverberated from his tent. Lars had disappeared.

"Would you like to forage for herbs?" asked Will with a smile on his face.

39

Meg and Asmud made their way back toward the camp by the river. Her herb basket overflowed and Meg anticipated sharing their harvest with Annie. At the onset, they had just wandered, enjoying the scenery and the luxury of space. The camp must be having a protracted *dagmál* as no other beings ventured up there. Although a small island, the vegetation varied as they moved north and changed from oak groves to spruce woods, divided by open grassy meadows decorated with dancing spring flowers.

Magnificent oak groves contained huge, ancient trees. One tree, largest in the grove, needed five or six people to circle its bulbous and gnarled trunk. Branches reached out over thirty strides in all directions, creating a sense of stillness and sacredness beneath its shelter. New leaves were sprouting and the ground crunched under their feet with last year's crop of fallen acorns. Meg gathered two large handfuls.

Eventually, they discovered a secluded spot by a grassy meadow, warmed by the sun yet sheltered. Asmud lay down his cloak and offered Meg a charming smile as an invitation.

Some time later, Meg, enjoying a languorous nap, became conscious of a rough tongue licking her face and the comforting sound of humming. She turned toward her new lover but instead, found her cat, Bea. Rosamund was sitting beside her friend, purring, and Asmud stood a little way off, an amused smile on his face.

"Time to go to work." Meg jumped up. "And you can stop smirking." She softened her remark by offering him a kiss. "First the meadows, lots of treasures there, between spring greens and roots, and then into the fur tree forest I see above us. There are so many uses for spruce tips and pine needles, and we can use the cones for fires. We should have brought another basket," she lamented.

"We can use my cloak and helmet," Asmud offered, responding to Meg's enthusiasm. They made up for their delayed start by working assiduously at hunting and gathering.

40

By the time Annie and Will made their way into the interior of the island they found they were a couple amongst many; indeed, it was hard not to stumble over bodies lying in the grass or under trees.

"We might have been better staying at the camp," she muttered to Will, "I bet no one is left there. Let's go herb hunting, maybe they'll go back to camp soon."

The beautiful spring day slowly ended and, unfortunately for the newly budding ardour of Annie and Will, no one was making an effort to return to camp—preparation of the *náttmál* could wait!

Eventually, hunger drove people back to camp to re-start fires in preparation for the evening meal, sending winding columns of wood-scented smoke into the air. The patchwork quilt of dried, sweet-smelling clothes had disappeared and griddles were loaded with fresh herring. Men who chose not to celebrate spring in the woods and meadows had gone net fishing and returned with a healthy catch of the spring migrating herring.

Thralls with flowers in their hair prepared platters of spring greens: dandelion leaves, purslane, scurvy grass, chickweed and stinging nettle. Once the fish had baked, cooks would be pouring fritter batter onto flat pans. Ale flowed and board games were in progress. An evening of feasting lay ahead.

Before Annie and Meg could relax and enjoy the evening, they had a commitment to their injured Varangian. They planned to compare notes on their plant collections afterward.

Sigurd's condition had worsened. He burned with fever, tossed restlessly and muttered incoherently. They could smell the pus building in his wound.

"This is beyond herbs." Annie shook her head. "Finne had said something about cleansing with fire."

She sent one of the sulky-looking thralls to fetch him. "I suppose these two have been stuck here all day and missed out on the holiday." She looked at Meg as she said this and they both smiled at each other.

Finne came quickly. He didn't need the two women to tell him the situation; he was familiar with purulent wounds. He called to two men by name. "Agne, Halsten, come quickly. Make a hot fire; use the bellows. These are good men. I have worked with them before on this type of wound." He waved his hands vaguely over Sigurd.

It was hard to watch. The two men had a fire burning fiercely in no time. Finne thrust his long knife, his *seax*, into the centre of the glowing coals. When he decided the time was right, he wrapped a piece of leather around the hilt and pulled his knife from the furnace. The blade glowed a dull red. Meanwhile, one of the men placed a rolled piece of leather between the delirious man's teeth and both held him down. Finne thrust the blade into the open arrow wound. Sigurd screamed, arched his back like a bow, and then, mercifully, fainted.

Two thoroughly shaken women dressed the now-blackened wound with Angelica and made a powerful poppy seed infusion, with instructions to keep offering the drink as often as needed.

The festivities were well under way when Meg and Annie returned to their friends. Each campfire appeared to offer a variety of activities: storytelling, tafl, poetry, and vigorous singing. Lars and Ivar, oblivious to their surroundings, focused on a game of *tafl*. Asmud and Will watched with deep concentration while Asmud explained the moves in a low voice.

"*Tafl* is a game of war. We take it seriously. The king's side wins when the king escapes to the edge of the board. The attackers win by capturing the king."

Meg and Annie also watched with interest, as they had not seen a *hnefatafl* board at such close quarters. When on the ship, they tried to stay as far away as possible from the players, in case of eruptions. Annie realized the game was similar to chess, not that she had ever been able to understand that game either. She recognized the king, the *hnefi*, the same piece as the little man Meg 'captured' from King Eiric's mead hall. Eventually though, they tired of watching and gathered their precious bundles of plants to one side to compare notes.

After five minutes of sorting, Meg and Annie looked at each other and burst out laughing. They had both collected the same plants—including acorns.

Meg began. "We're lucky to find these young comfrey leaves and roots, known as 'bone-heal' and 'wound-healing herb,' so early in the year. This borage is useful as a blood cleanser. This burdock root, mashed up, makes a great poultice for relieving pain and healing wounds—we can use this on our sick Varangian. Here's good old, ordinary daisy; it stops diarrhoea and works on aching joints."

"What a great collection," added Annie, "I'm not sure about the acorns. I know they can be ground—they are a nut—but I don't know whether the Vikings eat them. You can also make a drink from acorns; it's like a mixture of coffee and chocolate."

Meg looked puzzled. "What is this coffee and chocolate?"

Annie laughed. "I'll make you a drink when we get to Constantinople."

Asmud wandered over to them. "I heard you talking about the acorns. We believe acorns are a good luck symbol and will only eat them if there is no other food available. I'm sure the men will have collected their own acorns but to be given one by you two powerful sorceresses will have much more meaning. Give one to each of the men. They will love you for it."

The food tasted amazing; no fights broke out, and the good weather continued as the spring evening ended. Before darkness fell, Annie and Will took the opportunity to steal away into the meadows and 'pick more acorns' while they had the opportunity. Finne had been over to their fire and informed them of a change of plan. The leaders planned for the fleet to move on tomorrow at dawn.

"Everyone appears rested and we want to take advantage of the good weather. So be ready to go as soon as the sun shows its face."

41

Flowing toward the ocean, Dnieper River widened considerably, its banks friendly and accessible, unlike those granite schisms through which they had battled rapids and Pechenegs. Sails ballooned with spring winds, creating effervescent bow waves and the mood was light on Finne's ship, laced with a sense of anticipation. The Black Sea lay ahead, and beyond the sea, legendary places with legendary names: Golden Horn, Bosporus, Constantinople, and ancient Byzantium.

Agne and Halsten carried Sigurd onto Finne's ship so Annie and Meg could supervise his care. His fever had broken during the night and he appeared coherent but weak. Meg made up a stock of poppy juice before thralls doused kitchen fires.

Asmud became a travel guide again as Annie and the others stood at the prow, all commenting on the feeling of warmth from the sun's rays on their faces as it climbed higher into the sky.

"We will soon be in the wide Dnieper estuary: wide because two rivers flow into the Black Sea at that point. We will probably stay overnight at an island just close to where the other river enters the sea," he said.

"Another island!" Annie clapped her hands. "I like these islands in the river."

Asmud continued, "You'll like this island. Ruins of an ancient Greek town are still evident from long ago, at least five hundred years before your Christ's birth. If it is still light once we make camp, we can explore them. I have travelled throughout the Mediterranean and spent time in Athens where I read stories of Herodotus. He travelled here and wrote about settlements of Greek colonies along the Black Sea coast. He recorded Olbia as one of the first communities and said it had over thirty thousand inhabitants."

The estuary grew wider, as Asmud had described, and the ships stayed close to its coastline until a small island came into view. Circling its rocky shores, the convoy finally found a sandy bay. One by one, ships pulled in and anchored in the shallow water.

Annie felt like a child again waiting for Santa Claus to arrive. She had travelled to Greece before, taking advantage of cheap flights and package deals. Since studying Greece in her history classes at school, she felt an affinity with all things Greek. How interesting that Asmud had journeyed to Greece. He was a dark horse, she thought—he told them what he wanted, when he wanted.

At last, they disembarked and the usual routine began: privies dug and tents set up. Wood collected for kitchen fires, containers filled with fresh water from a spring, and a new task—men had to take down and store all of the sails and replace them with bigger ocean-going sails. Setting up this camp proved more difficult and time-consuming, as supplies had to be carried up a steep headland.

As the frenetic activity slowed, Annie walked away from the camp, drew a deep breath, and looked around her new, small island. She was standing in the north-east corner and could clearly see the wide estuary. Taking a breath deep into her lungs, she smelled the tang of saltwater mixed with new spring grass: the Black Sea must be tantalisingly close. A gentle breeze ruffled her hair. The only signs of wildlife were noisy seagulls curious about all of the activity below them. They wheeled around the cliff face, swooping over humans, and dive-bombed into the sea for fish.

Land above the cliffs was flat and green with new spring growth. Some windswept scrubby trees and bushes partially concealed low stone walls laid out in symmetrical squares. As Annie drew closer to the walls, she became aware of a vibration travelling into her feet. Rosamund and Bea were following closely: Rosamund looked up and meowed; she could feel it too. Aunt Meg came over to join her niece.

"Can you feel it?" she said.

"Do you mean the vibration?" Annie asked.

"I most certainly do! It tells me this island is a portal: an entry point to another world. Shall we go and explore?"

"What other world? We can't just disappear. We're looking for twins—remember?"

Meg smiled. "We won't be long, a couple of hours at the most. We'll ask the others if they want to join us."

Ivar refused the offer. "Why in Thor's name would a want to go gallivantin' off. Aren't we doin' enough travellin'? An' Lars is down at the beach helping Finne wi' t'sails. Just don't be long," he grunted. "A'll have t'stew cooking."

But when Meg explained to Will and Asmud what they intended; they both rose to the challenge. Asmud ducked into his tent and brought out his precious sword, strapping it around his waist. "Just in case…"

Will raised his eyebrows and retreated to the tent, remerging with his longbow and sheath of arrows. "Ready for anything, now".

42

Moving away from the campsite, the foursome made their way toward an outside circle of stones.

"These look as though they may have formed the outer defences." Asmud kicked a stone.

"Vibrations feel stronger here." Annie looked down at her feet. "They're actually making my toes tingle."

They came to a slightly raised square of stones between two parallel lines of stone blocks. Meg stood for a moment. "I know what I am about to say sounds strange," she said, turning back to the others. "Just do as I do but first form a line holding onto each other's belt, that way we stay together."

Feeling self-conscious, Annie clutched her aunt's girdle as Will took hold of hers.

Asmud laughed. "A chain of explorers."

Meg continued to walk forward and stepped into the square block of stones with Bea and Rosamund at her heels. She disappeared. Annie gasped and, closing her eyes, walked forward, acutely aware of Will's hand in the small of her back.

The sky looked just as blue as it had a second ago, and the air as fresh and warm. A tall, solid, stone-built wall loomed behind them. Will released his grasp of Annie's girdle and climbed steps cut into the side of a tower rising from the wall.

"I can see down to the beach where we anchored but it's much bigger and built up: I can see dockyards and little houses. Land seems to go out much further. Stone steps wind all the way up the cliff—"

"—Come down, Will. You've separated yourself from us. We can be seen." Meg's voice, urgent in tone, sent Will hastening down the steps and seizing Annie's girdle again.

"I should have explained before why we must stay close together. I have placed an invisibility shield around us. If we separate, even for a few hands' breadth, we will become visible and that may not be a good thing. We'll just have a look around and then leave. Annie, please put the cats in their baskets. See how the tower is marked." Meg pointed to a symbol cut deeply into the stone, Ωι. "Omega. We came through here and, most important, it's where we leave. Asmud, please make a scratch mark on the stone precisely where we came through."

Turning as one, they regarded the centre of this strange island. A green meadow spread out before them; grasses and spring flowers bobbing gently in the breeze. Beyond the flowers, a main street opened up, and buildings, shining white in the sunlight, beckoned them.

With Meg in the lead and Asmud holding the rear, the foursome crossed the meadow and stepped onto a road paved with stone. Large, impressive, stone-built houses lined the road: elegant columns in front proclaiming their importance. Blocks of smaller, single story, squarely built houses extended away from the road on narrower streets, laid out in a grid system. High stone walls, with towers placed at regular intervals, surrounded the town.

A busy thoroughfare flowed with people moving in both directions. Annie delighted in seeing crowds of people moving around them—not seeing them yet not bumping into them—more of Aunt Meg's magic.

A large square opened up.

"The *Agora*," murmured Meg. "The marketplace."

The agora appeared to be the focus of all of the comings and goings and provided a hub of activity with people shopping, talking and arguing, smelling fish at a fish stall, choosing eels from barrels, tasting wine and olive oil, and calling to children who had escaped their constraints. Stalls stacked with woodcarvings, pottery, bales of brightly coloured cloth, art objects, intricate metalwork and painted stone carvings, looked close to collapsing under their weight. Both men and women wandering around the stalls were dressed in draped fabric of different shades of yellow, yet the sellers wore greens and browns: the style familiar to Annie from her visits to museums in Athens. The brightness and variety of colours; however, surprised her. She thought all togas were white. Women, examining contents of stalls, wore elaborate hairdos, intricately braided on their elegant heads and displayed heavily jewelled earings and necklaces.

Men stood apart in groups, involved in earnest conversations, serious and grave or laughing at a witty remark. It was easy to pick out slaves: both men, women and young people, dressed far more soberly in undyed hemp and carried heavily laden baskets while standing quietly behind various individuals.

"It's a good thing they can't see us. We would really stand out from these people in the different way we're dressed," Annie said. "Look at all of the different colours of the people's clothing, so interesting. This is Olbia, isn't it? It looks so prosperous and, well, Greek."

Meg turned back to her niece, "I believe it must be Olbia, and, as Asmud said, this town thrived long before the time of Christ. Are we correct, Asmud? Are we in Olbia? Asmud, did you hear me?"

A long pause, then Asmud spoke for the first time since they slipped through the wall. He sounded tense, as though he was forcing his words out through tightly compressed lips. "Yes, this is Olbia,"

"Tell us more, Asmud, you know so much of Greek history." Meg laughed, "You're not normally so shy about sharing."

Asmud sighed. "I learned more of Olbia's history in Constantinople. Greek settlements populated this whole area around the Black Sea. Greeks worked closely with their neighbours, the Scythians, who grew wheat for them to export to Greece and provided slave labour—just as we use Slavs today—I mean in my time."

Imposing buildings surrounded the large square, complete with more columns to emphasize their importance.

"Tell us more, Asmud. What are these beautiful buildings?"

Again, Asmud seemed to be struggling with his voice: emerging from his throat sounding strangled and clipped. "The building across from us is a gymnasium. I recognize the design, and a theatre next to it. That huge building further down the square with the pillars in front is a temple complex. Apollo, God of Music stands in front."

"Look how brightly painted he is," Annie exclaimed. "All of the statues I saw in Athens were white. I never realized how much the Greeks loved colour."

Meg turned back to her niece. "I don't know if you know this, Annie, but Apollo's twin sister is Artemis. She is our Goddess of childbirth."

Annie raised her eyebrows. "I didn't know that. I'll pray to her next time I'm struggling with a difficult birth. I'm amazed at the sophistication and beauty of the architecture from so long ago and these people were pioneers. They must have been brave to move so far from home."

"I think it's time we headed back," said Meg. "We've seen all the main sites and I don't want Ivar to become more irritated than usual."

43

"MATIÁ! MATIÁ! LOOK! LOOK!"

Annie spun around, startled by loud shouting. People in the huge square pointed at them, all shaking their fists and yelling. What happened? People could see them!

Meg hissed in dismay. "My spell is broken. How?"

They looked behind. Will still held onto Annie's girdle but Asmud—Asmud was on his knees a few paces back. Will released his hold on Annie and stepped back to help Asmud to his feet.

"What happened, my friend?"

"I tripped."

As all their attention fixed on Asmud, no one saw the fierce-looking men who appeared from nowhere and surrounded them.

"Who are you? Where have you come from? Who are you spying for?" These men did not look Greek. They wore red tunics and carried big staffs, which they used vigorously to prod the four. Their language was not Greek either but Annie, with her new gift of languages, could understand them.

"They are telling us to give up our weapons."

Asmud quickly handed over his sword but Will struggled: no one was going to take his precious longbow from him. A staff rattled the side of his head and he fell to his knees. One of the men relieved him of his bow and quiver.

"To King Scyles," the leader growled. "There'll be a reward for capturing this lot."

The men with staffs led their four bewildered captives back to the main street followed by a crowd of jeering people. Annie held Will's hand as he still looked stunned and blood oozed down his face, soaking into his beard.

The ragged procession reached a large gleaming, white building protected by an imposing wall with elaborately carved, heavy wooden gates. When the lead guard rapped on the gates with his staff, they swung open and a tall man, wearing a red padded tunic and carrying a spear, stepped forward.

"We have brought you spies, found sneaking around town. Armed and violent too."

While all of this was going on Rosamund and Bea remained tucked tightly in their baskets, covered by a scrap of wool. Palace guards took the place of the staff-carriers, wearing red, padded jackets embroidered with a crown. They all carried spears.

After waiting for what seemed like an interminable length of time in a small, hot chamber, guards led the four, sweating and thirsty, through a long corridor. They entered a large, sunlit room.

"On your knees before King Scyles, wretches. Eyes on the ground." Rough hands pushed their heads down.

"Arise, mysterious beings." A cultured voice, speaking accented Greek, reached Annie's ears. She and Asmud pulled the other two into a standing position.

A solidly built man of early middle years sat on an elaborately carved wooden chair mounted on a dais. He wore a purple Greek toga and a gold laurel wreath circled his head, yet his features were not Greek: Annie thought he rather resembled their new guards. An elegant younger woman also draped in flowing purple robes and with strong Greek facial features sat next to him on an equally elaborate chair. Her black hair was styled in intricate braids and covered with a fine gold mesh.

Grey-haired elders, wearing yellow togas, clustered behind them. On either side of the dais, a phalanx of stern-faced guards stood to attention, wearing the ubiquitous red padded tunics, helmets and spears.

"According to our *rabdouchoi*: our rod-bearers, guardians of peace and keepers of law and order; you four hid in the Agora in order to commit mischief against our city of Olbia. The penalty for this act is death. How say you?"

Annie waited for Asmud to speak in their defense as he spoke Greek but he remained silent. She turned to him, frowning, but he looked straight ahead, his face set in a bleak mask. Taking a deep breath and offering a prayer to any Greek Goddesses who might be listening, Annie addressed the king.

"Lord, Majesty. I can only say we come in peace and wish no harm to this beautiful city."

"Whence came you and how did you arrive here?"

"We came by sea from"—wracking her brain—what places existed in this, actually unknown period—"Byzantium and plan to return there. We anchored in your harbour in order to replenish supplies and visited the Agora to do just that but were prevented from doing so by your efficient, yet overly-zealous, guards."

"We have many visitors from Byzantium, the Golden City, but no reports have arrived of your ship and we have not seen your style of dress before. In addition, we are curious about your weapons and wish to examine them further. If you are, as you say you are, innocent travellers, you will not mind if we detain you longer while we decide your fate. *Evzoni:* guards, take the prisoners to a secure place. Treat them with respect—for now. Give them food and drink."

44

JORVIK

"I have them this time, Gösta. There is no escape. The big Rus was easy to manipulate. I implanted a picture into his savagely simple mind of his companions slaughtered by his hand along with a compulsion to kill. He tried to prevent himself from committing such a horrendous deed by separating himself from his friends. Such a pity his timing was so wrong for them and so right for me. I really am the queen of sorcerers."

Gunnhild smiled into the hand mirror her servant held up to her face. Her hair had begun to grow again. That arrogant young woman would pay heavily for what she did to Queen Gunnhild's shining black locks—and payment might be coming soon.

45

Annie sighed with relief. Their guards offered a platter of flatbread, soft goat's cheese, olives and a thin, watery, red wine, although this might be the last meal before their execution. Palace guards had escorted their prisoners to a small room empty of furniture, with only enough space for four of them, two cats at their feet, and two guards at the door.

Once again, Asmud's behaviour intrigued Annie. He neither ate nor drank. His whole body language made her think of a turtle pulling itself into its shell, as though he wished not to touch them. While eating, Meg, Will and Annie spoke quietly in English. Guards stared at their mouths as though it might help them to understand what these strange creatures whispered to each other.

Annie's stomach unclenched. She now knew what to say next in her story to King Scyles. She had instructed everyone regarding their parts. Even the cats, also now fed, knew what they had to do. She hoped Asmud had paid attention, as he showed no response to her proposals.

Eventually, the guards led them back into the same sunlit chamber where they found King Scyles pacing up and down. His eyes gleamed when he saw them and he waved them toward the dais as he returned to his throne.

"We are intrigued. We have questions about your weapons before we share our deliberations on your fate."

One of the palace guards brought forward Will's longbow and sheath of arrows and Asmud's sword. He lay them reverentially at the feet of King Scyles.

"My weapons experts have examined these thoroughly. Explain to me what materials have been used to forge this sword."

On saying this, the king glared at Asmud, as though accusing him of a misdemeanor. "And, you," his royal eyes bored into Will's, "what weapon is this? It looks like a bow yet none of my men can pull back the bowstring."

Annie cleared her throat, thereby earning her own kingly glare. "Majesty, may I speak for both as my Greek is much better than their poor offerings. My fear and hunger prevented me from telling our true story before, but now I know of your wisdom and mercy and believe I can tell you of our odyssey."

King Scyles grunted but nodded his head.

Annie's heart leaped; she knew the Greeks loved stories and she was about to tell a whopper, albeit mixed with a little truth. They had cleared the first and biggest hurdle.

"We come from a land many, many leagues from Olbia, called Garðariki: our people are Kievan Rus. Garðariki lies north of here, reaching almost to a vast sea. We know of snow, of floating ice mountains, of white bears prowling the land, of sleek seals that bark like dogs, of houses made of ice, and of giant oxen with huge horns. Do you have knowledge of our people?" Annie paused.

Scyles grunted again and shook his head, waving her on.

"The King of Garðariki is a wise and able ruler. He is aware of the isolation of his kingdom and wishes for his son and heir, Prince Sviatoslav, to see the world before he becomes king—"

"—What is this to us, woman. I asked for information about weapons, not far-off kingdoms."

"Lord and Lady," Annie bowed her head, pausing theatrically. "Allow me to present to you his Highness, Prince Sviatoslav of Rus, heir to the throne of Garðariki and his aunt, Princess Olga, younger sister of King Igor. This man," she pointed to Asmud, who still stared straight ahead, stone-faced, "is tutor to the prince and I am handmaiden to the princess."

"You expect me to believe such a story. Why would a prince and a princess not dress and travel according to their rank? Why is it that you, a servant, can speak excellent Greek and these others do not? If they are who you say they are would they not speak fluent Greek?"

Annie bowed her head, her mind searching frantically for plausibility within this fantasy.

"Prince Sviatoslav is travelling, as you say, *agnóristos*: incognito, so he may experience the world more openly. As for my history: as a young child, I became a prisoner of pirates. My mother was Greek and my father Danish. The pirates killed them after seizing our trading ship. Kievan Rus then captured their pirate ship. I have been with them ever since."

Before the king could ask any more awkward questions, Annie reached into the cat basket and, as the two cats leaped out, creating a distraction, Meg threw her henbane seeds into the air. They burst into a fine red dust and gently drifted down onto the heads of the people present. Just for a few seconds, the kΔing and his court saw the prince and his aunt in their royal regalia.

Newly named Prince Sviatoslav, aka Will, looked magnificent in a heavily embroidered tunic of red and blue with jewelled collar and cuffs and draped in a substantial cloak of blue with an elaborate gold and blue woven border. A large golden brooch secured a heavy woolen cloak at his shoulder. Soft leather boots came to his knees and a bejewelled hat trimmed with black fur adorned his royal head.

Fake Princess Olga/Meg matched her nephew's sartorial splendour, sumptuously dressed in a blue overdress deeply edged with gold thread. The lower edge of a soft pink under gown draped over leather boots. An ornate gold crown adorned her head and an equally ornate gold necklace completed her ensemble, each inset with gems. Rather than a cloak, a silver fox fur draped casually over one shoulder. Rosamund and Bea grew to their panther size, wearing jewelled collars; sitting like statues at the right hand of the prince and princess.

Seeing this royal couple set the Greek court back on their heels and their mouths fell open. As the king's wife recovered first, she stepped down from the dais.

"I am Queen Chrysanthe. I have a question. This country of yours… it is not located in the Underworld, I hope. To us, your black cats represent the Goddess Hecate: Queen of death and witches. Black cats are an omen of death. Is that why you are here, to warn us of a death to come? Are you witches?"

"We are, as I said, Majesty, travellers from Garðariki only. We bring no omens of death. We prize black cats in our land and consider them to be lucky." Well, the last bit is true, Annie added mentally.

"If that be so then you are welcome to Olbia and to our royal court."

She turned to her husband who still looked dazed. "I do believe we will escort our *guests* into the *peristyle* for refreshments."

Taking full control of proceedings, Queen Chrysanthe held out her hands in a gesture of invitation and led her ex-prisoners into an open courtyard bordered by pillars, with a fountain in one corner and a colourfully painted statue of Apollo gracing the centre. Rosamund and Bea, back to their normal size, followed decorously. Green foliage from trees and low bushes surrounded the courtyard; a musician seated on a bench played his lyre, gentle notes floating on the air.

Princess Olga sighed. "What a peaceful place, your Majesty."

"I spend most of my time here," the queen said, "away from the pomp and ritual of court. My women and I often do our spinning and weaving here rather than in close confines of the *gynaikonitis*: the women's quarter. My husband, you may have noticed, is not Greek. He is of the Scythian tribe. His mother, however, was Greek, just as is your handmaiden," she turned to acknowledged Annie, "and she raised him to appreciate Greek culture, unlike his fellow countrymen. They neither read nor write, whereas he enjoys music and literature. Here he comes now." She laughed quietly. "He appears quite recovered from your presentation."

Queen Chrysanthe clapped her hands and servants entered the courtyard carrying platters laden with fruits and cheeses.

King Scyles seated himself on a bench and invited his new guests to join him. "Prince Sviatoslav, my apologies for your former treatment. Unfortunately, our suspicious nature is warranted: enemies may appear from anywhere. We will, however, attempt to make amends. I am most interested to know more of your strange weapon. I have never seen such an exquisite bow: it is so long and the wood…" Scyles shook his head in disbelief.

Annie, still wracking her brains to come up with an escape plan, had an idea.

She murmured into her princess's ear.

Princess Olga smiled. "My servant suggests Prince Sviatoslav would be most amenable to demonstrate his skill with the longbow."

Prince Sviatoslav spoke up for the first time. "Lord, I would be most happy to show you the efficiency of the longbow. You may even want to try it for yourself; however we would require a large open space in which to do so."

A long pause followed. Annie unobtrusively gave Asmud a sharp rap with her foot.

Asmud emerged from his trance, his voice strained. "I know the perfect place. Remember where we came up the stairs from the docks, close to the tower named omega; I noticed a long wide, grassy area where it might be safe to practice. Arrows will fly a long way and we wish to avoid endangering observers."

Annie continued to translate for them while her mind remained engaged in the delicate process of their escape.

The king looked interested, even excited. "And you—tutor to the prince—how do you come to have such an amazing sword in your possession?"

Asmud, sounding incredibly weary, told a story of warriors who came from the west long ago and settled north of the Black Sea.

"We warriors believe that if we die with our swords in our hands we will go to a place called Valhalla where we will live with our God Odin and defend him against the evil forces of the underworld. Our swords have magic powers and we name them for an animal spirit. I named my sword *björn-bitr,* bear-bite: after our great white bear. I am tutor to the prince because our people follow an old tradition: the prince must be educated in the ways of the warrior." He paused. "May I show you the beauty of this sword?"

A palace guard brought *bear-bite* forward and, keeping a firm hold on the leather grip, held it out with the point toward Asmud. Asmud explained that he did not have any knowledge of how the sword had been forged; only the maker knew and he had carved this name on all his blades. He showed a fascinated audience the name Ulfberht.

"This sword will bite through any sword or knife unless it carries the same maker's name; hence its name of *björn-bitr.*"

Now, Annie and the others stared in amazement as Asmud turned to King Scyles and offered him his precious sword as a gift. "Take *björn-bitr*, Lord, and know you own a weapon mightier than any in your kingdom."

46

While the royal parties sat on benches in the *peristyle*, nibbling fruit and sipping wine, the king's men were in town seeking old palm-wood casks and red paint.

Annie, although ensuring she looked calm in appearance, fretted inside and she could see Meg fidgeting. Asmud still wore his dazed look; Annie could not understand why: Will suffered a blow to his head, not Asmud. Asmud was acting so out of character—and the way he handed over his precious sword so meekly to the king—it just did not make sense. They had to get out of here. Ivar would be beside himself, roaming around the island frantically searching for them. Her escape plan held risks: they might all die—and this time, no magic was involved—mostly.

After an eternity, just when Annie thought she might scream from tension, a palace guard entered the *peristyle* and whispered into the ear of one of the courtiers.

It was time to go.

Marching back through the town provided a contrast from marching to the palace. Drummers and tambourine players led the impromptu parade, followed by a haughty marching palace guard. King Scyles and Queen Chrysanthe walked casually behind, acknowledging their subjects with an occasional wave. Will and Meg, wearing their new status but same old clothes, walked behind them looking drab beside the royal purple, and yellows of the entourage. Annie, clutching her precious cat basket, merged with palace servants in the rear. She had searched in vain for Asmud when they left the palace gates behind but could not see him amongst bobbing heads.

Arriving at the *Agora*, shoppers began following them, along with a majority of stallholders. Rod-bearers joined in, leaving market stalls and their contents to the mercy of the gods. An excited buzz almost drowned out the drummers and tambourines: people were visibly puzzled at the change in fortune of the four arrested a short time ago.

The noisy, enthusiastic, and increasingly disorderly parade arrived at the designated meadow. As requested, two casks rested on the grass, filled with sand; tiny red circles painted, somewhat shakily, in the centre, on one end, wet paint forming rivulets. Will instructed Asmud to pace off thirty strides from the omega tower, then twenty strides more, marking each spot with a rock. Slaves rolled the two casks to the thirty and fifty stride mark.

More slaves placed four chairs, carried from the palace, into a good viewing location for the royal party at the side of the green, away from the direct flight of the arrows. Annie's heart sank when she saw the chairs. Mobility was paramount to her plan. Will could freely move around as the star attraction but the placement of the royal viewers would trap Meg at the wrong side of the open space.

The throng increased in numbers rapidly as word spread throughout town. They crowded into the newly formed arena and lined the defense walls with some hardier souls climbing up towers. Shrieking children and barking dogs tore around. Spring grasses and flowers lost their jaunty bounce and lay flattened as the scene disintegrated into chaos. Palace guards and rod-bearers formed a protective half-circle around the royal chairs yet did nothing to calm the frenetic scene.

A loud voice arose above the hubbub.

"*Kairete Polla:* Citizens of Olbia; Many Greetings. What we are about to show you is dangerous. Guard your children. Control your dogs. Move away from these walls and come down from the towers. Be seated on the grass at the far side of the casks."

Annie translated: her voice heard clearly in the sudden quiet.

Will, standing tall and holding his longbow, repeated his words once, then again. His quiet demeanour and soothing voice calmed the multitude, which began corralling its children and animals. Rod-bearers came over to the wall and encouraged people there, with energetic use of their rods, to move to the other side and away from the barrels.

Finally, the stage was set.

Will stood alone with his longbow, by their omega tower, his quiver of arrows strapped around his waist. Annie moved to his right and Asmud to his left, their movements carefully orchestrated. Will surveyed all, bowed to the royal party, and then rechecked the whereabouts of Annie and Asmud. He visibly took a deep breath, then pointed his bow towards the ground and nocked an arrow onto its rest, lightly holding it against the bowstring. In one fluid movement, he raised his bow, aimed the arrow at the thirty-stride cask, pulled back his right arm, and released the bowstring. Flying faster than the eye could see the arrow pierced the tiny red circle. Just as rapidly, he fired off two more arrows in succession, each finding the same red dot. After a stunned silence, the crowd roared.

Will waited for people to settle down. Dramatically, he repeated his performance with three more arrows into the centre of the second barrel placed fifty strides from the tower. After more roars from spectators had abated, he turned toward the royal party.

"Lord," he called over to King Scyles, "would you or your men wish to try my bow?"

King Scyles shook his head hastily and no one else stepped forward.

"My aunt also shows some skill with the longbow. In our land both men and women, boys and girls, practice archery. Princess Olga, please come forward and show the people of Olbia what you can do."

Meg looked startled. This had not been in Annie's script, but she rose from her chair and approached Will with a confident step.

Will grasped Meg's arm and steered her closer to the omega tower. Annie continued to translate, hoping her voice would not display her nervousness. Her heart pounded so hard in her chest she was convinced people could see the fabric of her gown pulsing.

The moment of extreme danger had arrived.

Will addressed the crowd, raising his voice so all could hear. "Before I hand this longbow to Princess Olga I have one more task to perform."

Annie's translating voice developed a wobble.

Will spun around, hands blurring as he nocked another arrow to his bow. He raised his bow, the arrow pointing at the chest of King Scyles, ruler of Olbia.

"If anyone moves I will release this arrow into the heart of your king."

The crowd inhaled as one then quieted.

"My Lord King, we apologise for our rudeness and thank you for your hospitality but we must return from whence we came—NOW!"

The people of Olbia would talk about what they then witnessed for years to come: their story becoming part of the fabric of their oral history.

The four strangers turned and walked through the wall.

47

Meg's group had not noticed the fading light until they stood on the other side of the wall; only now, no high wall existed, just a line of stones half concealed by fresh green spring grasses.

Annie and Meg sank to their knees as they realized their safe return. Annie held out her open palm to her aunt and showed her a beautiful little, green, bronze dolphin.

"I found him on the floor in the peristyle. I hoped he would bring us luck and he did."

Will grasped Asmud by the shoulders and shook him: a big grin on his face. They all began to speak at once.

"Will, your skill with the bow"—Meg.

Annie—"I can't believe we're sa—"

Will—"what an unbelievable experi—"

Annie—"Asmud, you are not saying anything. Are you alright?"

Asmud had collapsed onto the bank, and to everybody's dismay, he covered his face with his hands and groaned. "I am so sorry for the trouble I caused but I had to save you. Even now, you are all in danger from me. I am fighting this with every bone in my body."

"What are you talking about?" Meg looked at him in alarm.

"This overpowering thought came into my head as soon as we went through the wall—I must kill them. I will cut off their heads: Will first; then Annie; and—may the Goddess Freyja forgive me— you, my sweet Meg."

He broke off as his body shook with a spasm of sobbing.

Annie could not believe her eyes. This man, who shared so little of his feelings and wore a mask of impassivity, had disintegrated in front of them. Meg reached out to comfort him but he drew away.

"Stay away from me; I am contaminated. I don't deserve your friendship or," he turned to Meg, "your love." He quieted and took a deep breath. "That is why I separated myself from you and gave up my sword—reducing the chance of my being able to use it against you. But you need to know, if I get the opportunity, I still wish to kill you, my friends, including you, my dear one." He looked at Meg.

Annie stared at the distraught man. Something was wrong, she thought. Asmud may act aloof sometimes but he was no assassin. When someone begins acting differently—think of Queen Gunnhild.

"Asmud, look at me." Her voice, strong and commanding, reached through to Asmud. He moved his hands from his face and stared at her. Annie narrowed her eyes and opened her arms wide. "You called on the Goddess Freyja, then so shall I—Lady—Goddess of Love; come forth and help us. Remove whatever venom is affecting this man."

A now familiar feeling encompassed her as her heart rate increased; electricity coursed through her body and sparks of light shot from her outstretched fingertips. Rosamund and Bea leaped from the confines of their baskets and yowled.

A cloak of falcon feathers floated down from high above them and wrapped itself around the kneeling figure of Asmud.

Annie's mouth opened and a voice emerged—not her own—but lighter; sounding like a spring bubbling over river rocks.

"My Varangian friend; you were deceived by a powerful sorcerer who continues attempting to prevent the success of you courageous searchers. She placed murderous thoughts into your mind setting you against your companions in order to end your mission. I commend you for your vigour in resisting carrying out her commands. My cloak of feathers will draw her poison from your blood. Be as you were.

"Remain vigilant. She will try again. I cannot prevent her meddling. Re-enforce your protective mantle daily."

Annie's eyes fully opened; she wrapped her arms around herself as electricity drained from her body and watched Goddess Freya's legendary feathered cloak float upward. Asmud stood and hugged each of his friends in turn, his beard soaked with tears.

"Time to find Ivar, I believe."

48

Ivar tasted the stew bubbling away over the fire. "Tha's just in time. T'fish stew's ready an' Lars is mekkin' up some oatcakes."

Will looked at the others and raised his eyebrows. "We thought you'd be out searching for us, Ivar. I am sorry we were away for so long."

"Nay, lad. Ave 'ardly missed thee at all. Tha can't 'ave seen much; short time tha's bin away."

Lars looked up from his oatcakes. "Aye, a were reight mad when a found out tha'd gone explorin' without me, but a can see tha 'asen't 'ad time to do owt."

Annie remembered that once before, Meg had explained that when a person steps out of time, time itself becomes undefined. The last few hours had seemed to them so agonizingly long, whereas to Ivar, cooking his fish stew, and Lars, busy with chores, hours had flown.

"Word is we'll be off at sunrise. Lars says t'sails are up an' ready to go. We'll soon sail into Byzantium and none-too-soon for me."

"Tell you what," Asmud offered an un-Asmud like grin, "we've got quite a story to share with you over your stew."

49

A robust wind filled the large, square sails of the fleet. High bow waves painted fragmenting rainbows caused by rays of early morning sun. Finne told them the current was strong off the western shore of the Black Sea and flowed from north to south.

"If this wind stays with us we will see the Bosporus in less than six days."

When Annie reflected on their voyage from Olbia to the mouth of the Bosporus, she could still smell herring sprats sizzling on grills and salivated at the memory of clam and shrimp soup with spring greens. She smiled remembering the dolphins diving through the bow waves and replayed many intimate moments shared with Will.

Those few days were a joy. The Black Sea, being shallower near the shore, warmed relatively quickly as they moved south, as did the air. From sunrise to early evening, ships took advantage of strong winds and made good time hugging the coast, salt spray cooling the travellers. Because winds were constant, merchant warriors lounged on deck, trawling for herring and mackerel. Only the tiller man worked. Despite a crowded deck, people found their own space; moods were light and the daily routine unhurried and pleasurable. When the sun had completed three quarters of its journey, the fleet would anchor by the accessible shore and strike camp. Once everyone completed their chores, all would head down to the water.

Bathing was the priority, although to Annie it seemed a frolic in slightly salty water. Then the serious business of food gathering began. The Black Sea was generous in its bounty and seasoned travellers knew where oyster beds grew. These oysters were not only flavourful but also pretty, their white shells lightly tinted pink or green. A few adventurous men, roped together, reached the rocky reefs lined with mussels just offshore, and with a sharp knife, soon had the mussels in a basket. Others waded deep into the water, casting fishing lines for mullet and flatfish. A few threw nets into the coastal shallows where huge shoals of Black Sea herring sprats gathered.

Annie and Will became experts at digging for clams in the shallow sandy bottom and finding crabs and shrimp amongst the rock pools. Rocky promontories formed small coves and they climbed over the rocky barriers with their bounty, finding private little stretches of warmed sand where the two of them lingered until sunset.

Because of this seafood bounty and an abundance of spring greens, the *náttmál* and the *dagmál* became meals of epicurean delight. A now depleted ale and wine store might have caused concern but fresh spring water always seemed available to fill the water barrels.

Rosamund and Bea also took full advantage of these halcyon days. Annie hardly saw them as the cats spent most of their time hunting in the long grasses or sleeping in warm sheltered hollows.

Given all the opportunity for rest and relaxation, balmy weather and abundant food, Meg and Annie's two patients returned to health. Daily bathing in salt water hastened the healing of both wounds and their wan faces regained colour—and not just them; when Annie looked around, everyone looked healthier. Traders had also taken to trimming one another's hair and beard in preparation for arrival in Constantinople. Even slaves, both male and female, took care of each other's grooming. Annie made a note to talk to Meg about giving one another a trim. Annie's bouncing curls had taken on a life of their own and needed taming.

The holiday ended when a shout came down the line—"Bosporus ahead". For a second Annie felt a deep twinge of regret that this special time with Will had ended. Then she remembered their mission—find the twins. A shiver went through her as she considered what might lay ahead for the searchers in Istanbul, Constantinople, Miklagarðr, the Golden City, Byzantium; so many names for one fabled city.

50

Rowers bent to their oars as tillermen steered south into the Bosporus. High rocky cliffs loomed on either side of the narrow strait. As the heavily laden ships moved down the seaway, Annie experienced a strong sense of déja vu. She had celebrated the end of her midwifery training with a week's holiday in Turkey along with a classmate: three beach days in Bodrum and two in Istanbul. They had crossed the Bosporus on the Galata Bridge to the Asian side after their hotel receptionist insisted.

"You must see the real Istanbul, not just the tourist places," he stabbed at a map of Istanbul, "and be sure to take a boat trip along the Bosporus."

All the photos from that trip were on her laptop at home: stunning villas, soaring bridges, defensive fortifications on high cliffs. This journey would be different. Ironically, they would see the 'real Constantinople,' not as a tourist mecca but as a living, breathing city.

Finne visited Annie and Meg, weaving his way between moving oars.

"Keep your eyes on the cliff top. Soon you will see signal fires lighted, to warn the Byzantine Navy we are on our way. Fortunately, they will greet us as friends and not as enemies. I'd hate to experience their Greek fire."

Only a few years earlier Prince Svetoslav's father, Igor of Kiev, had sailed a fleet of ships into the harbour at Constantinople. The Byzantium Navy, with a reduced number of available ships to guard the city, spread Greek fire across the water, setting fire to Rus ships, causing chaos, many crew choosing to drown rather than burn to death.

"To this day, no one knows how they made Greek fire. Its formula is lost in antiquity. King Igor may have lost the battle, but due to on-going threats from Rus leaders, the Emperor signed a Treaty, and that's why we are able to be here. When the Byzantine Navy arrives, we must show them a charter from the Prince of Kiev stating how many ships we have and how many people are on board. They monitor us carefully." Finne laughed. "The Greeks are still afraid of us."

Shortly after Finne alerted them to watch for the signal fires, Ivar, still unable to row though his arm was healing, pointed up to the top of the cliff. A plume of smoke rose into the air.

"There's them signals Finne told us about. Won't be long afore t'-navy'll cum to greet us."

As the slow-moving trading ships continued their passage down the Bosporus Strait, waves offered less resistance than in the Black Sea, and as a strong current flowed from north to south, progress remained steady.

When the lead ship steered toward a small bay sheltered by a rocky outcrop, the sun was well past its zenith. Ships followed like obedient ducklings and dropped anchor as close to shore as possible.

"We'll make camp here tonight so we can arrive in the harbour tomorrow with plenty of daylight left," said Finne. "Be prepared. We will have guests for *náttmál*."

Finne prophesied correctly. Thralls had just commenced preparation for *náttmál* when a sentry shouted, "*Skeid koma!* Warship approaches!"

Two dromons, both at least forty metres long, with two banks of oars working and three raised lateen sails, flew up the strait, bow waves high, Imperial Byzantine flag flying: a yellow cross on a red background. The large cannon mounted in the bow and archers clustered aft raised Finne's eyebrows.

"They're showing us they mean business."

The dromons slowed, bow waves diminishing. In an impressive show of seamanship, the crew lowered the sails, banked the oars and glided to anchor, one on each side of the Rus fleet.

"Quite the pair of bookends," Annie joked to Meg, then had to explain the meaning of 'bookends.'

Sailors quickly lowered the gangplank on one ship and a party of naval officers disembarked.

Asmud pointed to the colourful group marching smartly toward them. "That one with the red plumes is a *Kentarchos:* a captain. He's the man we have to convince we are traders only."

Annie immediately thought of a tableau of Roman soldiers: the officers' helmets adorned with plumes, their short skirts overlaid with leather strips and embossed metal breastplates. Of course, the Roman Emperor Constantine had founded Constantinople. Twelve formidable spearmen, complete with large shields, escorted the party. Farulfr, leader of the Rus, dressed in his Varangian finery, stepped forward to greet the naval officers and immediately handed over a rolled parchment, which the captain proceeded to read intently.

"That must be the charter from Prince Sviatoslav," Annie explained to Will, Ivar and Lars and related the background of Igor of Kiev's failed battle and resulting trade treaty.

As all eyes focused on the small group of men; water lapping onto the shore provided a muted backdrop. Even the seagulls remained quiet. After an eternity during which the traders held their communal breath, the senior officer rolled up the charter and reached out his hand to clasp the arm of Farulfr.

A cheer broke out and the atmosphere changed instantly. Invited to share the *náttmál*, helmets came off navy heads and thralls brought forward the last few flagons of wine.

As *náttmál* progressed, lamps glowed on the dromons' decks. Annie sensed hundreds of eyes watching as the Byzantine crew remained vigilant. Their officers might be consorting with the Varangians but that did not mean these traders could be trusted. Spearmen continued to stand to attention behind their seated officers. Eventually, after a long evening of feasting on the remaining Black Sea harvest, officers returned to their respective ships, having told the traders they would remain anchored all night and escort the fleet into harbour tomorrow.

Annie and Meg stayed in the shadows during the evening, 'keeping their heads down in the trenches,' as Annie quipped to her aunt, who had no idea what she meant. Thankful the long day was over; they crawled wearily into their tent along with Rosamund and Bea. Meg sleepily whispered good night then offered a prayer to the Goddess Hecate for good fortune in Constantinople.

51

Long before dawn, the fleet of Varangian trading ships began the final leg of its journey to Constantinople with a dromon positioned ahead and astern, the dromons engaging only a quarter of their oars in order to maintain pace with the slow-moving traders.

Will, Asmud and Lars rowed while Annie, Meg and Ivar sat back and enjoyed the scenery and balmy weather; the cats curled in their baskets. As the sun rose higher into a clear, blue sky, its rays warmed the non-rowers and made rowers uncomfortably hot. Moving further down the strait, shipping traffic increased with small fishing boats; trading ships heavy with goods; an occasional military vessel on manoeuvres and, more frequently, small craft coming out to join the cavalcade. Word was spreading that Rus' were on their way.

Up to now, Annie had enjoyed the fresh smell of tangy seawater in a light breeze but now a new mixture of smells was finding their way to them: spices.

"Cinnamon, definitely cinnamon," Annie sniffed.

"Cumin, I think," Meg countered, "with a hint of ginger."

"Tha can both shut up," grumbled Ivar. "Me stomach's rumblin' as it is. There weren't much food left for *dagmál* after that lot 'ad finished last night."

"Apart from finding the twins, I am looking forward to replenishing my stock of spices and herbs; not to mention the dishes we will get to enjoy." Meg's face lit up at the prospect ahead.

Annie smiled her agreement then frowned. "No one has said anything about where we will stay in the city. We have to talk to Asmud the first chance we get, and we will have to buy new clothes. These are almost worn out from washing," gesturing to her now ragged apron dress.

"You told me you had travelled on the Bosporus before, Annie. How are you finding it this time?"

Annie laughed. "Empty. In my century, it remains one of the busiest shipping lanes in the world. There is constant movement of trading ships travelling up and down as well as ferries and tour boats. There are soaring bridges and Ottoman fortresses and castles on either side. Palaces and villas line the shores and, as we get closer to The Golden Horn, there are outdoor cafés and restaurants. Topkapi Palace is visible for miles before we get there as it is set on one of the highest hills. Of course, we won't see that as it was also built by the Ottomans."

Ivar, listening to this conversation, looked at Annie in total disbelief. "A think tha's been dreamin', lass. There's no room for all that stuff—an' who the 'ell are the Ottapans when they're at 'ome?"

The three continued their conversation as they drew closer to the city. Even Ivar became more animated as anticipation grew. More craft surrounded the convoy, cheering and waving; welcoming their yearly visitors, in sharp contrast to the Byzantine Navy. Varangians began singing to the rhythm of the oars. Annie listened to the words—amazing exploits of warriors against their enemies—no love ballads from this lot. She and Meg drummed on the gunwale matching the rhythm. The last few miles sped by. An excited shout from a rower had every head swinging around. The mighty sea walls of Constantinople were coming into view.

Crenellated stone walls guarded Constantinople on both land and sea fronts. Annie couldn't see where the walls started and ended: winding into infinity. Across the Bosporus from the walled city, a tall tower stood on a hill, dominating the skyline. Asmud had mentioned this tower to her and Meg before they left on this day's journey.

Annie pointed to the tower. "It's called the Galata Tower and houses the mechanism for a huge underwater chain guarding the entrance to the Golden Horn."

Annie did know of the Galata Tower from modern times and had toured it on her visit; however, the Genoese built that particular tower in the fourteenth century after Crusaders destroyed the older one. This tower's life stretched, like the walls, back into antiquity.

To her surprise, the lead dromon did not enter the harbour of the Golden Horn but continued south, the entire city displayed on their right side. Just before they turned yet another corner, she saw a series of impressive buildings climbing up a terraced slope.

"The Great Palace," called Asmud from his place at the oars.

After they turned west, another huge, long building came into view. She waited for Asmud's call...

"...the Hippodrome."

The convoy continued past two large harbours and Annie commented that they were going to finish up out at sea again. Eventually, the lead dromon pulled into a sizable anchorage, the massive breakwater providing shelter for many ships. Another large tower, not as massive as the Galata, stood guard at the far end. Storage buildings and silos clustered around the tower, dwarfed by its height.

One by one, Varangian ships lined up at the wharf and tired rowers hopped out and secured their hard-working vessels front and aft. As before, the two dromons tied up too, one at each end.

"Back to the bookends," laughed Annie.

Seagulls wheeled above the now frenetic activity below them, curious at the goings on at the docks and looking for scraps. Annie, Meg and Ivor, the cats still safe in their baskets, had scrambled off their ship with the help of Lars and now stood watching, along with the birds.

All of the cargo loaded so many weeks ago in both the Baltic and Kiev was piling up on the wharf. Carts and wagons, pulled by mules, formed a line: their drivers shouting to each other and to the Rus to get their attention. Soldiers from the two dromons oversaw everything.

Finally, a sweating Finne came over to the small group. "We will be setting off shortly. Nothing can be left here or it will never be seen again."

"Where are we going, Finne?" asked Annie, anxious and hoping someone saw order amongst the seeming chaos.

"We are going to St. Mamas. St. Mamas is an area outside of the walls assigned to us in the last trading treaty. I will tell you more about it when we have time. Just stay close to our ship's group and don't wander off."

With those terse comments, Finne turned on his heels and went back to work.

Still apprehensive and more than a little helpless, Annie stood silently with the others amongst the hustle and bustle, their immediate future uncertain and unknown.

52

Annie regarded the tiny and windowless room in which she and Meg now stood and felt like sinking to her knees and crying. "Well, we're here the Golden City. I'm not sure I like it so far."

Aunt Meg looked like Annie felt.

Walking behind the carts and wagons from the harbour to the St. Mamas quarter had left them hot and dusty. Noisy onlookers lined the narrow street, excited to catch a first glimpse of the fabled Rus traders. Soldiers marching ahead and behind the cavalcade did not relieve any tension. Stern faces, chain mail body armour, belted swords and large axes made it clear they would tolerate no stepping out of line.

Meg put her finger to her lips and shook her head. "I'll check with Asmud about his plans regarding his guests. We may not even be staying here with the traders." She left Annie alone in the bare room to look after Rosamund and Bea who were complaining loudly about being constrained in their baskets for so long.

Meg returned with Asmud and Finne, both men looking exhausted.

"Where are Will, Lars, and Ivar?" asked Annie as soon as the two large men came in, filling all the space in the room.

"Still helping with unpacking," replied Finne. "I am here only as a courtesy to you, my friends. Those two trade treaties between our people and Byzantium laid down strict rules. The Byzantines will treat us well. They provision us with bread, wine, beer, fish and fruits. The first food supplies are coming in as I speak; that is the reason why I do not have much time right now. Access to bathhouses is free.

There is a small one just down the road from here so please go and enjoy the experience. Not the grandest bathhouse I have experienced but it will do. Here are some tokens.

"Now, as the Byzantines worry about us they have laid down strict rules. We must stay in the St. Mamas area unless trading. We can only enter the city through one gate—the Golden Gate—accompanied by a Byzantine official, weaponless and having registered our names first. I tell you this because these rules will affect the movements of your companions."

Annie's face must have portrayed her despondency. Asmud jumped in quickly. "Tomorrow after we have all rested and cleaned ourselves up, I plan to take you both to the market for new clothes. Then we will go to the Grand Palace. I will leave my letter of introduction from Princess Olga with the court officials. We play a waiting game until we hear back. I am hoping we will be able to stay at the palace as emissaries of the princess."

Sweat dripped off the end of Asmud's nose. Like a six-year-old, he wiped the drops off on his sleeve and Annie laughed, feeling lighter. "Sounds like a plan, Asmud. In the meantime, I think my aunt and I may take you up on your offer of cleaning up. I don't know what to do with the cats, though."

Asmud offered to take them into the area behind their building for some exercise. "You will find Constantinople is full of cats," he said, smiling. "Locals take good care of them as they keep the vermin down."

After Finne and the others left, Annie and Meg climbed down the outside staircase of their newly assigned building to seek the public baths. Apparently, the building's second floor provided living accommodation and shops lined the street level.

Constantinople air felt hot and dry, adding to their discomfort, but curiosity about their surroundings overcame misery. Narrow streets lined with arcades on both sides enticed, offering shade. Annie and Meg had to manoeuvre past piles of cargo which men were unloading from carts while weary-looking slaves carried large bundles of goods. Their travelling companions waved at them as they recognized the two völvas.

Annie was even hotter and sweatier by the time she and Meg saw the bathhouse, easy to recognize as an inscription on the wall written in Greek read, 'Κολύμβησης είναι καλό για σας'—'Bathing is good for you'.

The bathhouse also distinguished itself from neighbouring buildings structured of plain plaster. This edifice showed off its grey stone and red intricate brickwork with many arches and a dome in the centre. Another sign outside notified all that men had the use of the baths until noon and women until sunset on this day.

"I don't have a swimsuit, Aunt Meg." Annie dragged her feet in the entrance.

Meg took her arm. "I don't know what a swimsuit is but you do not require anything. Let's go; trust me, you will enjoy this. Don't be shy."

On hearing *that* piece of advice, Annie felt even more apprehensive. She was not parading around naked for anyone.

Annie lay on her belly, as naked as all the newborns she had ever delivered, a female bath attendant vigorously scrubbing her back with a muslin cloth. Aunt Meg lay on the next slab, undergoing the same treatment and laughing at Annie's scarlet face. They were in the caldarium: a room made hot and steamy from a large pool of hot water in the centre. Other women appeared to be having various treatments, either to their hair or to their skin. One woman yelled loudly as an attendant plucked hair from her armpits. Women ranged from young to old and appeared comfortable in their nakedness. Annie listened to their chatting; distancing herself from her current skin care. She heard snippets about the latest hairstyles; arguments about the fastest chariot driver… Florentinus the most handsome… who's master or mistress the most tolerant… when the next races were scheduled at the Hippodrome.

Annie surmised that many of these women were servants or slaves; this must be a 'working class' bathhouse.

Annie's skincare expert had completed her energetic administrations and Annie was enjoying the warmth of the warm stone slab melting the tension in her belly and slowly sliding into sleep when she heard a voice close to her ear.

"I 'eard my mistress talking about that rich Greek, you know, the one what collects things. Apparently, 'e's been showing off 'is newest find at the last games. Whatever it is, it's sure to be the colour of silver. You know how 'e is. I was at the races with my mistress when 'e brought his white monkey. 'E 'ad it on a gold chain, sweetest little blonde thing you ever did see."

Annie sat up abruptly, and, forgetting her nakedness, looked around for the owner of the comments but steam in the room seemed to deflect sounds. Anyone around them could have uttered those words. Surely, the woman must have referred to Ivar's twins. Turning toward her aunt who lay emitting gentle snores, she shook Meg's shoulder.

"Aunt Meg, we need to get out of here. I have just heard news about the twins."

Meg looked sleepily at her niece. "We still have to go to the frigidarium to cool down."

"How many rooms are there in this place?"

They had started in the apoditarium where, after offering the tokens given by Finne, an attendant helped them out of their clothes and gave them a tiny towel and wooden sandals. An utterly inadequate towel, judged Annie, exposed and vulnerable, and trying unsuccessfully to cover herself, but Aunt Meg seemed to take it all in stride.

Apprehensively entering the tepidarium, Annie found it comfortable enough, other than having too small a towel, as a gentle heat radiated from floor and walls. Women either sat or lay on stone benches, gossiping idly to each other.

Then they clattered their way into another room, round in shape, sandals protecting bare feet from hot floors and heat much fiercer. Annie was surprised to find no water here, just benches and braziers giving off heat from burning charcoal. A few women sat on benches and another attendant signalled for Meg and Annie to join them. This attendant: a large woman unconcerned by her own expanse of wobbly, exposed flesh began coating Annie with oil. Annie reared back, but the woman's large hands pinned her down. Then the same woman brought out a long curved metal tool and began scraping off the oil. Annie looked wildly around for her aunt; when she saw she was having the same treatment she relaxed a little. They had moved on from there to the caldarium with the communal pool.

Now they were in the frigidarium. Annie, enjoying her warm, glowing skin, cried, "You want me to jump in that cold water—now—after all that."

At last, they were dressed, albeit in soiled clothing, and sipping on a sweetened drink in a tiny tree-shaded patio, Annie still recovering from the shock of her first experience, not only of public baths, but also of public toilets—five seats in a row allowed for the further sharing of gossip. She had thought Vikings to scorn privacy, but Byzantines had none of her English inhibitions.

She recounted to her aunt the words heard earlier.

"This woman mentioned a rich Greek and something about his newest acquisitions. She said he shows them off at the Hippodrome. It sounds like it might be Gennadios of Mytilene."

"This is good news, and so soon after we arrived. We must tell Ivar."

After finishing their drinks, the two returned to the long narrow street. Annie was in the middle of telling her aunt how she had never felt so scrubbed clean when Will and Lars came running up the street toward them. The men had to wind their way through all of the obstructions and their faces reflected agitation and frustration.

"Ivar has vanished. We haven't seen him since we started unpacking. We each believed him to be with the other."

Annie and Meg looked at them in consternation.

"He'll be heading into the city," Meg raised her hand to her mouth. "Oh, poor Ivar. He must feel so close to his children. And we have news for him."

"But he can't get into t'city," said Lars. "Finne 'asn't 'ad time t'register our names yet. 'E won't get through t'gate."

Annie looked back toward the city. "Then he'll be following the city walls, looking for an opening. This could be bad. Those soldiers are pretty serious about keeping us under control."

Will touched Annie's cheek with his finger. "Go back to your room and check on the cats. Asmud will have left them fastened in there. Lars and I will walk around the wall. We'll ask people if they've seen a crazy Viking—I'm jesting, Annie. We'll find him."

53

Loud banging at the door of Meg and Annie's room startled them. Annie flew to the door, expecting Will and Lars. A furious looking Finne stood there, accompanied by a large Byzantine soldier who easily held a defiant-faced Ivar by the scruff of his neck.

"Didn't I tell you about the rules laid down in the treaty? You are all more trouble than you are worth. This *fifi*, this idiot, attempted to bribe a gatekeeper at the Golden Gate to give him entry into Constantinople. His actions could jeopardize our entire trade mission. The army is demanding we hand him over for suspected treason."

Annie stifled a desire to throw her arms around Ivar. She looked first at Finne and then at the soldier. His helmet's rim shadowed the soldier's uncompromising eyes.

"Sir," she said, having no idea how to address a soldier. "This poor man is searching for his children. I am sure he attempted to explain this but cannot speak your language. We have come all this way to your beautiful city to find his twin girls, stolen from him in far-away England, having information that they are here. He became distraught, knowing he was so close. We are awaiting an audience with your Emperor who we are hoping will be able to help us."

Annie watched the soldier's eyes but saw no change in the degree of coldness. She sensed Meg stirring behind her. A draught of warm air brushed her skin and flowed toward the three men.

For a few seconds the group stood frozen and silent, and then the soldier released his grip on Ivar's neck.

"I too, have children," the soldier's voice clotted with emotion. "They are far away from here with my wife and mother in Edirne. I see them rarely. I feel your pain, comrade."

He grasped Ivar by the shoulders and pulled him to his mail-covered chest. Snapping a crisp salute to an astonished Finne, the soldier wheeled around and left.

Finne stared at the two women. "You did something, didn't you? These soldiers are as hard as nails. I've never seen one behave that way."

Meg smiled. "A little compassion never hurt anyone."

Finne shook his head in disbelief and turned to Ivar. "You got away with being stupid this time. Do not let it happen again or we *will* abandon you to the authorities. When I have registered your names you may travel into the city as you will, until then, stay close."

After Finne left, there seemed to be more oxygen to breathe.

"How did you do that, you amazing woman?" Annie turned to her aunt.

"As I said, a little compassion never hurts. I just softened his soldier's heart so he could feel his own love and yearning for his children."

Annie had just finished telling Ivar of the conversation she had heard in the bathhouse when Will and Lars burst into the room.

"Tha'll never believe this," cried an excited Lars. "We checked with t'gatekeeper at t'Golden Gate—would tha believe it—he's frum t'Baltic region— and he told us that one of them new visitors tried to bribe 'im and 'as been thrown in t'guardhouse. It 'ad t'be Ivar—by Thor!—is that thee, Ivar?"

Lars and Will stared in amazement at their missing friend, looking abjectly miserable, crouched in a corner of the room.

Meg and Annie filled them in on the most recent events and on their bathhouse findings.

Will reached for Annie's hand and looked intensely into her eyes. "I think it's time to scrounge our evening meal and then get some rest. It's all up to Asmud now. I'm going to ask him if he can find a role for me if you all go to the palace. I don't want to let you out of my sight."

54

Although it was only mid-morning, Constantinople's heat already felt oppressive. Led by Asmud, the group appreciated cooling shade offered under long porticoes. The Mese, the main ceremonial road through the city, was lined on both sides by colonnaded arches. They were on their way to a shopping spree with money from Ivar's purse, given to him in Jorvik by Queen Iseabail.

Asmud had explained how the efficient organization of trading in Constantinople worked. "It's controlled by one man, the *Eparch*. He tells guilds what they can and cannot do; where they can set up their shops; even how they can display their goods. I swear before Odin you will see more shops than you have ever seen in your lives."

He looked at each of them and laughed. "You can't go before the Emperor wearing these clothes. It is imperative we look influential, as if we have power. I brought my court outfit with me. You all look like sad Slavs."

Annie looked down at her clothes. Her linen shift was in tatters, while her woolen apron dress sagged and bagged and, in this heat, felt like a blanket. Aunt Meg's flushed face showed the same effect. Annie blew black curls away from her damp forehead and resolved to remain positive. She had recently become aware of a rock sitting in her belly. It had sat there, she now realized, since landing on the wharf cobbles at Theodosius. She did not know why a rock was there, nor had she been able to put a name to it.

When they arrived at the stunning Golden Gate from the St. Mamas region, guards gave Annie and her aunt a strange look; Annie even detected a sneer from one guard as he checked their names against a list and searched the men for weapons. Another guard examined Annie and Meg, taking full advantage of running his hands over their bodies before allowing passage through.

Once Annie recovered from wanting to punch him in the face, she wished she had her phone with her to take pictures. The Golden Gate, Asmud explained, was built hundreds of years ago by Emperor Theodosius, as a triumphal arch through which he would pass with his armies on his return from successful battles. The three arches of the Gate were built of polished marble and covered with gilded metal and supported two winged females representing victory. Four bronze elephant statues graced the roof.

Will complained about not being able to wear his dagger; he felt naked without having it strapped to his side. Annie bit back a retort; wait until you hit the bathhouse—then you'll really feel naked. Rosamund and Bea trotted along behind, looking pleased to be free, navigating the crowded pavement with ease.

The Mese was wide but throngs of people, pushing heavily loaded carts or driving horse-drawn wagons, left little room. All were heading to the markets with their goods. Along the way, beautiful buildings helped take the travellers' minds off the long road. A monastery and a magnificent church, both built in a typical Byzantine pattern of many domes, elaborate brickwork, and pantile roofs, looked down at everyone.

Further on, a tall column rose high above and appeared to signal the Mese's termination, but as Annie came closer she realized they were entering a forum. What had appeared as walls from a distance were symmetrical arches enclosing a large public square. A rank animal smell seared her nostrils. Enclosures containing pigs or sheep filled the square. The animals milled around uneasily, making sounds of soft distress. Men shouted numbers at each another. Customers crowded around to inspect stock. No one paid their group any attention.

"It's a bloody meat market," Ivar commented, looking around.

"It's the most elegant meat market I've ever seen." Meg pointed to a tall, imposing column in the centre of the square displaying reliefs of soldiers in action, spiralling up to the top.

"By the Goddess," Annie pinched her nose. "It almost makes you want to be a vegetarian."

"What's a vegetarian?" asked Lars.

"Someone who doesn't eat animal flesh."

The four men looked at her and shook their heads in disbelief.

"This is the Forum of Theodosius," Asmud explained as they made their way through the sellers and buyers as quickly as they could and came out onto the Mese once more. "Now we are coming to the main shopping area. Stay close. This is a busy thoroughfare."

"As if the first part was not," Annie muttered.

As they grew nearer to the city centre, colonnades appeared on either side of the street, all with shops at their lower level and housing above. The noise level increased perceptively as traders shouted at each other and to customers in many different languages. Just as in Birka, people wore a variety of dress from simple linen shifts to exotic flowing robes. Annie attempted to guess the different nationalities of people but soon gave up. Church bells pealed above the hubbub. Smells of stale fish and rotting vegetables fought for dominance with aromatic herbs and perfumes.

"I had heard Constantinople was a heavily populated city but this is incredible. I have never seen so many people in my life." Meg had to raise her voice to overcome the clamour of street noise.

Colonnaded porticos continued to line the Mese but now had a grander look. Crowds were thicker here, mainly men, most of whom gazed curiously at Annie and her aunt. Their facial expressions began to irritate Annie. What was their problem? Had they never seen a woman on the street before?

Asmud marched purposely onward, denying Meg and Annie a chance to look at jewellery enticingly displayed or colourful bales of silk stacked high. An occasional bakery offered tantalizing smells with large round flat breads piled precariously out front. A leather goods shop had row upon row of soft leather shoes and boots. Annie looked down at her big toe sticking out of worn leather Birka bought shoes.

"Not far now," Asmud called over his shoulder. "The Forum of Constantine is ahead. That's our goal."

As Annie and Meg had begun to mutter at the sheer unreasonableness of Asmud passing by all of the goods on display, this was welcome news.

Asmud finally stopped at the end of a row of shops.

"This is a Syrian cloth shop, and, most important to us, the owner employs needlewomen who make up the clothes. We do not have the luxury of time to buy cloth and have you sew."

Annie and Meg spent the next hour in bliss, more so than their men, but they too needed new clothes. The owner of the shop was a small, voluble Syrian who ran his business with verve and strong bargaining skills. His assistants: two skinny young men and a pre-pubescent girl, all eerily stamped with the Syrian's facial features, brought out bolt after bolt of the softest wool and finest linen. His long, narrow workroom was dark so he ushered his buyers outside under the portico where he instructed them "to see the colours and feel the weave." His grasp of Greek was sufficient for Asmud and Annie to understand; however, when he became excited over a particular fabric or alarmed over a low bid from Asmud he would switch to Arabic.

The two young men and the girl flew to his bidding and offered small cups of overly sweet tea between opening the bales.

Serious bargaining began in the back premises so Annie and the others remained in the foreground and watched two experts at work as each claimed to be a poor and broken man if either accepted the other's offer. At the far end of the shop, positioned under a single, grimy window, three women sat cross-legged, sewing. Bolts of cloth surrounded them and half-finished garments hung from stools and wall hooks.

"Has anybody asked you what you want to wear?" Annie whispered to her aunt.

"No. I believe our Syrian knows what men and women wear here in Constantinople and that's what we are going to get."

As the wily experts continued haggling, the young girl came up to Annie and Meg and began taking their measurements using a strip of cloth as a measure. She worked quickly calling out numbers to her brother. The other brother performed the same procedure on Will, Lars and Ivar. Ivar's face presented a picture of misery but he suffered in silence. Clearly, he determined to undergo any amount of torture for his children. Eventually, bargaining ended and Asmud swept his group out of the Syrian's shop.

"Onward," he ordered. "Lots more to do."

55

Annie, Meg and the cats had arrived back in their cramped room, which was no longer bare but stacked high with packages. Rosamund and Bea inspected each package carefully: decorously sniffing and touching each with a gentle paw.

"What a day," remarked Meg. "Never in my life have I seen so many people, shops and goods on display. Nor have I eaten such an amazing variety of food."

Annie nodded. "How good was that cabbage soup we bought from the street seller? The biggest surprise to me, though, was the honey dessert. Asmud called it kopton but in my time, we know it as baklava. Can you believe those women sewed all of our clothes in the time it took us to do the rest of our shopping? They must have kept going until the light began to fade. Shall we have a fashion parade, Aunt Meg?"

Annie and Meg opened bundle after bundle; sorting out what each garment was and in what order it went on. The Syrian had kindly drawn pictures and labelled the garments, shaking his head at the ignorant barbarians. They were helpless with laughter by the time they stood, fully dressed.

Each wore a long linen shift called a camisias. Over that went a fine wool tunica and covering the tunica was a palla, a rectangular piece of material, which wrapped around the body, similar to a Roman toga. They must also cover their heads with it, as was the custom when outside; the Syrian had pointed out firmly, otherwise the men would view them as fallen women or lowly servants. Now, the attitude of the guards and men in the Mese became clear. Soft, pointed leather shoes adorned their feet and long, elaborately beaded earrings hung from their ears.

"I love the soft blue of your palla," Annie lifted the material and ran it through her fingers, "but not as much as I like my green one. Do you recognize the dyes they have used?"

As they embarked on a discussion of the various plants used in dying fabric, a knock came at the door and in marched three smart looking men wearing new wool tunics and softly draped trousers, unknowingly performing their own fashion parade. They pirouetted and pointed their toes, showing off their long leather boots. Even Ivar joined in the presentation.

"We've got cloaks as well but it's too 'ot to wear 'em," said a proud and beaming Lars.

Asmud, still wearing his worn travelling clothes and appearing quite drab in comparison to his friends, opened a sack and, with a flourish, pulled out a round of bread, figs, walnuts and a hunk of cheese. Will carried a flagon of wine so after they had admired each other, they sat and picnicked while reminiscing about their day of shopping and sightseeing in the Golden City. Rosamund and Bea joined in, being partial to cheese and bread.

"We never got further than the Forum of Constantine—"

"—Could you believe the colour of the silks they were selling in there?—"

"Camels! I counted five camels, and I don't know how many mules and donkeys pulling carts."

"What about those two huge oxen. They took up most of the road. The wagon was loaded with stone blocks—"

A wistful sounding Meg said, "I could smell the spices while we were in front of the forum but they must have been on the other side."

Ivar's voice broke in over the babble. "This isn't getting us closer to me babbies. What's to 'appen now?"

Asmud, who had been lounging comfortably close to Meg, sat up straighter. "Tomorrow we make ourselves ready to seek an audience at The Great Palace."

"I dun't see why we can't just go and see the thief and get the babbies back. Aye an' mebbe tek sum of our travelling mates with us. We *are* Vikings, by Odin. Why are we skulking around?" Ivar's relaxed moment had passed.

Asmud clapped Ivar on the shoulder. "If we did what you suggest, Ivar, we'll all be thrown in jail. This powerful man has the ear of the Emperor. We must be circumspect and follow the rules. Be as patient as you can, and we will return your children to you."

Annie listened to this conversation with increasing dread. Why was that lump of rock in her belly growing heavier?

Meg stood and brushed the crumbs from her new clothes. "We have a big day tomorrow, so off you go, my friends. We will see you when the sun rises."

56

Asmud looked resplendent in his court outfit, carried so far from Princess Olga's court in Novgorod. From his soft leather boots to his green and gold silk brocade kaftan; his scarlet cloak, fastened on his right shoulder with a bronze dragon cloak pin and topped with a fur-trimmed hat; he looked the essence of a representative of Princess Olga and now outshone his friends.

Meg looked at him admiringly.

Annie watched her aunt's face. How will she leave him when it's time to go? She looked at Will, saw the excitement in his eyes at the thought of today's adventure, and her heart squeezed painfully. She too would face separation again. Enough! Focus on finding the twins.

The elegantly dressed group, unrecognizable from yesterday's un-kempt lot, headed out—Lars leading the way, chattering about the Varangian Guard that he had spotted marching through the city. Annie carried the cats in their baskets, Will by her side; Asmud and Meg brought up the rear.

They followed the same, now familiar route, the only route to the Great Palace, along the Mese, which appeared just as busy. Weaving their way between hawkers and food sellers, carts, wagons and the occasional official-looking personage riding a horse; manure piles offered foul smelling traps to the unwary. They stood aside when a cohort of Varangian Guard marched along the road, appearing incredibly large, bristling with weapons and ignoring everyone.

When they came to the Syrian cloth shop, they stopped to show off their new clothes to the delighted owner who finally introduced himself as Sayid Anawi.

"My children," he said beaming, showing a mouthful of immaculate white teeth. Out came the girl, Ishtar, followed by her brothers, Bassel and Alaa. They all bowed and Ishtar offered tea.

"So sorry, we have no time," said Annie in their language, "but we wish to thank our seamstresses."

Mister Anawi called back into the store and the three women came out, blinking in the strong sunlight. They smiled, hiding their mouths behind their hands, but looked delighted at the *shukraan:* thank you.

After repeated goodbyes, Asmud led his flock onward toward the Forum of Constantine.

"Be prepared to be amazed by what you are about to see." He opened his huge arms wide. "You have witnessed nothing yet of the greatness of this city."

True to his words, they stood in awe outside the monumental gates of the Forum, entering timidly, humbled by the grandeur and sheer size of its entrance. A huge, circular space lay before them, bordered by two tiers of colonnades and an equally massive gate beckoned from the other side. A tall, pink marble column arose from the centre, a naked god perched at the top, the rays of the sun surrounding his head.

"That is Constantine, the first Emperor, representing Apollo. He raised that statue to himself."

Crossing the Forum, statues of other gods caught their interest. Asmud recognized Poseidon and Dionysios. Meg was thrilled to see Artemis and Athena. Annie delighted in a life-size statue of an elephant and a dolphin and had to explain what they were to the others. This area was not as busy as the Mese. Annie sensed a feeling of calm, of order, after the hustle and bustle of the street. Men wandered around, surveying the goods on display at the ever-present market stalls. Constantinople used every open space it had for commerce. No other women were in evidence.

Silk merchants displayed their colourful bales. Meg remarked on the much higher quality of the silk available in the Forum.

"I bet this is where Princess Olga obtains her silk," said Annie to Meg, remembering the main hall of Olga's palace in Novgorod, the walls lined with billowing silk. The only other stalls contained candles: piles of them, all different weights and sizes. The smell of exotic spices was overwhelming, but not to be seen at this market.

Ivar grew impatient again; he had no eyes for architecture and commerce. They passed through the opposite monumental gates and entered yet another open space. In the centre stood a square of four pillars connected by arches and covered by a pyramid shaped vault.

"Feast your eyes on the Milion, the Golden Milestone. It is the exact centre of the city and if we had time to look," Asmud offered Ivar a measured look, "we would see inscribed on the sides, the distances to all of the important cities of the empire."

They moved on into another large square, surrounded by more colonnades. This one had a golden column at its centre and, again, functioned as a busy market place.

"We are almost there, Ivar. This is the forecourt of the palace, the Augustaion. Over there," he pointed to a massive and stunning building, "is the—"

"—Hagia Sofia!" cried an excited Annie. "It hasn't changed, in all of these centuries, it hasn't changed." She paused. "Oh yes it has. It doesn't have minarets on its corners."

"What is a minarets?" asked Will.

Once again, Asmud surprised Annie with his depth of knowledge.

"When I was in Baghdad on a trade mission for Princess Olga, I learned something of the Islamic world. A minaret is part of their church, which they call a mosque. A muezzin, a crier, climbs these tall slender towers five times a day to send out the message to pray. Just like we hear the church bells ringing here, I suppose."

Upon hearing this piece of exotic information, Will looked appreciatively at Asmud. "You were in Baghdad?"

"We Rus travel frequently to Baghdad in order to trade, just as we do here in Constantinople. Baghdad provides us with much silver."

"So, what did you mean, Annie, when you said the minarets aren't here?" Will persisted.

Annie sighed. "Many, many years from now, Constantinople will be captured by the Islamic peoples. Hagia Sophia will become a mosque, hence the addition of minarets." At times, she needed to keep her mouth shut about her knowledge of the future.

Silence fell upon the group as they contemplated such astounding news.

"Well, we'll all be dead by then so who cares," said ever-effervescent Lars.

"Right now, in front of me, I see the spice market, in the shadow of *our* Hagia Sophia," Meg said.

Smells from stall upon stall of colourful heaps of spices, brought from all over the known world, wafted toward them. To Meg's frustration, that was as close as they got, as Asmud moved on.

"We will return, my Meg, have no fear, you will be able to fill your precious chest. Over here, leads to the Hippodrome." He pointed in the opposite direction. "Ivar, you will be pleased to see this; it means we have arrived." He pointed to another magnificent block of marble, "The Chalke Gate: the entrance to the Great Palace."

They turned as one and stared at the huge gate. Sentries stood on either side of the large bronze doors, diminished by the sheer size of the entrance. A gold lattice screen hung above the doors offering a contrast to the grey marble.

"We have more *gœfa*: luck," said Asmud. "These are Varangian Guards." He approached the guards, resplendent in chainmail, gleaming helmets, shields by their sides, swords in their scabbards and axes in hand.

"It's old home week," Annie commented to her aunt as Asmud, Lars and Ivar clustered around the two guards and they began conversing in some kind of pidgin Scandinavian tongue.

After he explained that he was an emissary from Princess Olga of Kiev to see the Emperor Constantine, one of the guards almost diffidently checked the men for weapons. The other guard rapped on the door with his axe handle. As the heavy door swung open, a beardless, chubby man stepped out. The guard spoke to him in a quiet and deferential manner.

"*Ostiarios*: eunuch, doorkeeper," muttered Asmud to his friends. "The officials who are not eunuchs are called 'the Bearded Ones.'"

The doorkeeper came over and, without speaking, held out his hand for the papers. Upon perusal, he curtly signalled with a pudgy hand to follow and, finally, they entered the door to the Great Palace of Constantinople.

57

At the end of a long day, Annie had begun to grasp the complexity of the administrative bureaucracy of the Byzantine Empire. The first official, *Ostiarios,* the doorkeeper, had quickly and with obvious relief, handed them over to 'a bearded one' called a *basilikos mandatōr*: the Emperor's man. He carried a red wand as well as a strong sense of his own importance. He examined Asmud's papers, frowning in obvious disapproval at the Greek letters written by a foreigner, and took them on another tour only to hand them over to another official. Each of these introductions to new officials took them from one pavilion to another.

The Imperial Palace consisted of many buildings, spread over countless acres, and occupied six terraces that led down a slope to the Sea of Marmara. Another palace, the Boukoleon Palace, sat by the shores of the Sea of Marmara, used by the Imperial Family as their summer retreat.

The whole complex created bewilderment: churches, courtyards, fountains and more fountains, administrative offices, rooms filled with soldiers, rooms filled with clerks. Everyone appeared to be wearing different distinctive outfits, almost like uniforms and often complemented with large hats. Annie's impression was of a gigantic beehive with not even a queen bee in sight, and as she and the others grew increasingly tired and hungry, she had the wry thought that in her time, women had to contend with the glass ceiling, whereas here; they were invisible.

Their last official had deposited them in a shady corner of one of the many courtyards. Ivar muttered away to himself. Will voiced his concern that the officials had abandoned them. As the sun was beginning to descend over the Sea of Marmara, another beardless official walked over to them.

"*Éla:* Come." He swung around, his soft leather slippers making no sound and his white kaftan swirling around him. He led them into yet another antechamber, told them to wait—*periménete,* and left.

"We're gettin' nowhere," growled Ivar. "These buggers are just fobbin' us off."

His words had no sooner echoed around the small room than a tall, bearded and elegantly dressed man entered, wearing a large hat and a richly decorated tunic, covered at the front with a jewel-encrusted tablion, a rectangular panel denoting his importance. Two clerics carrying writing tablets and a palace guard accompanied him.

"I am known as Vassilios. Do you understand Greek?" He paused. When Asmud and Annie nodded, he continued. "My title is *Logthetēs ton dromou;* I am the Chief Minister, head of the Diplomacy department, amongst other responsibilities. I see you bring word from Princess Olga of Kiev; we hold her in high regard. She requests that you have an audience with Emperor Constantine. Please explain to me who you all are and why you wish to petition our basileus?"

Asmud introduced each of his company in turn: Ivar Ivarsson, a Viking from Jorvik in England and central to their petition. Mistress Meg Wistowe, a midwife, wise woman and close family friend of the Ivarsson family, Mistress Annie Thornton, apprentice to Mistress Wistowe, William Thornton, brother to Mistress Thornton and her protector, Lars Larsson, apprentice to Ivar Ivarsson, also a protector of the ladies. Finally, he bowed. "I am Asmud of Novgorod, Varangian Rus and tutor to Prince Sviatoslav, heir to the throne of Kiev, and emissary for Princess Olga of Kiev." Having planned their roles prior to coming to court none of their new titles or relationships, came as a surprise to the group. Each looked firmly into the eyes of this important man.

Vassilios looked intently at each petitioner. He raised his elegantly plucked eyebrows when Annie and Will were introduced as brother and sister: he with his blond hair and she with her black curls.

Asmud continued. "At the beginning of our spring in the northern lands, two beautiful children of only seven summers were snatched from the heart of their home in Jorvik, England, by thieves in the pay of a highly ranked person. We have followed these thieves through the Baltic region and into Rus lands. Word came to us that a man now of Constantinople bought these beloved children. He is a collector of precious objects, be they in human or animal form."

Asmud paused. "We know his name to be Gennadios of Mytilene. He lives here in your city. Their father," he nodded at Ivar who was now on his knees, his head bowed, "wants to take these children home, back to their grieving mother."

Vassilios nodded his head. "I know of whom you speak. He is a well known, respected and powerful man here. He is also rich. You have, I fear, many challenges ahead of you. What is it you require of our Emperor?"

"We wish Emperor Constantine to intercede with the Greek collector to give back the children," said Asmud. "We are able to recompense him for his loss."

On hearing this, Ivar stood and glared at Asmud, his cheeks wet with tears. "No, we cut 'is throat."

One of the clerics quickly translated, his face turning pale.

Will and Lars reached over and grasped Ivar to them.

The official frowned. "I understand your feelings my friend, but it will not further your mission to offer violence. I think you, personally, will not go before the Emperor. So, this is what I will do for you. I will arrange rooms for you to stay in the palace. Tomorrow morning you will wait in the anteroom of the Chrysotriklinos in the hope of being called before Constantine Porphyrogennitus. If he chooses to hear your petition, so be it. Wait here, someone will come for you. Please enjoy our hospitality. We will have food sent to you in your rooms and do enjoy the Baths of Xeuxippos."

He bowed, snapped his fingers at his small escort and left the room.

58

JORVIK

Queen Gunnhild smiled at her man Gösta. "It is good that our king is away raiding. It gives me time to think about my plans for our little friends in Constantinople, particularly the dark one who was responsible for burning my hair. Speaking of dark, I am thinking her life is about to become very dark, and as a result, knowing Gennadios, she will become very light.

"It is also good that we have time for other endeavours." She reached for the hand of Gösta and led him to a bank of furs on her bed.

59

Logthetēs ton dromou was as good as his word and the petitioners soon found themselves in private rooms at the Palace of Daphne. Although this address sounded impressive, Annie and Meg agreed their surroundings were surprisingly shabby as they shook a fine grey dust from the coverings, albeit brocade, on the couches.

In fact, the whole building appeared to be undergoing reconstruction. The chatty eunuch who brought their food, "call me Narses", told them that the building, now ancient, had fallen into disrepair.

"Our Emperor, may he be blessed by all the saints, ordered Daphne restored. So we 'ave to put up with all the bangin' and 'ammerin', day an' night. Well, not at night actually, 'cos the Emperor and Empress's bedchamber is close by."

They dined most royally on flatbreads and cheeses, small bowls of walnuts and olives, a dish of lamb meatballs simmered in a vegetable loaded broth smelling of basil, and small honey and sesame squares, aromatic of oranges. A red wine, which Asmud identified as Macedonian, washed everything down. All this feasting took place in a small dining area in their rooms. They lay on their sides on couches to sample the dishes on a central table.

"Just like the ancient Romans," Annie proclaimed, lounging dramatically.

Ivar did eat and managed to drink copious amounts of wine but refused to lie on a couch to eat. "T'aint right, layin' down to eat. T'aint natural. It's all reight for them soft buggers, not for proper men though."

After Narses returned with lemon water to wash their hands and take away the dishes, they lay back and contemplated their day.

"Asmud," said Will, "what did the official called the Emperor, Porfo-something?"

Asmud, also having imbibed the ruby red contents of a few goblets, spoke carefully, emphasizing each word. "Constantine VII is known as 'the Purple-born' as he was born in a specially created room of purple marble to prove his legitimacy as future Emperor. He has been Emperor in his own right for a few years, only. Apparently, he loves scholarly pursuits and the arts. He writes books and leaves his wife, Helene, and the bureaucrats to run the empire. I know nothing of his connection with our Greek collector. I only hope they base their relationship on business alone.

"Why do you say that, Asmud?" asked Meg, hypnotized by the flickering shadows made by the candles on the ceiling.

"Friendship might interfere with decision-making".

As everyone contemplated such a sobering thought, Will jumped up, startling everyone. "I'm for the Baths," he said. "Does anyone want to come with me? It's a while since I swam in the Black Sea."

Ivar surprised everyone. "Aye lad, I'll cum with thee. I stink like a pile o' dead 'errings."

Thanks to Ivar's eloquence, they all jumped up and made ready to explore the sumptuous and famous Baths of Xeuxippos.

Between the baths Annie and Meg had visited in St. Mamas and the Baths of Xeuxippos, there was no comparison. Annie looked around in wonder. The walls and floors were of luxurious marble; massive chandeliers with hundreds of candles hung from the ceilings. Numerous fountains and statues, featuring fish, nymphs and mythical creatures graced every open space. A huge dome sat atop the Baths ringed with more statues, mainly of athletic, naked men. Each room had a heated or cold pool. Attendants almost outnumbered patrons. Aromatic oils scented the air. Musicians played softly in the background.

"I've died and gone to heaven," Annie said to her aunt after an attendant had given her a vigorous massage, following the usual treatment of being covered in olive oil and scraped down with a strigil. Her earlier prudery had fled back to the twenty-first century.

Annie and Meg reclined in the women's section of this amazing public edifice, in the caldarium: the hottest room of the baths. She hoped the men were having as good a time in the men's section, and that Ivar had relaxed. The women who lounged around them were of a different class than the women in the previous baths. Even naked, they seemed worlds apart. Annie could hear their polished speech as they discussed the business of their neighbours, the gossip of the Court and she smiled at the discussion about who was the best-looking charioteer—not too different then from the chatter of servants and slaves. For the first time she heard reference to the Blues and the Greens: apparently rival chariot teams. Perhaps women could attend the events at the Hippodrome; they certainly spoke with assurance about the games.

After cooling down in the frigidarium, they made their way back to their rooms in the Daphne Palace. A full moon was high in the sky to light the way and the air was heavy with the scent of jasmine and early blooming roses.

As the men had not yet made an appearance, Meg and Annie began rearranging couches. Two couches remained in the *triclinium*: dining area, for Ivar and Lars, and more couches found their way into two different rooms.

Aunt and niece smiled self-consciously as they said goodnight.

60

After rising early and enjoying a breakfast of fruit, olives, bread and cheeses brought by Narses, who raised his eyebrows at the rearrangement of sleeping couches but made no comment, another palace official took the petitioners to the Chrysotriklinos.

"Is there no end to the incredible beauty of Constantinople?" whispered Annie, completely overwhelmed by their surroundings. They had passed through yet another garden courtyard, filled with fountains and newly blooming flowers.

They arrived in time to witness the ceremonial unlocking of the Chrysotriklinos palace doors by the *Papias,* a beardless official of obvious high status defined by his heavily embroidered clothes and, of course, a large hat. Guardsmen stood on either side of the doors: their swords unsheathed and wearing their signature red-plumed helmets.

The outside of the Chrysotriklinos palace, when seen in the early morning light, was a typical Byzantine building: reddish brick and stone, an octagonal shape with many windows and a large dome. It sat to the south of all the other pavilions, close to the seawall and overlooked the Sea of Marmara, glittering in the sun's rays. The air was fresh, smelling of the sea, and they all took deep breaths before they entered the building.

Another eunuch led them to a large antechamber, the pantheon, where they stood for a long time, huddled together, ignoring the looks being given them by other well-dressed petitioners.

Ivar looked twitchy. He knew he would not be allowed to enter the main hall following his earlier violent outburst, but he was muttering to himself and tapping his foot agitatedly on the marble floor.

"Steady, my friend," said Asmud, placing his hand on Ivar's shoulder. "We are almost there. We are only asking for an opportunity to visit the Greek. If the Emperor chooses to add his request to ours for the release of the twins, so be it."

"I feel so helpless, so useless," muttered the Viking. "This talk, talk, talk, is not my style." He offered a bitter smile. "Maybe I need my old raiding partner with me."

"Who is that?" asked Annie.

"Eiric Bloodaxe, of course." Ivar smirked at his own joke and appeared to relax a little. They had agreed beforehand that Will and Lars would stay with Ivar, both to keep him company and to ensure he stayed out of trouble. After that remark, Annie figured they had made a good decision.

Abruptly, the low buzz of conversation around them ceased. A sense of renewed energy swept through the increasingly stuffy antechamber. The *Papias* came into the room. "Emperor Constantine VII, Porphyrogenitus, and the Empress Helena Lekapene have graciously agreed to hear your petitions. The Imperial Audience has commenced. When I call your name, be prepared to enter the Golden Reception Hall."

Annie immediately felt the knot in her belly tighten. They had come such a long way. What would they do if this powerful man turned down their request? Anxiety must have shown on her face as Meg reached for her hand and gave it a squeeze.

Another hour went by. The official called names and men went through the imposing doors, individually or in groups. When they returned, others watched their faces. Success or failure? Their faces frequently told the story.

"Asmud of Novgorod: emissary to Princess Olga of Kiev: present yourself."

Annie took a deep breath; so much counted on the next few minutes; however, she held her covered head high and she and Meg followed Asmud through the doors.

61

The Golden Reception Hall offered the solemnity of a cathedral as, at the same time, both colours and patterns dazzled: walls of yellow and black marble, the floor a swirl of geometric mosaics, more mosaics of saints and apostles.

The Imperial Throne sat on a raised dais with a yet another mosaic, this one of Jesus hanging above. Three porphyry marble steps led to the throne. The Golden Reception Hall clearly indicated the association between Christ's court in heaven and the Byzantine Court on earth. Large circular candelabra studded with candles, illuminated the Hall, emphasizing yellow in the marble and gold in the mosaics.

As previously instructed, the petitioners prostrated themselves on the mosaic floor. When Annie finally stood, she absorbed the tableau above her.

Emperor Constantine lounged on his wide throne which Annie noted resembled a modern day bed, except flanked by golden lions. Dressed in a purple toga over a heavy brocade and jeweled dalmatica, he was not a pleasant looking man, despite his ornate attire and crowned head. Evidently enjoying food and drink, his toga did nothing to hide a magnificent potbelly. Helene, his wife, sat by his side; her crown set upon elaborately styled upswept hair. Heavy gold and ruby earrings framed her delicate features and aquiline nose. Her purple toga draped elegantly over a bejeweled tunica. While the Emperor lounged, boredom written on his face above a wiry, black and bushy beard, a scroll close to hand, his wife looked alert, her sharp eyes missing nothing.

Palace guards stood on each side of the dais, swords in hand. The

Papias stood to one side with scribes behind him, writing tablets poised. A smell of heavy incense caught in Annie's nostrils; the room dwarfed her, making her feel insignificant and powerless, the design's intent.

The *Papias* spoke. "I present Asmud of Novgorod to your Majesties. He brings greetings from her Highness, Princess Olga of Kiev, and wishes for good health to you both. Speak your truth, Asmud of Novgorod."

Asmud cleared his throat nervously and, taking a deep breath, he began his plea. "Jorvik is the seat of King Eiric, son of King Harald Fairhair of Norway. King Eiric rules a large area of England. Jorvik is a prosperous and rapidly growing centre for trade due to its easy access to the North Sea and many trade routes across our world. Ivar Ivarsson, formally a warrior and now a peaceful fisherman, married an English woman. Twin girls, known for their shining, fair beauty, blessed their union and sadly became their only issue. Others recognized their uniqueness and snatched the two children, of only seven summers, off the streets of Jorvik in full daylight. We have followed the trail of the thieves across the Baltic and through the lands of the Rus'.

"In Novgorod, Princess Olga heard of our search and offered to write to her trading partner of many years, Emperor Constantine, asking his help to find and return the children to their grieving parents."

As Asmud told his story, beautifully, Annie judged, she realized she had dug her nails deeply into the palms of her hands, blood leaked from the imprints. She risked looking at the faces of the Emperor and Empress. The Emperor still looked bored, but the Empress looked puzzled.

"We appreciate the grief of the parents but two questions must be asked." Empress Helene leaned forward. "Each spring we welcome our Rus traders who bring us so many beautiful and precious goods; amongst them, amber, furs and slaves. We recognize the Rus for their trade in slaves. The slaves are a much-needed commodity in our Empire. Why then, is this event so different? Moreover, why would the Princess Olga choose to become involved in this minor matter?"

"As to the first question, Majesty, this was not a raiding party, neither a form of tribute, and these were not children who had been abandoned. The crime here is that a person of high standing in England sought payment in gold by seizing these children to sell them, as we have since discovered, to a man known as Gennadios of Mytilene who now resides in Constantinople. This is not slavery but theft, a crime punishable by law."

At this, the Emperor finally lifted his head, boredom gone, and looked closely at Asmud.

"From reports I have received of conditions in Britain; these children will have a much better life here than there. I understand people still live in round mud huts. Are you demanding that we convict one of our leading citizens of Constantinople of theft? Gennadios is an artist to our court. He makes the gold plate from which we eat. Look around this room. He creates the magnificent metalwork you see using gold and cloisonné. We frequently commission him to make icons for our churches. Few men can create such art. Yet, you accuse him of *theft*." The Emperor's manner remained courteous, but the narrowing of his eyes did not denote a good outcome.

Asmud stood his ground. "Our understanding is that these children were not stol—brought here—to be raised as this man's children, but to become part of his collection; to be exhibited, shown off."

Emperor Constantine grunted and shook his head.

Annie groaned inside. It was all going terribly wrong.

Meg took a tiny step forward. She looked at the Empress Helene and held her eyes.

"Majesty, I am Margarette of Wessex. I am a close friend of the family from whom these children *were taken*. In answer to your question as to why the Princess Olga chose to support our quest, I must relate a story of happenings in Novgorod.

"I am called Knowledgeable Woman in the Scandinavian countries. My skills relate to women and women's concerns. Before we left England, Queen Iseabail financed our journey. Her husband, King Eiric, has assisted us since on a number of occasions. They have done this because of their horror of the crime committed on their land."

Annie listened with some apprehension. She and her aunt had discussed the next part of the narrative in detail. The Greek Orthodox Church did not hold with magic so they were treading on dangerous ground here.

"When Princess Olga became aware of our presence in Novgorod she requested that I attend her court. During a private conversation with her Highness, it became clear to me that the princess harboured a deep desire to embrace Christianity. At the conclusion of our discussion, she told me she had made up her mind to do so and would bring Christ to her people. She told me I had been constructive in her decision-making.

"As she holds your Majesties in such deep regard, I am sure she will be contacting you with her mission to bring the word of Christ to her people. In gratitude for what she saw as my help in clearing her mind, she offered to ask for your assistance in returning the children to their parents. She even sent her son, Prince Sviatoslav's tutor to assist in our endeavors."

Now Annie could see that Meg had the full attention of the Emperor. Nothing would be dearer to his heart than spreading the Greek Orthodox faith. Empress Helene leaned forward once again.

"How is it that you two women travelled alone across such harsh and dangerous lands to seek these children? Where are these loving parents that sent you into many perils?"

"We have travelled all the way from England with the children's father, also with two more protectors, my apprentice's brother, and a young Viking. They are waiting in the antechamber."

The Empress turned to the *Papias*. "Bring them into our presence."

Will, Lars and Ivar followed the *Papias* into the Golden Reception Hall, their faces reflecting a mixture of fear, confusion and awe.

After making their clumsy prostration to the Imperial couple, Asmud introduced them. Emperor Constantine looked long and hard at Ivar Ivarsson and, to his credit, Ivar looked straight back at him, not with his usual Viking pugnacity but with a sense of steadfastness. Annie's heart swelled with pride.

Emperor Constantine looked briefly at his wife and gave an almost imperceptible nod of his head. Again, the Empress spoke. "This is what we shall do for you, Ivar Ivarsson. Because you have displayed such Christian love for your children—even though you are a barbarian—and because your endeavors have attracted strong and powerful people to your cause, we will request that our friend Gennadios receive you at his home so he may listen to your plea. We can do no more than this."

Even as the group began to mumble their thanks, they were ushered backwards out of the throne room by the *Papias*.

62

Now all they had to do was wait… wait… and wait.

Will, Ivar and Lars returned to St. Mamas and brought back everyone's possessions, reporting on the activities of their former travelling companions. Finne was as big and blunt as ever, busy setting up his shop in one of the alcoves along with the other traders. The traders were also occupied with taking their slaves in small consignments to the slave market in the Valley of Lamentations. Lars glanced at Annie as he recounted this, remembering Birka.

One of the items they brought back was the *Hnefatafl* board and a marathon of *Hnefatafl* began; the men only stopping to eat, drink, and leave the rooms to relieve themselves.

It seemed that Rosemond and Bea had decided to do their own exploring. The cats only returned to the rooms at nighttime, looking sleek, fat and ready for bed.

Annie and her aunt agreed to copy their example and explore the area around the Great Palace. They asked Narses how they might travel openly through the markets. He suggested that, if they go no further than the square in front of the Hagia Sofia, and cover their heads, he would ask permission to accompany them. Meg's eyes lit up. Finally, the spice market, and surely, they could go inside the magnificent basilica.

Annie and Meg did things backward. They hit the spice market first. Stalls were busy with buyers mingling, tasting, smelling, and talking, all men—no women. They received the usual curious looks but were oblivious. Annie visited the Grand Bazaar when she was in Istanbul in the twenty-first century. She had marvelled then at the colourful display of brilliantly hued spices from around the world. This ninth century version was no different. Aromas of cinnamon, cardamom, coriander, cumin and peppers battled one another; fighting for supremacy in the nose, vying for attention. Buy me; buy me—and buy Meg and Annie did. Traders knew a good thing when they saw one and, despite the fact that they were dealing with women, and foreign women at that; they laughed, gestured, weighed and bagged precious seeds and powders. When Meg, Annie and Narses could carry no more, they reluctantly left and moved across to the great cathedral.

"This Hagia Sophia," Annie told her aunt, "is the third one on this site and was built by Emperor Justinian in five hundred and something."

Meg looked at her niece and smiled. "How is it that you are an expert on this building?"

"I toured it when I was in Istanbul. By then it had become a museum—I mean, in the future—confusing isn't it, this time thing?"

They walked slowly up to the basilica. Its proportions were overwhelming: the huge dome arching overall, semi-domes, solid blocks of evenly cut masonry and decorative red tiles and brickwork; no wonder it was the world's largest building at the time.

Walking inside, they carried the smells of spices with them, which immediately vied with odours of incense swirling around in the vast space. Light poured in through multiple windows, softening edges and creating a sense of otherworldliness. They lifted their eyes to the huge dome above their heads and gasped at its enormity as well as its beauty. Hagia Sofia was a Greek Orthodox Church and priests, dressed in distinctive black garb and hats, moved back and forth on their busy church business. One of them came hurrying over to the spice-smelling trio.

"Ladies are not allowed in this space," he said. "You must go up there, up into the gallery."

Annie remembered a story her mother told her of an officious man telling her to refrain from playing billiards in a British Legion Hall in her youth. When she indignantly asked why, he said rules forbade women from playing in case they ripped the cloth. Annie knew just how her mother felt.

Heavily laden with spices, they returned to their rooms in the palace and after Annie spoke at length about the stupidity of men throughout the centuries, she contrarily announced to an un-caring and non-listening, hnefatafl-playing male audience that she was going to make them all coffee: a drink of the gods.

63

Narses professed curiosity as he lit a small charcoal stove in a corner of the courtyard. He had taken a large vessel of water out previously following Annie's instructions. Annie opened her sack of precious acorns she had garnered with Will on their special island, her cheeks growing warm at the memory. Meg followed every step along with Rosamund and Bea.

Annie showed Narses how to remove the white caps from the smooth brown nuts then placed the acorns in a metal pot and boiled the water, repeating three times.

"We are removing the tannin, the bitterness," she told her fascinated companions. As they watched bubbles break the water surface, Narses told them of his previous life and of how he became a eunuch employed in the Imperial Palace. Annie expressed amazement that the young man showed no resentment at the circumstances bringing him here.

"I was a boy when my parents had me castrated. I am the youngest son. I can build a fine career here in the Grand Palace and bring power and prestige to my family if I succeed. As a eunuch I can never seize the throne so I pose no threat to politicians. I am trusted and the more I can prove my loyalty, the higher I rise." Narses shrugged his shoulders. "You may not understand our customs, but they work."

After the third boiling, Annie decreed they were ready for the next stage and described what she required. Narses took them through numerous winding corridors into another of the many palace courtyards. This one was smaller with a round, bricked kiln in its centre.

"Not many people know about our little place. We bake bread for our own use and warm up food we liberate from the kitchens."

He soon had a small fire burning and when only red embers remained, they laid out the acorns on a shelf above the coals to cool.

A quiet oasis, the courtyard sat in the middle of the noisy, bustling and sprawling palace. Even in such a tiny space, clay pots overflowed with multi-coloured flowers. As the acorns dried, they rested in companionable silence, enjoying the rare peacefulness. Rosamund and Bea found a beam of sunlight and sprawled in total abandon.

"Now for the tricky part," said Annie. They laboriously peeled the acorns and laid them out again to be roasted. A distinct aroma of roasting acorns began wafting across the courtyard and escaped. It was inevitable that the smell attracted attention, and soon some of the palace servants drifted in to the courtyard.

"What is that smell?"

"Nars, what are you making?"

"I want whatever is in the oven," and so on…

"It is an experiment. May be good, may be very bad."

They took the roasted acorns back to their rooms and Annie showed her assistants the last steps. Grinding the acorns in a stone bowl with a pestle did not disturb the hnefatafl-players for a second.

Returning to the little courtyard, they boiled the acorn grounds in a pot on the charcoal burner. This time an even larger crowd of palace employees gathered as the coffee aroma filled the air. No one was wearing a large hat so Annie guessed their audience to be lower civil servants. She added a pinch of cardamom and cinnamon to the bubbling liquid.

"Whatever that is we want some," someone in the crowd shouted.

"So sorry," said Narses, not looking sorry at all. "This is destined for our *Logthetēs ton dromou*: our Chief Minister.

He carried the precious pot back into their rooms and disappeared briefly, only to return with a set of exquisite drinking cups with a green and yellow glaze and white interior. "I borrowed them from the big kitchen, only the best vessels for nectar."

Finally, the smell of coffee reached the players who ambled over to find the source.

"What do you call a drink from the gods?" asked Ivar, his eyes wide with wonder as he sipped the brown liquid.

"'I call it coffee," said Annie, delighted with her experiment.

Narses, after sipping his drink, asked, "May I make coffee for the Emperor? He'll elevate me to the position of chief eunuch."

Annie did not get a chance to answer as a loud knock came at the door to their rooms.

A beardless one entered, a scroll in his outstretched hand, but before he handed it over, he sniffed deeply. "What is that smell? I have never smelled that smell before."

Annie smiled. Maybe she should open a coffee shop in Byzantium; she would make a fortune. Then she realized this man could be bringing news.

Asmud read out the contents of his scroll, his audience holding their combined breath.

"Gennadios of Mytilene invites the party of Asmud of Novgorod to attend his country home at the ninth hour on the day of Titre."

Narses translated: in one day's time in the mid-afternoon.

No one spoke. They had travelled a long way for this moment.

64

Walking from Constantinople in early afternoon heat required some fortitude. Annie and her party were heading northwest, leaving city walls behind. Two palace soldiers led the way and two followed, the vibrant red plumes of their helmets standing out against the brown and green tapestry of the countryside. The second hill of Constantinople was surprisingly steep. Unlike their toiling owners, both cats snuggled in their baskets, enjoying the ride. Annie had informed them of this momentous day and asked for their help in untangling the twins from the Greek Collector; unaware she was the one who would need untangling.

When Asmud had finished reading the brief directive on the scroll brought by a beardless one to their palace rooms, Annie expressed irritation that the Collector did not advise them of his address.

"Are we supposed to know? Is he so arrogant he assumes everyone knows where he lives?"

Narses cleared his throat. "Everyone *does* know where Gennadios of Mytilene lives. His townhome is located near our University and the Imperial Park called *Philopation* shelters his country villa."

Narses explained the Emperor and Empress held Gennadios in such high regard they gave him permission to build his country villa in the park where the Imperial Court went every day to hunt or enjoy the gardens. "Not too many citizens are allowed live up there."

"What does the man do to make him so powerful?" asked Will.

"Gold is his plaything. Gennadios makes icons of the saints for the Emperor—may they bless us and keep us safe"—Narses genuflected—"and jewellery for the Empress and her ladies. Any more questions, because I've got jobs t'do."

Small fields on either side of the dusty road were neatly tilled or being tilled by field workers, always with a single ox and a small wooden plow. Some of the neat furrows already showed green shoots pushing through light, sandy soil. They walked past a small village consisting of a few houses clustered together. Goats and sheep grazed in the distance and, scattered around an olive grove, were beehives.

All kinds of travellers used the road, both in and out of the Great City; Asmud informed them the large harbour of Prosphorion lay north and goods from around the world arrived there, all destined for Constantinople. Amphorae piled high on donkey-drawn carts trundled by them, their iron wheels raising even more dust. Men carrying large bundles on their backs called to each other in a variety of languages. A herd of goats offered some light relief as the curious animals gathered around Annie and the others, exploring the texture of their clothing before handlers herded them away. Dejected groups of slaves, chained together and escorted by heavily bearded men in long, white, flowing robes, shuffled along, heading, no doubt, for the Valley of Lamentations.

Annie looked down at her new leather, now dust-coated, shoes, thankful for the cloth covering her head, protecting her from the sun's rays. She tried to analyze the strange sense of foreboding she had felt since arriving in Byzantium even though events so far had worked in their favour. Now they were on their way to see an eccentric old man who collected people, accompanied by an escort from the palace, no less. She was not sure if the soldiers were there to protect them or police them. So, what was causing her anxiety—Queen Gunnhild? Annie had not thought of her for a while, but she needed to be on her guard.

Fields on their right gave way to a high, curving stone wall, seemingly going on forever. Eventually, an elaborate gateway, wide enough to admit large carriages, broke the monotony. Two sentries, supposedly fierce and equipped with shields and spears, but looking hot and bored in the afternoon heat, guarded the gateway.

Their escort stopped and crisply saluted the sentries. "We request entry in the name of our Emperor. Party to meet Gennadios." After handing over a closely examined stamped disc, the sentries waved them through.

Annie's soldiers moved through the gateway with ease of familiarity. Once inside, the lead soldier turned to his group.

"This is the Park of Philopation known for containing both beauty and danger. Wild animals live here. Stay close together and remain alert."

After hearing those terse orders, the soldiers' party moved on, leading a party of highly nervous visitors.

65

Constantinople could have been a million miles away. Bird song was the only sound breaking the stillness. They walked along a wide paved path shaded by silken canopies, the soft leather soles of their shoes making no sound on paving stones. On either side of the path, verdant land fell away in undulating waves, creating small hills and hollows. A narrow, shallow canal wound its way before them.

"This is a hunting park," the same soldier turned back again. "The Emperor and his party enjoy coming out here to hunt the wild animals. As you can see, there are not many trees, so the architects designed these hiding places for the animals."

"What wild animals are we talking about?" asked a nervous Meg.

"Roe-deer, wild boar, antelopes."

"They're not so terrifying," Ivar sneered.

"How about lions and tigers then. Will they suit you?"

The group walked on in silence but with heads rotating. Every little bush became menacing even if draped in innocent blossoms.

As they moved deeper into the park, a refreshing sound of fountains became more prevalent; pools of water shimmered in sunlight. Landscaped borders lined the pathway. Perfumed roses and lilies distracted Annie and her aunt sufficiently to stop peering around for wild animals.

Ornamental pavilions came into view, their silken awnings moving gently in the warm air. "Resting places for the hunters," said their soldier/guide.

"I'm ready for a bloody resting place," grumbled Ivan, *sotto voce* to Will. "What a waste of good land."

The group circumnavigated a huge palace of classic Byzantine architecture: its high walls hiding what lay behind. Formally laid out gardens with numerous colourful statues surrounded the buildings. Statues offered a selection of Greek gods and various animals, including graceful storks and pugnacious pigs. The only other humans they saw were men working in the gardens, trimming, pruning and weeding.

Taking a side path, the soldiers moved up into the upper left corner of the park. "Nearly there," the chatty one said quietly. "Pretty fancy place we're coming to. Best mind your manners."

There it was, the country home of Gennadios of Mytilene; stealer of children; collector of objects, human or not.

They paused to take in the moment.

The wide, rambling group of buildings was again, classical Byzantine, with rounded walls of smooth stone and elaborate red brick trim. Large and small domes topped various edifices. Rows of rectangular flowerbeds laid out like freshly dug graves in a meticulously manicured graveyard and covered with waxy, lily-white flowers, lined the front aspect.

The soldiers led their charges through an imposing stone gateway. Ten guards were waiting inside, five on each side of a paved walkway; in regulation dress—but white: white plums on their helmets and white leather strips on their skirts; swords unsheathed and raised.

Annie gulped. She looked quickly at Will. His face reflected total astonishment. His hand reached to his side, grasping the empty space where his dagger usually sat, left behind at the palace, following instructions from an official. Asmud and Ivar also looked stunned—a trap—they had been led into a trap!

Just as Lars opened his mouth to yell—what, they would never know—one of the white plumed guards stepped forward.

"Welcome to the home of Gennadios of Mytilene. He awaits you in the Garden of a Thousand Gardenias."

66

At first, Annie had difficulty seeing Gennadios of Mytilene. A thousand white gardenias greeted them, a garden aptly named. Numerous fountains around the exquisitely enclosed garden spouted a creamy, white and frothy spray. More white flowers covered bushes, shrubs and trees. She found the smell of the perfumed air overpowering, almost repellent. A male peacock, surrounded by his wives, grazed amongst the bushes; they provided the only colour Annie could see.

In the centre of all of this whiteness stood a small man with long white hair and an equally long white beard. Dressed in a simple white toga, his only adornment was a small white monkey perched on his shoulder. A gold chain linking the animal to its owner stood out against the white background.

"Welcome to my home," he said, his arms outstretched in the traditional way. "*To spíti mou eínai spíti sou.*"

"My home is your home," muttered Asmud.

Annie could not help thinking back to her first impressions of Princess Olga's great hall in Novgorod: coloured silks and white clothing. What was it with these rich, entitled people?

Gennadios of Mytilene clapped his hands and three male, beardless, white-clad servants entered the garden, their arms full of trays of bread, olives, fruit and cheeses, and tall goblets of liquid.

After arranging seating and placing food platters on various small tables, the servants positioned Annie and Meg on either side of the Greek on carved wood chairs, which looked to Annie remarkably like modern deckchairs. Gennadios lounged on a long, white silk-clad couch with his monkey. Asmud, Will and Lars sat directly facing him on rustic benches. Ivar stayed where he was, standing and, surrounded by the red-plumed palace guards, no doubt following orders. White plumed guards stood in a circle behind Gennadios, swords still drawn.

When Gennadios' guests refused his offers of refreshment, he opened his arms in a gesture of acceptance and spoke. "Why are you here?"

His eyes twinkled as he said this. Annie stared at him in disbelief. He looked the image of a kindly grandfather.

Meg responded. She spoke in an even, calm voice. "May I introduce—"

"I know who you all are and of your journey to get here. I repeat, why are you here? What do you want of me?"

Meg continued as though he had not rudely interrupted her. "We believe you have in your collection twin girls, purchased by you in Jorvik, England, a business transaction between you and Queen Gunnhild, wife of King Eiric of Jorvik."

"What you say is true. Queen Gunnhild and I have conducted many business transactions over the years, to our mutual benefit. I enjoy a similar relationship with our beloved Emperor and Empress." He paused, with the obvious intention of allowing his comments to register. "Why you have taken it upon yourselves to make such an onerous journey puzzles me. I bought these jewels in a legal transaction. They are come to a better life, away from the mud huts and the diseases of that poor benighted country whence you came."

Ivar lunged forward with a roar. Immediately, one of the red plumes grabbed him by the scruff of his neck and both red and white plumes closed around the group, their swords pointing menacingly like the spokes of a wheel: the five seekers becoming the hub.

In the sudden silence, the song of a bird warbled, its notes rising and falling. Another bird joined in the song, then another and another. Rosamund and Bea brought their heads above the cover of the baskets, their blackness striking amid the pristine white world.

"My rash friend; your impetuosity has startled my beautiful songbirds. I have nightingales, blackbirds, goldfinches and linnets, amongst others. I cannot tolerate this behaviour. My feathered companions live a life of captive serenity. Let us all breathe deeply and inhale the peacefulness of my world. Those cats I see in your baskets, Mistress Thornton, must go. They have the same blackness of your hair. Black is anathema to me. I have created a world of light. It soothes me. White is pure, as is the element of gold.

"You stare at me in amazement. I assure you Gennadios of Mytilene is sane. I am an artist, a creator, in fact, a genius: and, as Aristotle said, 'There was never a genius without a tincture of madness,' so let us be peaceful together. If you give your bond to remain calm, I will release you from your temporary prison. I do insist; however, we remove those cats. They disturb my equanimity. Guard, be so kind as to take the baskets away."

Annie looked wildly around and pulled her precious cargo to her chest, to no avail. A white plume stepped forward and placed his hands on the basket.

"They will remain safe, mistress. You may have them back when you leave." He tugged at the basket; Annie tugged back.

He spoke quietly into her ear, "You have my word as Dexios of Petra, captain of the guards."

Annie caught a quick nod from her aunt. She released the basket. The white-plumed guard Dexios walked away with Rosamund and Bea.

"Good." the Greek Collector reached over to one of the platters and carefully selected a few grapes, which he slowly fed to his monkey. "Honoured guests, meet my friend Argyros, a blue monkey from Africa; regard his whiteness, a rare deviation of nature. Argyros means silver. You must agree he is beautiful." He stroked the little monkey's head. The monkey—his face disturbingly similar to a human's—grinned. "I appreciate deviations from nature, so I collect them." He chuckled: a warm, rich sound. "A deviant collector. I like the title." Then, as though hosting an afternoon tea party, he turned twinkling eyes back to his guests.

"I understand your interest in my collection and that you might wish to collect something for yourselves—guards! If that man continues behaving badly, pierce him through or take him out of my sight.

"Do you wish to see my porcelain collection? It is so fine, so thin; you can see your hand through the china. I know of no other porcelain outside of China. Alternatively, we can visit my herd of white gazelles or my white tiger. No? You might want to wander through my rooms of oddities. I have a three-legged man from Arabia; a woman with three breasts from Africa; a perfect man only forty-eight *daktyloi* high, three measurements of your foot, young man." He paused and pointed to Asmud's shoes. "As you can see, I also like the number three; it fascinates me. In our Greek stories of the Gods, three brothers, Zeus, Poseidon and Hades each ruled their worlds. I, too, rule my world and all the creatures therein.

"I am teasing you. I am sure you anticipate seeing see my delectable look-alikes: my most recently acquired jewels. We are fortunate that they are safely here with me. I understand that a number of attempts were made by the unscrupulous crew of my good friend, Captain Abdul Azim to take them for their own profit. In fact, when their ship docked in Prosphorion harbour, the slave woman looking after my jewels took a man overboard who was trying to steal them away. Both died. It is sad that people cannot be trusted these days."

The air in the garden seemed trapped in a heavy layer, pressing the cloying perfume of the flowers into Annie's nose. This man's insane chatter filled her with even more dread. She broke out in a cold sweat and her head swam. Meg came across to her, calling for water and lowering her niece's head. "Listen to me; the cats are safe, I placed a protection spell upon them. This man is quite mad. Mayhap we can use his madness to our benefit."

When Annie eventually raised her head, Gennadios clapped his hands. "Good, I am pleased you are recovered. And now, please observe my treasures." He clapped his hands again and two of the beardless ones walked to the far corner of the garden where a small, circular, silk-walled pavilion nestled amongst the shrubbery. Drawing back a silken wall, the servants revealed a charming yet macabre tableau. Annie drew in a sharp breath. Her friends did the same.

Two children sat on a couch inside the gently billowing silk. A young female accompanied them, all three dressed in white, classical Greek chitons. The two girls, identical in their profiles, focused on a tumbling group of white, fluffy kittens. The minder looked on, her hair an unyielding pile of flaxen coils, offering a sharp contrast to the free, bubbly, blond curls of the girls. A fair-haired boy, also dressed in a classic Greek chiton, perched on a stool behind them playing softly on a harp.

Annie quickly comprehended the paradox facing her. What appeared to be a tableau of gentle beauty and harmony was, in fact, an image representing dissonance and immorality. The figures—real, living children—were all slaves, captured and taken from their homes. She turned to look at her aunt. Do something. Say something. Release us from this craziness.

Again, Aunt Meg gave a slight shake of her head.

"So, what do you think of my lovely look-alikes? Are they not exquisite? Of course, as they came to me as heathens, I will have them brought into our faith. As I cannot tell them apart, I have given them one new Christian name to share, *Krysanthe*: golden flower. They have settled in well. Of course, they still receive a few drops of the poppy daily to help them adjust. I will reduce the amount slowly as they become used to seeing me as their *Bampás*, their Papa. I have already taken them to the Hippodrome to display to the common people. I must humbly say they received more attention than the Emperor's elephants and giraffes."

He smiled fondly at his new acquisitions and turned back to his incredulous audience.

"Again, I ask you, what is it you want from me?"

"As much as you believe you purchased these children in a legal transaction, you need to know they were not for sale. They lived in their own home with a loving father, mother and grandparents." Meg continued to speak in a quiet, calm voice; her hands remained loosely clasped together in her lap; her grey eyes regarded Gennadios without flinching. "Their loving father is the man you have removed from your sight. Two ruffians snatched the children from outside their home in full daylight. They were taken by force and without permission by order of Queen Gunnhild. They are children, not exhibits and need to be at home with their parents."

"Where is your proof? How dare you accuse a person of royal blood with such a heinous crime? Only the fact that my Emperor requested that I see you guarantees your safety here."

Asmud leaned forward. "As you have stated, you know who we all are; so you know I am here as a representative of Princess Olga of

Kiev. She, too, is a friend of Emperor Constantine and a strong trading partner to the Byzantine Empire. She also supplies his Majesty with his Varangian bodyguard, whom he values most highly. Princess Olga is most concerned that these children return to their rightful parents." He paused. "As soon as possible."

Asmud's emphasis on his last remark was unmistakable. Annie watched a red tide of anger rise up the face of the Greek, made more vivid against a white backdrop. He stood abruptly and stalked off toward the main building, shouting commands.

"Guard these barbarians with your lives. Remove my jewels. I have important business."

67

Will spoke first. "Now what; that didn't go too well. Perhaps we should just snatch the twins and run, not that we'll get too far."

"I hope Ivar is safe," said Lars. He hadn't spoken for so long, his voice sounded rusty.

"We will remain here, calm and orderly," said Meg. "That abominable man will return and he will want to negotiate. The last thing he wants is to have his reputation tarnished. At least, we can see the twins are alive and safe, even though they appear benumbed. Meanwhile, let us take advantage of his absence and take some refreshments."

"How do we know the food isn't poisoned or drugged?" asked Asmud.

"He fed grapes to his monkey, we'll eat only those."

Meg was, as usual, right. The sun had begun to move further west and the shadows were gathering in the garden when Gennadios returned, rubbing his hands together, and smiling as he sat. Argyros no longer sat on his shoulder.

"I have consulted my Oracle," he giggled. "She suggests the following to solve our little dilemma. I will return the children to you in exchange for Mistress Annie Thornton, whom I understand to be a Viking völva of great repute."

A deep and stunned silence greeted his proposal.

Will and Asmud leaped to their feet, prompting the guards to step forward, swords lifted.

"Never!" shouted Will.

"This is not a joke, sir," said Asmud, attempting to maintain a measured voice. "We are willing to pay you whatever you paid for the children."

"Sit. Sit. I am not interested in the money. I can buy any human being I desire. A child costs only ten *nomismata*, and a castrated child, thirty. I look only for the satisfaction of owning incomparable objects. I believe a captive witch outweighs even these two jewels. So, take them away with you, and leave me your völva. However, this is the condition: she must come willingly and bind herself to me for all time.

"Let me, Gennadios of Mytilene, reassure you; I appreciate and follow Plato's definition of *Éros:* contemplation of the beauty within the person. The ownership of a powerful völva will lead me to a higher plane of spirituality. She shall remain as pure as light."

"Let me stay with you instead." The still, calm voice of Meg floated above the tension. "I tell you I am a much more powerful and experienced sorcerer than this child. Between us, you and I can achieve greatness."

Asmud turned and looked at Meg, his features etched deeply with anguish.

Annie looked at Will and then turned to Gennadios. The heavy rock lying in the pit of her stomach since arriving in Constantinople melted away. She felt so light she believed she could float.

"Thank you for your offer, Mistress Wistowe. While you have been a good teacher, I, your pupil, have now surpassed you in my powers as völva. You are growing old, while I still have the gift of youth. Take the children and go. See that Ivar and his little ones are united and returned to their home."

Annie reached for Will's hand. "Go back to Hallamby, my friend. We *will* meet again in another life." Smiling serenely, she turned away and moved toward Gennadios, not turning to watch as her stunned friends left the garden with the twins in the arms of Ivar and Asmud.

68

Annie remembered the joy on Ivar's face when the guards brought him back into the garden and took him, along with Meg, to his children. They looked puzzled when Ivar called them by name but came willingly to him, asking if the kittens could come too.

So, they had accomplished their mission, and she, Annie, was no longer needed. It felt right to be here with Gennadios. She had come to her rightful place. All would be well.

A small frown marred her brow. Where had Rosamund gone? She was not used to being without her. The white-plumed guard, Dexios, had come to her once Gennadios left the garden and told her the cats were not in the baskets when he went back to retrieve them. "They must have left of their own accord," he said. "I will watch for them."

Annie looked in a burnished copper mirror at her silvery curls and traced her finger along her gently arched, blond eyebrows. How different she looked! Female slaves had spent hours grooming her. She had soaked in perfumed water, had her skin scrubbed with a strigil, her hair treated with an unknown, strong smelling substance, unwanted body hair plucked, her nails shaped and painted. The slaves finally wrapped her breasts in a *strophion*, then dressing her in a soft, linen chiton. Only the glow of gold set in her pearl earrings and holding a giant pearl ring on her finger deviated from her whiteness. Soft, pearl-covered leather sandals adorned her feet. Two girls still threaded snowy, silk ribbons through her hair.

"Stop fussing," she laughed and pushed them away.

When her handmaidens paraded her before Gennadios, he praised them for their fine work, and then dismissed them.

"Now you are worthy of Gennadios," he purred. "Come; turn around for me, my captive Viking völva. How the throngs of Constantinople will admire me at the Hippodrome when they see my newest possession. The exchange was to my advantage. You need a new name for your new life. Annie is so plebeian. I name you Alina, meaning 'light'.

69

The twins lay sleeping on a couch in the rooms of the Great Palace. They curled around each other as though mimicking the two sleeping white kittens they had brought back with them. Ivar sat at the end of the couch, silent and watchful.

When everyone had eaten and drunk their fill of food and watered wine, having eaten only a few grapes all day, they sat and stared at each other.

"Now what do we do?" Will asked.

Meg observed him with concern. He looked haggard; his eyes sank into his skull and the skin on his face had shrunk so it looked stretched over his cheekbones.

"We have much to do. I must find a way to return Ivar and the children to Jorvik. Then we can focus on rescuing Annie."

"How do we know she is safe with that crazy man?" Will, the powerfully-built ex-soldier, looked close to tears.

"Gennadios himself reassured us he looks for spiritual enlightenment through his possession of Annie, not of seeking carnal pursuits. I believe we must take him at his word; otherwise, we will go crazy too." Meg turned to Will, Asmud and Lars. "Be reminded, Annie has many skills. She is resourceful. Last year an unscrupulous man in our village imprisoned her. He planned to have her burned as a witch but Annie was able to escape and expose him using her many abilities. I am impressed with how serene she looked. In fact, that's the least worried I've seen her look since we arrived."

Will did not appear appeased but Asmud looked relieved. "Well, on to our other issue. It will be hard to find a ship going north at this time of year. We might be able to locate a captain willing to take Ivar and the twins through the Sea of Marmara into the Mediterranean Sea. Trading ships travel constantly between Constantinople and the Greek ports. Some will go on to London and the north. It is a long and dangerous journey, though. Pirates abound there too."

"I was thinking about something a little quicker, like shapeshifting." A frown appeared between Meg's eyebrows. "I need the cats, but as they decided to leave their baskets and disappear, I'll have to manage without them. I must leave you, my friends, and consult the Goddess."

70

Gennadios played with Argyros, throwing grapes and pieces of orange for the creature to catch in his mouth; Argyros missed none. Songbirds trilled their morning arias in the *peristyle*, the walled garden in the country villa.

The new Alina watched with quiet amusement. Actually, he's not a bad old sort, she mused, once you got past the fact that he collected people. She could learn to love this eccentric and slightly mad old man.

"How is my Alina this beautiful morning? Are you feeling well?"

"Quite well thank you, Gennadios. Do you have any plans for today?"

"Today Emperor Constantine and the Empress Helene may visit the Park of Philopation. They come out here most days to hunt and enjoy the gardens. I beg of you to stay in this garden, as the men will release wild animals. I include lions and tigers as well as deer."

Alina shuddered but said nothing.

"After hunting, their Imperial Majesties may honour me with a visit. I will show you off to them; therefore look beautiful for me. One important note," Gennadios paused to feed his monkey more grapes, "only I know of your special skills. Our culture does not tolerate witchcraft, even though the poorer people amongst us practice magical beliefs. Our Holy Mother Church views the practice as a sin. So… not a word to anyone; our little secret—oh, and how I acquired you." He smiled, holding an elegantly manicured finger to his lips.

Alina returned the smile but his remark about 'being shown off' bothered her—she hated being the centre of attention. Still, she realized she wanted to please the old man and how did he, as he called it 'acquire' her? Her mind appeared to be made of thick fog when she tried to remember the past.

The captive völva spent most of the day bathing and enjoying a vigorous massage, followed by another top-to-toe skin treatment. Water flowed everywhere in Constantinople, Alina had discovered, and proved no different here in Gennadios' sumptuous country home. Creative and efficient plumbing provided fountains, both inside and outside the villa; Fresh water flowed freely through copper taps and elegant spouts shaped as birds and animals. Terracotta pipes transported waste from yet another communal lavatory.

Her handmaidens dressed her in a white silk chiton. This time Alina paid special attention to this clever and ubiquitous garment worn by both males and females. Consisting of a long tube, it was secured along her upper arms and shoulders by fasteners then flowed to the floor. Excess material looped through a belt and draped gracefully over her hips.

Two giggling young girls worked hard attempting to control Alina's unruly blond curls. They managed to pin her hair into an upswept style controlled by a pearl band. Wayward tendrils lay at her neckline and ears. Gennadios had created her earrings and provided the only colour. Alina watched the light catch garnets set in an exquisitely painted enamel base and jiggled her head to make the pearls dance on their gold chains. She regarded her hands, both bedecked with large gold, pearl rings.

She pirouetted before the mirror. Strange, she had not thought of friends for a while. Somehow, they seemed to be fading, their faces indistinct.

Alina turned again to her reflection in the full length burnished bronze mirror. The likeness reminded her of something, an image— an image from her previous life, yet even the memory of that life was diminishing.

Aha, the memory returned.

When visiting Athens on a cheap package trip, she brought home a statue of a caryatid. A caryatid was a Greek maiden transformed into a column supporting a porch in the Acropolis in Athens. She looked like a caryatid! Alina frowned, wrinkles spoiling her perfec-

tion. Where was her statue now? How strange to have difficulty remembering life before Constantinople.

No matter! *Now* is important. Posturing in front of the mirror,
she had never been aware of her beauty before. This is so much fun.
Maybe she'd never go home. She laughed. Of course, Alina would go
home… but not yet… not for a while.

71

Alina was resting on her day couch in the women's quarters when the trumpets blew.

"Who is making that noise and why?" she asked the young hand-maiden who was desultorily waving a fan over her blonde curls.

"Oh, that'll be the Emperor and his lot chasing the poor animals, again. They're always at it. They come here most days. It's nothing t'do with us unless they decide to visit the Master." Walking over to the open window, she complained, "It just means more work for us if they do decide to call in."

"When will you know if they decide to visit?" asked Alina remembering Gennadios' words, 'I'll show you off'.

"Usually, they arrive as the sun moves over the tops of the trees and the heat drops a bit."

Alina's heart-rate increased. "Do I look alright?" She saw puzzlement on the young slave's face. "I mean do I look presentable?"

The slave girl, with eyes huge in her pinched face; fair hair sticking out in all directions and a drab, colourless tunic hanging from her skinny frame, looked down at Lady Alina lounging on her couch.

She stammered, "M-my Lady, you look beautiful—a Goddess— Dexios already adores you," lowering her head. "I want him to look at me like he looks at you; but he don't even see me."

For an instant, Annie felt ashamed. This child was a slave whereas she had everything her heart desired since deciding to live with Gennadios. A beautiful home, slaves to attend her, a kind and loving papa—what did Gennadios call himself— Bampás. She would look her best for the Emperor, to please her Bampás.

Gennadios' senior eunuch, Castinus, knocked gently on the door of Alina's room. "The Master requires your presence in the reception hall, Lady Alina. We are blessed with the presence of their Majesties, the Emperor and Empress."

Alina carefully made her way to the reception hall. Two white-plumes stood outside the doors leading into the hall, one of whom was Dexios who winked at her as she passed.

Annie stiffened. How dare he wink at her? The man was impertinent. She took a deep breath and walked into the luxuriously appointed room.

The Emperor and his wife lounged on a white silk couch, gold en-crusted goblets in hand, and impressive amounts of food spread before them, served on gold plates. Their colourful and bejewelled outfits stood out in a room draped in white silk. Gennadios' only concessions to colour were icons of saints. Huge vases filled with boughs of white flowers perfumed the air. A delicately carved ivory triptych behind the Royal pair's couch showed Jesus, surrounded by his saints. For a split second, Alina reverted to Annie and wondered how many elephants had died in the making of the piece; however, the thought passed in a flash as she prostrated herself before their Majesties.

"Arise, child," Empress Helena spoke. "We do not stand on cere-mony here with our dear friend Gennadios. He has been showing us his designs for a new necklace for me. It is in the shape of the Cross of our Lord with emeralds set in gold. We are well pleased."

The Empress signalled to a slave to bring forward a stool. "Come; sit at our feet so we may see you. Gennadios has told us of your beauty. He has not told us of your uniqueness, and I know this man well. You must be unique or you would not be here."

Alina moved to perch on the tiny embroidered and gilded stool, her eyes cast down, limbs trembling and heart pounding.

"You look familiar to me. Have I met you before?" The Empress reached down and, using a perfectly manicured finger adorned with a richly enamelled ring, hooked it under Alina's chin, and lifted her face upward.

"I have no memory of meeting your Majesty."

The Emperor stirred. "Were you amongst the party who petitioned me to speak to my friend, Gennadios, about something or other?"

"I have no memory of such a meeting".

"Now we have the pleasure of the company of this lovely young woman. I repeat, what makes you unique?"

Alina wracked her brain. What did make her unique?—apart from the fact that she was a witch. Her brain froze. Silence grew so loud, it became deafening. Gennadios shuffled on his couch.

A picture began to form in her head. Triangles folded and unfolded. Numbers swirled. The high pitched, feline voice of—was that her cat Rosamund?—sounded in her ear. Of course—The Pythagoras Theorem!

"Unlike your revered philosopher Pythagoras, numbers are a mystery to me; however, like Pythagoras, I have been gifted with the ability to talk to animals."

If royal jaws could drop, theirs did. Even Gennadios looked at his captured witch in awe—and some disbelief. Emperor Constantine had actually stopped eating during Alina's revelation. He spat out an olive stone into a gold bowl held at the ready by a slave. "You say these things. Prove it."

Another image came into Alina's head. She was standing in a square, stamping her staff on the ground and flash-freezing two men. She remembered how powerful she had felt. Yes, she could do that again. She didn't need anyone else to help her; she was all-powerful.

"As I said, Majesty, I can talk to the animals; I can make them submit to my will."

"What powers do you use to do these things? I smell demonology here." The Emperor turned to Gennadios. "I do hope you are not becoming involved with sorcery, my friend."

Annie interjected. "Majesty, I do not invoke the devil, nor do I use trickery. My unique gifts came with me from my mother's womb and my Bampás here has been astute enough to sense this."

"I wish to see this 'talking to the animals' skill, right now, here." The Emperor looked agitated, his face reddening.

Alina took a deep breath and closed her eyes. Then she walked behind Gennadios and, standing where neither he nor the monkey could see her, she sent the monkey a message: help me and I will feed you the most luscious fruit I can find. She spoke softly. "Argyros, can you hear me?"

The little monkey, who had been sitting on his master's lap, swung his head around, but he could not locate the source.

"Argyros, please choose the finest grape and give it to your master."

With great delicacy, the monkey picked over the bunch of grapes and, having chosen the largest one, placed it deftly into the mouth of Gennadios.

Emperor Constantine and his wife clapped their hands in delight. Argyros grinned.

"Argyros, take off your beautiful silk cap and place it on the head of your master."

When the monkey did so, the royal couple clapped again.

Alina became bolder. "Argyros, take the dish of grapes and offer it to their Majesties."

The monkey's gold chain was not long enough so Gennadios had to stand and follow his pet over to the royal pair. With great ceremony, Argyros offered the dish to the Empress and then bowed.

Their applause was loud. Alina could see the look of pride on the face of her Bampás.

"I have an idea," said Gennadios, his face alight with excitement. "When we next attend the chariot races, we will provide a spectacle the people of Constantinople will never forget. Imagine Alina standing alone in the centre of the Hippodrome, a tiny figure in shining white. Two lions enter the arena, just as happens with convicted felons, but this time goodness triumphs over evil as Alina calms the beasts and walks away. The crowds will go crazy."

72

Alina stared at the wall in her room. What had she done? Her Bampás chose to have her eaten by lions so he could gain more fame. How could Gennadios, who professed to love her, do this? She had nowhere to turn for help. Sighing deeply, Alina anticipated her coming demise, wondering how long it took a lion to eat her, limb by limb.

A light knock at the door broke into her gloomy thoughts. Dexios entered, a finger held to his lips. He flashed a charming smile at Alina's slave girl and gestured she should busy herself elsewhere.

"Lady, I know of your concern that your cats were not in the baskets when your friends left here. I want to ease your mind. I have seen them and am putting out food and water. They remain close by in the gardens."

Alina stared at the young and handsome guard. "What do I care of cats? I am about to die for sport in your stupid hippodrome. Have you not heard?"

"I have, Lady. We all have heard of your great gift and pray we will attend in order to see you tame the beasts."

"Out! Out idiot! Leave me in peace."

Sunset had arrived when another knock disturbed Alina's melancholy thoughts.

"I hear you are refusing food, my dear. What is the problem? What concerns you?"

Gennadios looked genuinely worried as he crossed the room and sat by Alina.

Alina stared at him in amazement.

"As much as I love you, my Bampás; I cannot understand why you want to kill me by feeding me to the lions?"

"Oh, my child, you have the skills to perform this amazing feat. I am well aware of your power and of your achievements in the past, and think of the glory, of the adulation I will receive as a result of your performance."

An icy wind blew across Alina's face.

"Why are you aware of my power and past achievements, Bampás? I have no memory of sharing them with you."

"My Oracle tells me everything," he responded with a chuckle. "She told me of your coming here and of your many gifts. You may feel better knowing she also informed me you have already shown remarkable abilities in another arena far from here."

"That knowledge certainly makes me feel better. Who is this all-knowing oracle you consult."

"She appears in the form of a raven—a white raven—so rare and beautiful; I almost wish I could include her in my collection. Impossible, of course."

Gennadios' words hit Alina like a blow to her belly. Although her recent past had begun to fade, as a creeping mist blots out everything in its path, all came rushing back. Gunnhild! Gunnhild had done it again: she had subverted Annie's defences and bewitched her. Retribution indeed.

73

Mistress Meg Wistowe came back into the room and watched the three men entertain the twins by juggling their morning fruit. Gales of childish laughter met frequent scrambles for rolling oranges, figs and grapes. Will however, sat alone, staring into space.

"I am concerned." Meg walked over to Asmud and held out her hand; a small, wooden figure rested in her palm. "Twice before, I have used my *hnefi*, my king piece from the *Hnefatafl* board, to summon help from King Eiric. Now, I want to send a message to my friend Gytha, using King Eiric once again as the medium, letting her know her babies are safe and will return home. I cannot even get the piece to stand up, it just topples over."

Asmud reached for the intricately carved king and examined the base. "It seems smooth and level enough. I thought it may be damaged from its travels." He carefully placed the king piece on a small table and watched as it fell, headfirst.

"No, something terrible has happened to King Eiric. I believe him to be dead." Meg began pacing up and down. "Now I worry about what that means for Jorvik and my friends." She looked across at Ivar, attempting unsuccessfully to throw grapes into his daughters' mouths, allowing herself a small smile, thinking that they may not yet remember their father but as they wean off the poppy juice, memories will return.

Will approached Meg, "What of your talk with your G-Goddess." His stutter as he asked the question showed his awkwardness with Meg's witchy ways.

"I haven't yet spoken with her; I became so distressed at the action of my *hnefi*."

Will frowned and shook his head. "It's a game piece, Meg, what of it." He began pacing up and down the room. "My concern is for Annie. I feel so useless. We must save her from that man. Although he appears not as other men, I do not trust him."

Meg observed the strain on the young man's face. "I will g—"

A tap at the door and Narses bustled in, excited with his news. "Everyone in town talks of nothing else. Gennadios brings his latest jewel to the Hippodrome tomorrow. Apparently, she is an amazing conjurer and can talk to animals, bending them to her will. She will show everyone she can tame tigers and lions."

The only sound heard in the room was the laughter of the children and even that sound faltered as a shocked silence descended.

Will turned to Meg; his face betrayed his anguish. "I knew something terrible would happen. My beloved Annie is in danger." He spun around to Ivar and Lars who stood as if turned to stone. "It's time we stopped behaving like scared chickens and become men again. We must rescue her. We can find a boat and... and..." His voice trailed away.

"Will, Will, that won't help. They will come after us. Annie is safe for now. We need to think calmly and I really must find out why my *hnefi* is behaving this way. Ivar and Asmud please comfort Will until I return—I may be a while."

When Meg returned a long time later, the sun had set and the twins were fast asleep on their couch. Her face revealed the extent of her exhaustion. Asmud poured a goblet of wine. As Meg took the goblet from him, her hand trembled, spilling wine down the front of her palla.

"My sweet, what is it? You have been away all day. You have more bad news?"

74

Turmoil reigned in Gennadios of Mytilene's country villa as slaves prepared to return their master and his latest jewel to the city. In the stable yard, slaves feverishly groomed horses until their matching grey coats gleamed and struggled to secure silver plumes onto tossing heads. Energy swirling around the yard created more tension and the sound of hooves pawing flagstones added to the din. Grooms waited impatiently to harness the team to a large wagon as slaves crawled all over, waxing and polishing. Sporting wooden wheels, a curved roof and a padded, silver brocade-covered interior, the elaborate wagon offered a unique sight around Constantinople. More slaves piled various goods and chattels onto a second utility wagon where a mule, already harnessed, brayed hoarsely.

Annie sat immobile, away from the chaos, while her thoughts tumbled around in her head like clothes in a dryer—no beginning, no end—just a circle of panic and despair. She had lost her friends through inattention to the power of Gunnhild. How stupid of her to remain unaware of the possibility of revenge—and revenge this certainly was—for thwarting the Queen's plans to destroy Will and Lars to prevent them from continuing their search. Annie vividly remembered being in the hot, crowded square in Novgorod; Will and Lars locked in a battle to the death. She had been strong then, her borrowed staff giving her power to break the spell.

Of course, the Queen would retaliate. Knowing Gunnhild's pride, singeing her locks when she was flying overhead as Raven had created even more vitriol. Annie had not given the possibility a thought. Where had her brains been? Why had she slid so easily into the role of Gennadios' new acquisition and had even begun to care for him, forgetting both her beloved Will, her aunt and friends in the process? How weak was that? She chided herself continuously.

Worst of all, she had discovered she really was bound to this crazy old man. After Gennadios told her of the white raven, Annie ran from the room and out of the building. She almost reached the gates leading out of the courtyard before she came to an abrupt halt, choking, her hands clutching at her neck. Two white-plumes came up to her and gently escorted her back into the presence of Gennadios who chuckled—a rich, warm sound.

"My dear Alina, do you not remember the terms of our agreement? In exchange for the children, you agreed to be bound to me for life. And you are. My Oracle made sure of that. You may not be able to see the chains, but just like my little Argyros, we also are attached."

Castinus tapped on her door. "Time to go, Lady." He escorted Annie down the stairs and out into the courtyard where Dexios and the other white plumes stood to attention.

Gennadios came bustling out of the ornate entrance doors, shouting incomprehensible instructions and startling the horses. His monkey sat on his shoulder as usual.

"There you are, my dear. Into the carriage with you. We have lots to do to prepare for tomorrow. As the Romans said, '*Tempus Fugit!*'"

Dexios stepped forward to help Annie climb into the small space. Openings on either side of the carriage let in some light and air, but Annie immediately found the space claustrophobic. As Dexios was about to step back he whispered in her ear. "Your precious cats are in the following wagon. I will care for them in Constantinople."

Annie remembered how imperiously she had behaved and bowed her head at her cold-heartedness, toward both him and Rosamund and Bea who had stayed nearby. Somehow, once back in the city, she would find a way to contact her aunt. Dexios might help her; he appeared to be a friend. A sudden thought struck her. What if her dearest aunt and friends had left Constantinople already and this was to be her life from now on: a puppet witch, on display for a psychopath who could jerk her strings whenever he desired?

75

When Meg had finished talking, her four companions looked at her with shock written across their faces. Lars spoke first. "Mistress, you say King Eiric is dead and t'Anglo-Saxons 'ave taken back Jorvik?"

Ivar, trying to comprehend her words, blurted, "What of Jorvik? Is me city at war? Me wife, 'er parents, our 'ome—all gone?"

Meg held up her hands. "Please, calm yourselves. When I left you, I accomplished two things. I shapeshifted into a golden eagle and flew to Jorvik. I realize that sounds strange to your ears but it is something a völva can do. I rode the wind on powerful wings making my journey swift. I spoke with your wife, Ivar. She and her parents, now knowing you and the twins are safe and coming home, have replaced sadness with joy.

"Gytha told me all of the news. Details of the king's death remain vague. He and his jarls rode north, possibly into an ambush. Queen Gunnhild has fled with her sons. The word is that she has sought refuge in Denmark. Gytha knew nothing of Queen Iseabail; mayhap she has returned to Scotland. I pray for her safety, a good woman, and kind to us. An English king has taken control and Jorvik is once more part of England. I also communed with the Goddess Hecate."

"What of Annie?" Will cried.

"Annie's situation is interesting and—I have to say—predictable. Queen Gunnhild slipped through our defences again. She stayed in close touch with Gennadios. He sees her as his 'Oracle'. Gunnhild devised the whole strategy of exchanging the twins for Annie, retribution for what Annie did to her: searing her 'feathers' in the square at Novgorod."

"Speak plainly, Meg, I beg of you." Will became more distraught, pulling at his hair and pacing.

"She, Gunnhild, has bound Annie to Gennadios with invisible bonds so she cannot ever escape him."

Will howled like a wounded dog and fell to his knees. Lars reached down to his friend and held him.

"All is not lost, Will. Listen to me." Meg's voice sharpened. "Listen to me. Those bonds can be melted by total immersion in pure water: water coming from the clouds, so the Goddess spoke."

Will looked up; hope beginning to shine from his eyes. Then they dulled again. "How do we accomplish such an act before she is eaten by lions?"

Asmud had remained quietly in the background during the drama. He now stepped forward.

"I believe we need to manage one event at a time. Routine at the Hippodrome is always the same: the circus performing first. Then the Emperor parades his exotic animals; after that, the jugglers and acrobats perform and, I believe Gennadios's exhibition may be next. Chariot racing comes last."

"What did Narses mean when he said, 't'conjurer can talk t'animals'?" Ivar raised his eyebrows. "What does Annie know of talkin' to animals? Perhaps it's not Annie, but some poor addled-brained thrall."

Meg shook her head. "If this scheme involves Gennadios, Annie is his prize piece. Why she says she can talk to the animals, I do not know, but if she says she can, then she can and we need to help her in any way possible. Asmud is right. We require a plan to help her survive the Hippodrome, and then we can move on to melting her bonds.

"In the meantime, we have to send Ivar, Eydis, Eyia and Lars back to Jorvik. I wanted to shapeshift you and the children, Ivar, but I do not have that much power. I can shapeshift myself, but not others."

Asmud reached out and clasped Meg's hands. "I've been given your shapeshifting much thought. We change them into something they are not. Is that not shapeshifting?"

He had everyone's attention but Lars, looking embarrassed and with red-tipped ears poking out from his hair, blurted out, "I'm not goin' back. I 'aven't 'ad chance to tell you with everythin' goin' on. I'm going to stay 'ere and become a Varangian guard. Ivar 'as promised me the coins to pay me entry fee. A might 'ave to join an ordinary regiment first but it's what a want to do."

"What about your parents?" Meg looked worried. "We said we would bring you safely home."

"Am of the age to move on. They know that. A would 'ave gone araidin' with King Eiric this autumn. A'll go 'ome when am rich."

"Good for you," Asmud nodded his approval. "I can guarantee you will enjoy the life. Now listen to my shapeshifting idea."

Asmud had just begun talking when a tentative tap on the door interrupted him. Sighing in frustration, he opened the door, Meg at his shoulder. A young man dressed in a plain brown tunic and looking vaguely familiar stood there. He had an anxious expression on his face.

"What business do you have with us?" asked Asmud.

Meg spoke first. "I recognize you. You were the guard at Gennadios' place. You took the cat basket from my niece. Is—Meg's voice broke—"is she all right?"

"My name is Dexios, chief guard in the employ of Gennadios of Mytilene. I come to you with a message from your friend Alina."

"Alina? We have no knowledge of such a person." Asmud's voice betrayed his hostility.

"She lives with my Master. You accompanied her to his country villa. I repeat; I bring you a message from her"

Asmud reached for Dexios' arm and, rather than reacting in a hostile manner, a grin appeared across his face as he pulled him into the apartment.

"Will, we have a messenger from Annie!"

Everyone began firing questions.

Meg laughed, shushing the others and led the guard to a couch.

"Sit Dexios; Lars, bring refreshment to our new friend and saviour. Asmud, please translate our visitor's Greek."

Dexios stared at her. "I had anticipated some hostility, even violence, but this reception has me bewildered."

As he sipped on his wine, Meg spoke. "My name is Mistress Meg Wistowe. Annie, or Alina as you appear to know her, is my niece as well as my apprentice. We are anxious for news of her. That is why we welcome you. Please tell us Annie is well and why you are here."

"Your Annie is well but sad and frightened. She's going to the Hippodrome tomorrow to face the lions."

"This we have heard. How did such a monstrous idea come to be?" asked Meg.

Dexios told of the visit to Gennadios by the Emperor and Empress and of the Empress's demand Annie speak of her uniqueness.

"I was on guard duty outside the room and could hear the conversation. Later, one of the slaves shared with me the amazing feat your niece performed. How the monkey did all she commanded, even feeding grapes to their Majesties. It seems that my Master was so pleased with her talent he decided she should appear at the Hippodrome and repeat her performance, but with lions." Dexios looked apologetic. "He loves to reap the praise from the crowds. Do you think she can do the same with the lions: make them obey her? She is so beautiful, so perfect. I cannot bear she should be harmed in any way."

At this impassioned statement, Will stood—this young man was in love with his sweetheart.

"Has your master or anyone else harmed her in any way?" Will spoke roughly, stepping forward, his fists curled.

"No, no, we all love her and, to my Master, she is precious. I have come here at the request of Alina—your Annie. She wishes to know if you remain in Constantinople and, if so, how can you help her. I also brought your two cats back from the country. They are safe in my room at the town house."

"It seems we owe you a huge debt of gratitude, Dexios." As Meg said this, she looked at Will with a slight shake of her head. "I know Annie is capable of taming the lions." She turned to her companions. "I ask you to take your minds back to the square at Novgorod and visualize the scene when Will and Lars were, hmm, wrestling: how she prevented catastrophe. That is the skill Annie can use tomorrow; she just needs a little help from her friends."

76

Constantinople's famous Hippodrome had created a cauldron of noise, heat and smells, all rising upward. Annie sat with Gennadios in the *Kathisma*, the Emperor's Loge. The Loge held seating for the Imperial Family, hundreds of imperial courtiers and invited guests, accessed via a private passageway from the Grand Palace.

Two elaborate thrones sat in the centre of rows of brocade-covered seats awaiting arrival of the Emperor and Empress. Luxurious purple hangings and intricate tapestries hung on the back wall. The *Kathisma* sat above the common herd who filled marble stacked rows surrounding a long u-shaped racetrack.

When Annie and Gennadios first took their places in the Emperor's Loge, Annie was appalled by the mass of faces staring at them—at her—and the ripple of sound sweeping through the crowd: they were chanting Gennadios, Gennadios.

Had she not felt so apprehensive she might have enjoyed her first sight of the famous Hippodrome of Constantinople. Prior to their arrival, Gennadios had given a detailed history of the Hippodrome's past. How it had been at the centre of the Nika riots in AD 532 when political manoeuvring between plotting senators resulted in hostility between rival factions of the chariot teams, which exploded into riots lasting days, resulting in 30,000 deaths. How the Hippodrome was the one special place where people could see Emperor Constantine. How it was the centre of social life in the city… and on and on.

Annie had to admit; it was a spectacular place. The track must have been nearly fifteen hundred feet long and over four hundred feet wide. Over one hundred thousand people would attend today's event. She could see no empty spaces on the tiered seating and people were clinging to and hanging off various columns and ledges. When she expressed curiosity about why all the spectators on the west side wore blue and the spectators on the east side wore green, Gennadios explained they were the supporters of the rival chariot teams and separated to reduce the risk of fighting breaking out.

Just like our football fans, Annie mused. Nothing had changed over the centuries.

A barrier ran down the centre of the sand-based track and held a variety of statues, seven being of Porphyrios, a legendary charioteer, so Gennadios informed her. A tall obelisk decorated with plates of gilded bronze stood at the centre of the barrier, its gleaming panels catching the sun's rays. Statues of gods, Emperors and heroes were everywhere. Annie even recognized one of Romulus and Remus, the founders of Rome, with their she-wolf mother. At the far end of the racetrack, a row of twelve boxes provided the charioteers entrance, not unlike the starting gates of modern horseracing. High above the boxes, on the roof, stood four magnificent copper gilded horses.

Food sellers, trays filled with small bowls of *kakavia*, a fish soup; *dolmades*, stuffed grape leaves; *yuravalekia*, grain dumplings, and grilled sardines mixed with fried onions, navigated the many stairs. Other sellers carried baskets of oranges. Wine vendors ladled out wine from large amphorae. The combined smell of all these foods floated up to the *Kathisma* mixed with the heat and odour of thousands of over-heated bodies. Annie could understand why courtiers busily waved fans across their faces. Her nausea increased with each breath.

Observing a number of entrances, Annie wondered from which gate the lions would enter but refused to ask.

"Our Emperor placed that obelisk there." Gennadios leaned over, pointing at the bronze obelisk, oblivious to Annie's distress. "His name is on a plaque at the base. All the statues around the arena are of famous charioteers from the past; those on the roof too, celebrating their achievements. The tall obelisk you see there on the *spina*, the barrier in the centre, came from Egypt and travelled down the Nile River on a specially constructed raft. Emperor Theodosius transported it here in 390, the year of our Lord."

Annie looked down at the crowd, seeking distraction. They did not seem to be paying any attention to the statues but having a great time feasting and drinking, throwing dice, arguing, laying bets and generally enjoying their day at the races.

"Not too different from Epsom or Ascot, except that people aren't eaten in those racecourses for public enjoyment," she muttered to herself.

Annie startled as the shrill sound of trumpets pierced the clamour, which lessened slightly and, as one, faces lifted to gaze at the *Kathisma*. The Emperor and Empress entered with their entourage, surrounded by a Varangian Guard detail. Once Emperor Constantine Porphyrogenitus decided he was comfortable, he waved his hand.

The circus began.

A large entrance known as the Black Gates faced the *Kathisma*. A trumpet blew, quietening the hubbub and heavy wooden doors slowly opened, pushed by two giants wearing only loincloths, their heavily muscled bodies gleaming with oil.

The huge arena quickly filled with a myriad of dogs dressed as people from different countries; acrobats vaulted and cartwheeled.. Wrestlers covered in oil, and then, inevitably, sand, grappled one another. Crocodiles paraded on leashes held by muscular attendants; the crocodiles massive jaws bound with leather straps. Behind them walked elegant, loping giraffes with huge soft eyes, followed by elephants linked, trunk to tail. The crowd howled at the antics of the performers and pointed in awe at these strange and exotic animals owned by their Emperor.

Once the first act had cleared the arena, and the second act commenced, Annie had to close her eyes, as, to her horror, this performance glorified hunting and death. Again, the trumpet sounded to begin the session and, from the same entrance, dogs raced to bait bears, and cheetahs to attack antelopes. Two male lions attacked a bull, tearing out its throat before taking huge bites. Each time an animal died, crowds responded with cheers, reveling in bloody carnage.

Sweepers came and dragged dead carcasses away, raking over bloodied sand. Now the metallic smell of blood joined all the other smells wafting their way upward. The crowd settled down. Once the arena was clear, a sense of anticipation grew and faces lifted again toward Gennadios.

A chant began, growing in volume: Gennadios, Gennadios. Constantinople's goldsmith and collector of people stood and waved. Bowing first to their Majesties, he then turned to Dexios, standing at attention behind them. "Dexios, take Alina to the arena. Do good work for me, my Alina, and you will be well rewarded." With that, he sat down, a big smile on his face.

77

Annie could not move. Her legs seemed to have disconnected themselves from her brain. Oily fish and fried onions wafted across her nose and a burst of acid-filled saliva erupted from her throat, burning like liquid fire.

A gentle hand reached down and clasped her arm. Dexios whispered softly into her ear. "Come with me, Lady, your friends await. All will be well. Remember our plan."

Annie's sense of walking down stairs and into the tunnel behind the Emperor's box was dream-like. As her disordered mind tried to grapple with the reality—she was about to be eaten by lions—a giggle burst from her lips. This wasn't happening to her, a midwife from Yorkshire. She'd wake up in her own bed tomorrow and tell her friend Mary about this crazy dream—no—nightmare.

Meg, Will, Asmud, and Lars stood quietly behind a tall pillar. Asmud had tied a red rag onto a pole and held it high above his head. They, too, had watched the circus and had been appalled at its display of cruelty. Meg remarked that the reactions of the crowd disturbed her most.

"They thrive on the spectacle of suffering and death. It feeds on something loathsome within them."

Asmud nodded. "That's why they come here and the Emperor knows it. He gives them what they want and the circus keeps the masses quiet and compliant. I think this is Annie's appearance time," he continued. "Chariot races are the main event so she'll provide a perfect pause in the action."

"I hope Dexios can find us in this crowd," Meg looked anxious. "It's hard to believe there are so many people in one place."

"Here they come now," Lars had to raise his voice above the hubbub. "I can see the white plumes on his helmet above the heads of the people crowding the end of the tunnel."

Asmud began waving his pre-arranged signal banner.

Dexios pushed hot and sweaty bodies out of the way: not too gently either. As he saw Alina's friends he turned and, protecting her with his arms, moved toward them.

When Meg witnessed her niece's bleached white hair and eyebrows and her pale, tense face, she had to suppress the overwhelming urge to burst into tears; however, Annie needed all of the strength she could muster and seeing her aunt break down wouldn't help.

Meg reached out and embraced a now sobbing Annie. Will, looking shocked at the appearance of his beloved, also reached out his arms and wrapped them around both niece and aunt. Both began muttering endearments into Annie's ears. Annie eventually shook herself free and laughed shakily.

"I thought you'd all gone away and left me. I behaved so badly. I was so selfish—"

"Hush child. Gunnhild bewitched you. In fact, you still are bewitched. We will deal with that piece of mischief later. Right now my favourite niece and apprentice, and skilled völva in her own right, must get ready to entertain this crowd. We have brought everything you require to tame those beasts. Are you ready?"

78

The crowd in the Hippodrome grew restless. The arena remained empty of entertainment. Nothing happened. People began throwing objects onto the racetrack: mainly dead fish and rotten fruit, no doubt brought for such an occasion. They raised their fists and shook them at Gennadios. Mocking laughter broke out.

The trumpet blew. Nothing happened.

Pandemonium erupted again. The trumpet blew once more, sounding harsher this time.

Silence came abruptly in the Hippodrome as a small figure, dwarfed by enormous space, walked slowly into the centre of the arena. A concerted intake of breath from the spectators greeted two large, sleek, black panthers flanking the blue-cloaked woman, her hair hidden by a hood of animal skins. The woman stopped when she reached a statue of an angel, in the centre of the spina, who was holding a rearing horse and rider in her open palm. The angel's size made the hooded and cloaked woman appear even smaller.

Lifting the hood from her head, white curls sprang free, gleaming in sunlight. Glass beads around her neck caught the light and a white, silk chiton showed briefly beneath the cloak. She held a sturdy staff in her right hand: small stones held by ropes decorated the top of the polished wood.

Annie's heart beat so hard it pulsed in her ears. Fierce anger surged through her, making her gasp. How could that abominable man do this to her? Why would the Christian Emperor allow him to collect people? What sort of a place was Constantinople that it allowed such cruelty to exist? Adrenalin began to surge through her body, washing anger away. Her limbs trembled and her stomach clenched. Breathing deeply, she willed her pulse to slow down. Her vision cleared and became acute.

Annie blinked.

A face she recognized came into sharp focus amongst the amorphous mass of faces. Sitting behind the barrier facing her was Finne—not only Finne but also a whole crowd of the Rus traders with whom she had journeyed from the Baltic. All were dressed in their most magnificent finery, with beards braided and bejewelled, and, as they became aware that she had seen them, they stood as one and raised their right hands to their hearts.

Annie walked slowly over to Finne blinking away tears; two panthers close behind.

"I have something for you, Ani," whispered Finne. 'My wife gave it to me when she left us at Novgorod. She said I must return it to you."

He held out his hand and sitting in his large palm lay Annie's locket. 'Take it, and know this; we have all taken a vote and made you an honorary Varangian.' Now show these *fifl:* idiots, what you can do."

As Annie's hand closed over her locket, she realized she had found herself again. Alina had disappeared. Nodding solemnly to Finne and her fellow travellers, she turned back to the centre of the arena. One hundred thousand people were silent.

Annie Thornton, midwife, witch and consummate völva, raised her staff and looked toward the four bronze gilded horses, glowing golden in the sun. The crowd turned as one and gasped again. A Golden Eagle perched on the head of one of the horses: the symbol of old Rome. With a flap of his huge wings, the eagle launched himself from his perch and soared into blue sky. He used his enormous wingspan to wheel and dive over the heads of spectators. He swooped toward the Emperor's Loge and turned away at the last moment. After giving the Hippodrome crowd an aerial exhibition the like of which they had never seen before, the eagle landed gently on the left shoulder of the small, cloaked woman.

People stood, cheering and shouting, throwing hats, cloaks—any loose thing they could find—into the air.

As before, in the square at Novgorod, Annie felt a surge of electric energy but this time it emanated from the eagle. The surge passed through her arm into her body, into her right arm, her hand and into her staff. Her hearing became acute. A soft warning growl emerging from the throats of both Rosamund and Bea hurt her ears. Both panthers moved to take defensive positions in front of the völva.

Annie sent the two familiars a message. *Be still, my friends; remain calm. The Goddess protects us.*

Sensing the intake of breath from the crowd and seeing their faces turn toward the Black Gate, the völva saw that two large male lions had entered the arena. She could even see them blinking in the strong sunlight. The pair stopped as they left the gates and looked around as though to get their bearings.

The lions' strong, compact bodies looked to be about ten feet long and their shaggy manes and fur reddish-brown; however, they looked thin, under-nourished, coats dull and ragged. As soon as they spotted Annie and the two large cats, each pulled back his lips to show huge yellow teeth. Simultaneously, each lion lowered his body close to the sand and moved forward—slowly—stalking.

Annie watched them with narrowed eyes. She sensed Rosamund and Bea's agitation and sent them another message to remain calm. Both panthers lay down at her feet. The Golden Eagle remained motionless, its yellow eyes also watching the lions with intense focus.

People were silent.

As the huge beasts came closer, the primitive part of Annie's brain screamed NOW! Her völva instinct said *not yet*. The lions, still moving slowly toward their prey, began to separate, each approaching from a different angle. They came within thirty feet—Annie could see their eyes glowing a soft orange; she watched the long, lean hind muscles of each lion tense—then they launched themselves at her with a mighty leap.

She slammed her staff into the ground and shouted, *"PAVO"*: **"STOP."**

The two beasts halted in mid-leap, their hind legs just touching the sand, jaws wide open.

Annie signalled to Rosamund and Bea and the cats lazily rose to their feet and circled the unmoving lions before returning to lie at her feet.

The crowd went crazy.

Annie looked up at her master, Gennadios, and stared at him. She walked forward and circled the lions, the eagle still perched on her shoulder; flanked once again by her two black panthers.

Had there been a roof on the Hippodrome, it would have blown off from the cries of adulation. Now the ecstatic spectators threw flowers until the sand lay covered in flowers of every hue but mainly blues and greens. Charioteers would be lacking a flower tribute this day.

Annie walked slowly back to the entrance to the tunnel. She turned back to face the arena; the eagle flapped his giant wings as the panthers rose on their hind legs. The völva slammed her staff into the ground again, and in the blink of an eye, they disappeared from view.

79

When the völva and her menagerie disappeared so spectacularly from the arena, the lions came to earth from their leap and looked around. Dexios, who stayed back for a second to watch, remarked they had a puzzled look on their faces. *Where did our dinner go?* He told Annie a goat was quickly hustled into the arena to replace their missing meal and a dozen brave handlers with long poles had to force the lions back through the Black Gate.

"Mind you," he smiled. "I think the lions got a better deal. More meat on the goat than on you."

The rest of the day was an anti-climax for Annie, although she felt strong and whole again inside. Before they parted, (Meg now back to being Meg and not a Golden Eagle) had reassured her the plan they conceived for ridding herself of ties to Gennadios was foolproof and only required execution.

Gennadios greeted her effusively back in the Kathisma and escorted her to the Emperor and Empress. Annie made the right noises but had no respect for people who applauded such cruelty. She knew she had to be aware of not judging people from another culture regarding their different practices, but it was hard.

All she could remember from the chariot races following her performance was the yelling of the crowd, screams of colliding horses and the bravery of charioteers who each steered their four horses at impossible speeds around the oval track. The small, vulnerable chariots careened wildly on the tight corners, where most of the collisions occurred. When charioteers were thrown from their chariots and dragged along the sand, in danger of being crushed by the galloping horses, the crowd grew noisier and wilder.

That evening, the performance of the Conjurer of Gennadios, Annie's new name, became the talk of Constantinople. Even the chariot races palled beside her exploits.

Back in her room in the town house, Annie clutched her precious bundle given to her by Meg which she had carried from the Baltic on her journey with the traders. Her thoughts clung to the memory of Will's embrace before they parted. Rosamund and Bea had chosen to return with Meg but Annie felt comforted knowing she had the friendship and protection of Dexios.

She fingered her locket and thought of Finne and the Rus traders with affection. That was quite a tribute the traders had offered her, they, so courageous themselves, making her an honourary Varangian, and Finne's wife, sending back Annie's precious locket—such a thoughtful and generous gesture. Knowing her aunt had a plan to help her niece escape sent Annie into a deep sleep with a smile on her face.

80

Asmud poured the Macedonian wine into elaborate glass goblets Narses had brought from the kitchens before leaving.

"We salute you, O Eagle Goddess," he said, laughing and raising his goblet."

"Shush," Meg admonished him, laughing also. "Thin walls. We don't want our secret known."

"Tell us again," begged Ivar. "A wish 'ad been there to see it all."

Will raised his glass; he was trying the Retsina wine from Greece. "I also honour you, Mistress Meg. You are an amazing woman. I will never doubt your witchy ways again." He took a big drink of his wine. Everyone broke out into loud laughter at his sour face.

"An acquired taste, my friend," Asmud smiled, sipping his Commondaria wine, the best available in Byzantium.

When Lars had stopped laughing, he told Ivar about Finne being in the Hippodrome with the Rus traders. "All dressed up in their best clothes, Ivar," he said. "A were that proud of 'em an' when they saluted our Annie, a though me 'eart would burst."

He turned to Meg. "Mistress, a think when Ivar leaves and Annie is free, am back to stay wi' Finne. A'll apply for me ticket to join Varangian Guard frum there. By eck, Ivar, tha should 'ave seen 'em guardin' t'Emperor. A really want to be one of 'em."

"Back to work," said Asmud. "Do you all remember me saying I could perform shapeshifting? I never got chance to tell of my excellent idea because Dexios came to visit. I can't turn Ivar into an eagle but I can make him and his children unrecognizable."

He pulled out some sketches he had made and showed them to

his friends.

"Asmud, you are so clever," cried Meg.

The sketches showed a Greek Orthodox monk with two small acolytes by his side. Each wore a long black robe. A cowl covered the monk's head and concealed the upper part of his face: only his beard showed. The two small acolytes' heads were bare of hair.

"I have spoken with our Syrian cloth merchant and he will make up the garments. The children will lose their blond curls for a while but hair grows back. I have also spoken with a sea captain about a passage to Crete. Ivar will have to arrange his own passage from Crete to England."

"You forgot something," said Will, a big smile on his face.

"I believe I have thought of everything," Asmud retorted, bristling.

"You need to put a gag in Ivar's mouth. I do not think monks have a mouth on them as he does. Mayhap he needs to practice being humble and penitent."

At the thought of Ivar demonstrating either, everybody started laughing.

"Why does he need a disguise in the first place?" asked Will. "He's done nothing wrong. Would he and the children be prevented from leaving Constantinople?"

"I do not trust Gennadios. He will feel beaten and may plan revenge when we have Annie back. The ship's captain seemed most eager to transport a monk. I think he believes he will gain much favour when he finally reaches his heaven."

"Timing is so important," said Meg. "I'm sure Annie wants to say goodbye to Ivar and to you too, Lars. Asmud, it will all depend on when we find out about the sailing day and I suppose that will be weather dependent. This is going to require detailed planning. Annie needs to make up her special drink as soon as possible."

81

A smoky, smelly and dark taberna offered a perfect rendezvous. Fishy aromas competed with a simmering pot of cabbage soup. Although tables were set outside in the soft evening air, the two men had opted to sit inside where they might be less conspicuous. Will picked at his bowl of mussels. Dexios had recommended them as a speciality of the taberna. Unfortunately, a putrid fish sauce called *garum* coated them, supposedly flavourful, but Will decided you had to grow up with the taste, somewhat like Retsina wines.

Dexios could not stop talking about Annie's performance at the Hippodrome. He spoke in awe of her 'special gift'. "…and I've never seen a live eagle before. We have falcons for hunting but I have seen only marble eagles."

Will understood Dexios did not know of Meg and Annie's witchy side, as he called it.

Dexios tossed back his watered wine. "Another one," he said, pointing at Will's empty cup. "You won't get drunk on this stuff. It's against the law to sell undiluted wine; it's supposed to prevent fights breaking out."

He signalled to a small boy, hovering in the background and once the boy refilled their cups, the men got down to business.

Will leaned forward. "Mistress Wistowe has concerns Lady Alina is greatly stressed by recent events and needs to be cleansed by bathing in pure water, a common cure in our country. Alina plans to ask your master if she can visit your Basilica Cistern next to Hagia Sophia. We understand the cistern is full of water brought down from the hills north of the city. If he allows her to go, will she be accompanied by guards?"

"I'm sure Master Gennadios will insist on guards. Lady Alina is too precious to go out alone. Anyway, I don't see why she has to go to the cistern, a dark and eerie place, all that water underground and great big pillars supporting the roof. The sound of water coming into the cistern and water dripping from the roof makes a strange music. If she needs to bathe, why can't she go to the public baths? They've got those fancy ones near the palace."

"Pure water, remember. Water in public baths is definitely not pure—all those bodies floating in it. I appreciate that people here do not normally bathe in the cisterns so we need your help to make this happen."

Dexios' eyes narrowed and he leaned closer to his drinking companion. "What exactly are your plans following this 'cleansing'? Alina will return to the town house, yes?"

"Why do you ask that?" Will raised his eyebrows, stalling.

"I can arrange that I take her but if I do not return with Master Gennadios' jewel, as he calls her; my life and another other guard's life will be forfeit. We will end up in the Hippodrome as dinner for the lions. And, just to remind you, I can't talk to the animals."

"Of course Annie will return with you. She has suffered a distressing experience. She needs to recover. You will be doing her a great favour by ensuring this happens."

"Then I shall. I will choose Nikkos to go with us. He is willing but not too bright. Now, what exactly do you want me to do?"

82

Gennadios radiated goodwill. He ordered Castinus to bring Alina into the small, heavily perfumed *peristyle*, the walled garden in the centre of the town house. A dolphin-shaped fountain provided a soothing background noise and grapevines climbing cane supports vied with lush patches of herbs and vibrant rose bushes. Caged song-birds sang arias. The air remained fresh in the late morning and a few bees worked open blossoms, their combined buzzing adding to the ambiance.

Goldsmith Gennadios and owner of the most famous woman in Constantinople, plied his jewel with olives preserved in thyme honey, with a sweet drink made from crushed Thassian almonds and with squares of konditon, which Annie recognized as baklava.

Immune from all of Gennadios' blandishments, the end was in sight; Annie took a deep breath and proceeded with 'the plan.'

"Bampás, you have been so kind to me; I want to do something special for you."

"Light of my life; you have already done much for me. My star is so high in the sky; the people of Constantinople venerate me even more than before. The Emperor and Empress have invited me to a special banquet tonight in order to celebrate my acumen in—shall we say—in acquiring you. I can ask for no more."

"Am I to attend with you?"

"Of course not, my jewel. The banquet is for me and me alone. I have earned the honour."

Annie smiled. "In order to demonstrate my love for you and to thank you for, as you say, acquiring me, I want to make you a special drink—a drink unknown in the Empire—a drink even the Emperor has not yet tasted. If you enjoy it, then you, and only you, can take it to their Majesties and gain even more glory."

Gennadios stopped smiling. His voice became silky. "And you, my jewel, you will drink this drink with me, or better still, before me?"

He thought she was trying to poison him. "Of course, my Bampás. Believe me; your mouth has never tasted such delight as is in store for you. I know you will be busy in your workshop for the rest of the day. I shall spend my time preparing the ambrosia. Shall we meet before you go to the palace?"

After Gennadios left to go to his workshop, Annie took a big gulp of the sweetened almond drink to wash the taste of her fawning of Gennadios out of her mouth.

Chief eunuch Castinus expressed surprise and bewilderment at Lady Alina's request to enter the kitchen and take control of creating a dish for the Master. "The kitchen is no place for Lady of the House," he protested. "It is totally unacceptable for you to work with slaves. It is also a hot, dark and smoky place."

Alina insisted and he had no choice but to take her there. Although familiar with the location of the dreaded communal toilet and bathing area, Annie had not been aware the kitchen was next to it, due no doubt to both areas needing running water.

Castinus was right about the dark and smoky atmosphere. Logs fuelled a built-in clay oven and, as there was no chimney to direct the smoke, it made its way out through any cracks and crevices. The top of the stove held a variety of iron pots and when the Lady Alina explained to much-discomforted kitchen slaves what she wanted to do, they showed her how they shovelled hot coals from the fireplace and placed them under the iron pots on top of the stove. Acorns soon boiled away.

Once the kitchen slaves relaxed slightly after recovering from the shock of Lady Alina's presence, a couple of them offered to help, so she put them to work peeling and grinding acorns into a reasonably fine powder. Once that tedious job was completed, she spread the powder on a flat iron sheet and placed it in the oven to roast. As the smell began to permeate the room, more slaves popped their heads around the door, asking excitedly what the Lady was cooking.

Annie enjoyed her time in the kitchen; she had had enough of being a princess. She endured the smoke and heat and spent the rest of the afternoon watching the slaves prepare her evening meal: lamb infused with rosemary and a fresh salad of greens from the garden that included sorrel, spinach and early spring nettles, garnered from the countryside.

As the dinner hour drew near, Annie asked the slaves to boil some water. She added some of the roast acorn grounds to a small jug and poured the water on top; a pinch of cardamom completed the ambrosia. Once again, the aroma of coffee created a similar reaction she experienced in the palace.

"I have left enough for you all to taste. Enjoy and thank you for your help."

Annie left behind a happy but bemused group of slaves—a gift and a thank you!

Castinus accompanied her to Gennadios' workshop, carrying the jug and two bowls.

Annie had not visited Gennadios' workshop before. How large and busy it appeared. Workers were everywhere, all performing different tasks. Gennadios sat at a long table littered with the tools of his craft: small hammers, chisels, files, wires, clay tablets, sheets of silver and gold foil.

Beads of sweat popped up on her forehead. This workshop was also hot. A furnace in the far corner, presided over by a slave wielding a small hammer and tapping on an anvil, revealed the source of the heat. Gennadios appeared so absorbed in his task he did not see her for a number of minutes.

"Ah, there you are my jewel. I had not become conscious of the late state of the day. Come and see what I am creating for my Empress Helena."

Annie recognized the exquisite gold crucifix set with emeralds from the sketch she had seen when their Majesties visited them in the country. Gennadios explained he was attaching tiny pearls to the outside of the cross.

"It requires my absolute total concentration. Why are you here to bother me?"

"I have brought you your ambrosia, my Bampás, I call it coffee. May we go into the peristyle; it is so hot in here?"

Gennadios shook his head and sighed deeply at being disturbed, then shouted some instructions to his foreman and led Alina into the relative coolness of the peristyle.

Once his Master and the Lady had seated themselves, Castinus poured bowls of coffee for both. Gennadios took his bowl and held it steadily in his hands while looking intently at Alina. "Go ahead, my dear. I wait with anticipation."

Annie smiled and sipped her now cooling drink. Gennadios waited for a few beats and, when she did not fall to the ground writhing in agony, he sipped. He sipped again. His eyes widened. He sipped repeatedly until his bowl was empty.

"My jewel, is this more of your magic?"

"No, my Bampás, this is no magic. I made it for you with my own hands. More?"

As Gennadios savoured his coffee, Annie took a deep breath. "If I have pleased you once again, Bampás, I have a small request. I am so bored. I have nothing to occupy my time. When I spend time with you, it passes quickly, but otherwise, time drags painfully."

Gennadios waved his hand dismissively. "Do what I imagine other women of high social standing do in our society: spin, weave, pray, organize the house slaves, look after their husbands and children. I know they do not go out in public unless it is to go to the Hippodrome or to the Baths. What do I know or even care of what women do to pass the time?"

"Bampás, it is more than likely I will have no husband or children, only you. I have to find something to do or my life will become empty. I have seen so little of Constantinople, this most beautiful city. Do I have your blessing to visit some of the wonders, such as Hagia Sophia; one of the many monasteries, perhaps; the Bucoleon Palace and the Basilica Cistern?"

He laughed. "The Basilica Cistern! Why would you want to see that? It's just an underground water storage system. Moreover, I just told you; women of a higher class do not go out in to public."

"I understand the cistern to be a great feat of engineering. I would also like to see the Aqueduct of Valens and see how the water travels as far as it does. I believe it delivers water to the Great Palace from many miles away. We have nothing in our world to match it."

"If it pleases you, only because I am the most generous man in Constantinople, you may have one outing each month, provided you dress discreetly and cover your head and face. Ask Dexios to arrange an escort. You may be away from the time after the mid-day meal until before the evening meal. You will, of course, return, as you have no choice." He chuckled. "I must prepare for my banquet to celebrate your success at the Hippodrome. I will save your ambrosia as a gift for another time."

83

Will rushed back from the taberna. "Tomorrow, it is tomorrow, Dexios says. They are going to the Basilica Cistern tomorrow after midday. We must prepare." His flushed face betrayed his excitement at the thought of Annie being free.

Meg caught his arms. "Settle down Will. All we have to do is watch and provide a small distraction at the right moment. In the meantime Asmud, what is happening regarding Ivar's journey?"

"It is all as we have planned. Our Syrian has completed the robes. I am to pick them up later today. The captain will send me a message when he plans to weigh anchor."

Meg nodded her head in satisfaction. "I have the last few seeds of henbane and I shall instruct Bea and Rosamund on their roles."

84

Annie didn't have butterflies in her stomach; she had snakes—hundreds of them—all fighting to get out. She had attended the hated communal bathroom so many times she had become an embarrassment. Her handmaiden had to fasten Annie's cloak broach and tie the hood over her mistress's head as her hands trembled so much.

"Lady, I can ask Castinus to give you his special medicine. He makes it from the bark of brambles. I know it works. We have all used it many times."

Annie could only nod her head. She had no strength left for anything more physical yet had a vigorous few hours ahead of her. When her aunt told her of the plan to have Annie become totally immersed in water, she had not taken into account that not only could Annie not swim, she feared the water having experienced a frightening incident during her school swimming lessons. A push by a feckless boy into the deep end left her with an abiding fear of being underwater.

Fortified by the Rubus elixir, as Castinus called the bitter drink he gave her, and with her gold locket now hanging around her neck, but still feeling depleted and afraid, Annie left the town house with Dexios and Nikkos. She had never talked to the young guard before; he always stayed in the shadows. Even now, he hung his head, looking bashful.

This was good. Annie sent the young man a strong message: keep those eyes pinned to the ground. What did they say in Yorkshire—see nowt, say nowt?

They walked from the town house without incident. The Mese was crowded as usual; the market stalls busy, smells of perfume and spices overwhelming the senses. Dexios told Annie the stalls had been placed there by order of a previous Emperor to block the city's less aromatic odours from the sensitive noses of the Imperial Family in the Great Palace.

The Basilica Cistern was located just off the Mese on the left of Hagia Sophia. Annie caught a glimpse of the Milion monument ahead of them, the Byzantine zero-mile marker, the starting-place for the measurement of distances for all the roads leading to the cities of the Byzantine Empire. She remembered Asmud saying the Milion signaled the end of the Mese. The Baths of Zeuxippos and the Grand Palace were south of them. She felt a pang; her loved ones were not far from her but she wasn't able to be with them—yet. She paused in her morose thinking. Somehow, the 'yet' lifted her spirits and her step became lighter. Dexios walked ahead, Nikkos behind. Annie's small stature and covered head made her almost invisible to the crowds of people. No one recognized her as the famous 'conjurer' from the Hippodrome.

The entrance door to the cistern was of marble with elaborate carvings and ancient script adorning its surface. Behind it loomed a high stone tower, its purpose, Dexios explained, for adjusting water pressure. "Those Roman engineers thought of everything," he said with awe.

"How deep is the water?" Annie whispered.

"Oh, quite deep, I understand, it's always higher at this time of year due to the heavy spring rains."

Dexios used a flint to strike a spark and light the torch he brought with him, not aware his comments had increased Annie's fears tenfold. He opened the heavy door and peered inside. "It's pitch dark in there. Stay close to me: you too, Nikkos."

The three cautiously stepped inside and found themselves on a broad stone platform. As their eyes became used to the flickering circle of light from the torch, they saw they had company. Stone steps led down to the water from the platform and two men perched on them close to the water. Another person stood in the shadows.

"You men, what are you doing? Why are you here?" Dexios' voice sounded abrupt and echoed across the cavernous space.

"Checking water levels, officer," came the response. "'Ave to do it every day and report back to our master."

"Slaves," muttered Dexios to Nikkos. "So, Lady, this is the Basilica cistern you asked to see. I spoke with a friend at the palace who works in the office responsible for the city water supply. This is what he told me." He cleared his voice and began to recite, sounding like a child repeating his lessons. "The water in this cistern travels along the Valens Aqueduct from springs in the hills far from the city. Emperor Valens built the aqueduct over five hundred years ago. The cistern can hold up to eighty thousand cubic metres of—In the name of J—"

His recitation came to an abrupt halt as the shadowy figure on the right moved forward and threw something toward the two white-plumes. Annie expected this so was prepared, but not prepared for the resulting effect.

The cistern filled with a diffused light, illuminating a forest of el-egant marble pillars supporting the many arches of the roof. The light danced across the arches, creating strange shapes and changing colour. Red, green, blue and violet swirls vied with each other.

Aunt Meg had surpassed herself; she created the Aurora Borealis in an underground cathedral. For a fraction of a second, Annie forgot her fear.

Her two guards stood rigid, hypnotized by the light show.

"Now, Annie. Now. Come down these steps and into the water. We have a rope anchored for you to hold."

Will's urgent voice broke through Annie's lethargy. Removing her cloak and sandals, she began descending the rough stone steps. The rough surface of the stone bit into her tender feet and further awoke her to what was about to happen. Before Annie could turn and run back up the steps to safety, a strong hand clasped her arm and wrapped her cold, numb hands around a thick, rough rope. A gentle hand in the small of her back propelled her forward. Her feet found the water. Slowly, Annie descended, feeling the cool water climb up her body, inch by painful inch. She hesitated when the water reached her chin, her limbs trembling. Taking a deep breath, Annie surren-dered her fate to the Goddess and climbed hand under hand on the rope to pull herself under the water. Immediately, she panicked, her heart rate doubling and mind screaming to get out. Get out!

Two small splashes created waves on either side of her head.

Opening her eyes, startled, and fearing an attack by some subterranean monster, Annie almost opened her mouth to scream as Rosamund and Beà swam into view. Her startled brain screamed *cats don't swim—you're hallucinating.* Rosamund's high-pitched voice came into her head. *Oh, yes we do— when we have to. Enjoy the ride.* The two cats swan around and around, creating a vortex with Annie in the centre. Annie began to spin within the vortex. The cats swam faster. She kept spinning, until, like a dolphin leaping out of the ocean, she shot out of the whirlpool into the arms of her beloved Will.

"I've got you," he cried, his voice thick with emotion. Will carried Annie up the steps to Meg who wrapped her niece in dry linens and soon had her changed into a warm, dry chiton and cloak. Will and Lars, meanwhile, prudently watched the light show along with the hypnotized white-plumes, remaining oblivious to the other scene playing out before them.

"By the Goddess, Annie, your hair has returned to black!" Meg looked in horror at her niece's transformation back into herself. "We must wrap your head and keep it wrapped until you escape. Even your eyebrows are black again. We'll just have to hope no one notices them."

Meg gave Annie a fierce hug. "You are free of the restraints put there by Gunnhild. We still have to get you safely out of the Collector's house. Be patient."

Will and Lars approached the women now Annie was decently dressed and both hugged her. Two wet, furry shapes wound themselves around Annie's legs. She picked up the cats and buried her face in their wet fur. "Thank you, thank you, my brave friends."

Meg towelled the cats until they looked like cats again and not skinny, wet rags.

"One more thing, Annie. When you leave here, you will meet a travelling monk and his two acolytes. Say your goodbyes."

With that cryptic remark, Meg clicked her fingers. The Aurora Borealis disappeared and the cistern returned to darkness.

Dexios spoke. "Damn, the torch went out. Have you seen enough, Lady? This is the most boring place I have ever been in; I hope you found it more interesting. By all the Saints, where is the door?"

85

When the two white-plumes and Annie emerged into the sunshine, blinking against the light, Dexios leaned down and whispered, "A strange experience, Lady Alina, I lost track of what happened in there. Did you manage to bathe in the water? I know Will helped. Do you feel better?"

"Thank you, Dexios, I do. What do you mean: you lost track of what happened?"

"I feel as though we were only in there for a few seconds. I remember going in and I remember coming out, but nothing in-between. I've been working too many hours or drinking too much wine. I'll talk to Nikkos later about it. I'm not sure what he saw or heard."

They made their way back through the square in front of Hagia Sophia. It only seemed like minutes to Annie since they entered the cistern but the sun had passed over the stunning basilica and the Milion monument cast its shadow across the square. Even so, people still milled around stalls; cats of all colours were underfoot; traders still shouted their wares. A phalanx of Varangian guards came from the direction of the Great Palace, boisterous and noisy, as usual, caring little for the people in their path.

Annie walked between her two guards, made insignificant by their size. A large, broad-shouldered, heavily bearded monk, robed in black, materialized in front of Dexios, two small acolytes hanging onto his robe.

"Officer Dexios, Am Father Ivar. Am a close friend of Mistress Wistowe. A've cum to give Mistress Annie me blessing."

When Dexios moved quickly out of the way, taking Nikkos by the arm and murmuring into his ear, Annie looked curiously at the heavily hooded monk. "Did I hear you say Father Ivar?"

"It's me, tha daft lass. Ave cum t'say me goodbyes 'cos me an' babbies are goin' 'ome to Jorvik."

Annie's eyes grew as big as an owl's. "You've become a monk? You, Ivar?"

"Not a real monk. A'm pretendin'. So as we can get out of 'ere safely. It works, dunt it. Tha didn't know me, did tha?"

Annie flung her arms around him. "Oh, Ivar, I shall miss you so much. How will you travel?"

"On a ship, through t'Mediterranean Sea. It'll tek a few weeks."

"Is Lars to become a monk too?"

"Nay, lass. 'E's not goin' back with us. Lars is stayin' 'ere. 'E's goin' to be a Varangian guard. The lad's set 'is 'eart on it."

"Oh, his poor parents; they'll be so upset."

"Nay, they're Vikings. That's what young-uns do. If he were back 'ome, 'e'd be off fighting, cum end of summer."

"We've had quite an adventure, haven't we," Annie said, "and soon the twins will be back home with their mother and grandparents, and you'll be a fisherman again. It has all been worth it. Give your wife and parents a huge hug for me. Do you have the Scottish Queen's magic box with you, the one that saved you before?"

When Ivar nodded and patted his chest she stepped around the large monk to hug Eydis and Eyia, tears in her eyes. "Ivar, what happened to their hair; they're as bald as a billiard ball!"

"What's a billiard ball, Annie? You do say sum daft stuff. We 'ad to do that. It were them blond curls got us into trouble at beginnin'. Anyhow, t'curls'll grow back."

Dexios stepped forward gesturing with his hand. Annie found it hard to let go of Ivar and the twins but people were beginning to pay attention to a young woman hugging a priest in front of the Hagia Sophia. Although happy for Ivar and his family, Annie's heart squeezed painfully as she watched the three disappear into the crowd. She would never see them again.

As the white-plumes escorted their ward to the town house, Annie realized her goodbyes had started. Soon it would be Lars and Asmud, even Finne, and then—by the Goddess—Will and her aunt.

Annie shook away the thought of saying goodbyes again, despite knowing she would have to return home soon. Her life back in Yorkshire seemed to belong to someone else, but it was *her* life, her midwifery practice, her parents and friends, and—Adam—she'd forgotten all about Adam!

As they grew closer to Gennadios' home, Annie started to think about her escape from her collector's luxury prison. She must not involve Dexios, or any of the house slaves, for that matter. If Gennadios found any of them to have assisted, the punishment would be swift and brutal. Moreover, she wanted to teach the old man a lesson; one he would remember. An idea began to form in her head. She smiled.

86

Meg, Asmud, Will and Lars stood on the quayside at Prosphorion Harbour. They had left the Grand Palace at dawn, telling Narses they planned to visit the famous harbour and buy seafood at one of the many warehouses surrounding the quay.

A man-made seawall formed a natural inlet and protected the harbour. The Prosphorion provided a hub for all the wares brought into Constantinople from trading routes in Asia, the Black Sea and the Mediterranean. Narses had informed them that the harbour's glory days were over, as constant battles to reduce silting had proved ineffective. Nevertheless, Prosphorion remained a busy place.

Ships of every description lined its quay and gangs of slaves carried sacks, barrels and hundreds of amphorae both on and off the ships. A long line of carts pulled by mules waited patiently for heavier items. Ships entering the opening in the huge sea wall anchored in the centre awaiting berths. Seagulls wheeled and cried, searching for breakfast. A fresh breeze brought the now familiar tangy smell of the Bosporus to Meg and her companions: a mixture of salt, fish and spices.

Asmud's plan had been to arrive at the Prosphorion before Ivar and the twins so no one would make a connection. They had found the northern road busy as ever with travellers and traders going in both directions.

As they stood there, reminiscing about their earlier journey down the Bosporus, Lars spied the monk and his acolytes. Ivar was making his way along the jetty, asking for Captain Biros.

They had all said their goodbyes earlier, in the privacy of the palace rooms. Asmud wanted only to ensure Ivar embarked safely onto his ship. The four watched their friend and his precious children board the trading ship and disappear below.

"I am filled with both happiness and sadness at the same time," Meg said. "We did our job. The twins are going home. Now for the last part of the plan." Meg turned to her companions. "I wonder what Annie has in mind for escaping the Greek Collector. She knows she must not involve any of his household staff."

Asmud looked at his lover with sad eyes. "I hate to hear you use the word 'last', he said. " What does that mean for us? We know Lars will be off now to his Rus friends; I will return also and travel to Novgorod with them after the summer—and you Will—I suppose you will return to your inn. What are your plans, my *Ástvinur*: my darling?"

"Not yet, Asmud, too much still to be done, then we will talk about the future. For now, we buy some fish and return to the city. Annie will get in touch with us when she is ready."

87

Annie's dip into the pure waters of the Basilica Cistern had become last night's memory as she sat in the peristyle with Gennadios, his pet monkey Argyros on his usual shoulder perch, grinning at Annie. As usual, the air was fresh; bees buzzed in the herb beds; caged birds trilled and the dolphin spouted its water into the shallow basin below, creating a relaxing background to their conversation.

"Your celebration banquet went well, my Bampás?"

"It did. The Emperor and Empress hold me in the highest esteem. We must think of more conjuring feats for you to accomplish in the near future. You are a good investment, my jewel. By the way, that is a most remarkable way you have arranged your head cover. I have not seen that style at court, not worn by our women, anyway."

"It is called a turban, my Bampás: a fashion from my country. It creates a mystery, don't you think? What might be hidden behind it?"

"It certainly changes how you look. There is something different about you today; I cannot put my finger on it."

Annie smiled to herself. It wasn't just that physically and psychologically she had escaped from Gennadios' bondage. In desperation, she had painfully plucked every hair of her black eyebrows, not having the wherewithal to find the dye used on her hair previously.

"Bampás, have you ever thought about how it feels to be owned by someone?"

"What a strange question—of course not! Slaves run our empire. We cannot exist without them. It is their misfortune to be captured or born into slavery."

"I was thinking more of how you collect people. I know you collect prized objects and animals that look different, but you also collect people—like me—like the twins. Do you see me as a person or as an object; a 'thing'?"

"What has got into you today? You are a possession. I own you. You are mine to do with as I wish and if you insist on asking such questions you will find yourself on bread and water for a while."

In his agitation, Gennadios stood and began pacing around the small square garden. "Haven't I given you all you desire? I even allowed you to have a day out yesterday. I am the kindest of masters. Everyone knows that."

"Then give me my freedom."

Nature paused, awaiting an answer from Gennadios. Bees stopped buzzing; the sound of the fountain and the songs of the birds faded away.

"Have you lost your mind, child? Why, in the name of all of the saints in heaven, would I do that?"

"Because you love me. We have a saying where I come from, 'if you love someone, set them free.'"

"I have never heard such rubbish. I don't love you. I OWN YOU! Moreover; remember you are bound to me forever."

"I thought I would ask, Gennadios, before—"

"—Before what? You ungrateful wretch. You are a pathetic example of a völva. My Oracle told me as much. The Empress Helena made it clear I had no choice but to give up those beautiful twins and look what I received in return. Return to your rooms while I think of a suitable punishment for you." Spittle formed at the corners of the old man's mouth, he was so angry.

"As I was saying Gennadios, before you so rudely interrupted me; I believe it is time you learned what it means to be owned, to be collected, and to be viewed as an object."

Annie stood and, staring intently into the eyes of her master, reached behind a climbing vine and brought out her staff and blue cloak, which she slowly draped around her shoulders.

"I call forth Freyja, Goddess of Love and—you will appreciate this Gennadios—of Gold, to assist me in teaching Gennadios of Mytilene humility and empathy. By the way, Gennadios, The Goddess Freyja also loves cats."

Gennadios stared back at Annie with a look of disbelief on his face, quickly followed by a flash of fear as the atmosphere in the peristyle grew heavy and the sunlight faded.

He looked down at the back of his hands. Thick black fur sprouted. He turned his hands over. Pink pads formed on his palms. His nails grew long, curved and sharp. He lifted his paw to his face and felt the fur, the whiskers, and the delicate little ears. He opened his mouth and felt the needle-sharp teeth with his long pink tongue. He looked behind and twitched his long black tail. He regarded his monkey in shock. They were both the same size! He sat down and began compulsively cleaning the fur now covering his cat-like body.

"Are you listening to me Gennadios? You are now my cat. You are also my female cat. I have changed your name to Genni. I like the colour black so I have made you black. I will teach you to do tricks. You will follow me everywhere I go; sleep under my bed; eat when I choose to feed you. If you misbehave, I will reduce your food. I may even whip you if I so choose. Do you understand what I am saying to you?"

The un-catlike brown eyes of Gennadios looked out at Annie. Genni's mouth opened; she meowed.

"Good. I'm glad you've got the message."

Annie removed the collar and gold chain from Argyros and attached the collar to Genni. Argyros leaped into the nearest tree and sat there chattering. Annie knew the monkey would not stray far; he knew where his food came from.

"Let us go for a walk, Genni. If you behave, I will give you a sardine."

Annie led her new pet around the walled garden, thoroughly enjoying herself.

88

Annie called for Castinus who hurried into the peristyle.

"You called, My Lady?"

"I plan on going for a walk. Please ask Dexios to accompany me."

"Lady, does the Master know of these plans?"

"Oh, yes, he knows. He may even go with me."

Dexios walked ahead of Annie and her new pet along the Mese. He expressed surprise that the master had allowed the Lady Alina to own a black cat, given his dislike of the colour.

"He could not refuse me as he has such a high regard for my powers. Is that not so, Genni?" She tugged on the gold leash, just a little.

They passed through the Chalke Gate without hindrance, the guards recognizing the great and famous Gennadios' white-plumed guard, and entered the Grand Palace. They did not recognize the great and famous Gennadios though; Annie giggled to herself.

Annie's joyous reunion with her aunt, Will and Asmud made them all misty-eyed. After Dexios ate and drank with them, he left, citing people he wanted to visit in the palace.

"I'll be no longer than one hora," he said. "I would not like to experience the wrath of our Master if we are away longer."

Annie could hardly wait until Dexios left the room. She appreciated his friendship and still had to protect him. "I would like you to meet *my* Master, Gennadios of Mytilene," she said with a flourish and held up Genni for inspection.

Rosamund and Bea came into the room. When they saw another cat, they did what all cats do: they came over to inspect, sniff and challenge. Genni cowered down on the floor but Rosamund and Bea, being smart cats, walked away bored. Clearly, even though this cat might look like a cat, it did not smell like one.

Meg, Asmud, Will and Lars peered down at the cowering cat, exclaiming at the strange phenomenon of the brown eyes of Gennadios looking anxiously at them.

"What is the purpose of this inspired act of *seiðr*, of shape-shifting?" asked Meg.

"I am teaching my Master how to be humble and empathetic. Is that not so, Genni? He is learning how it feels to be owned—changed into something at the whim of another. You are learning that, aren't you, Genni? If not, you will remain a cat forever, not as a pampered cat but a feral cat, out in the streets of Constantinople, and as a female, you can expect to have lots of kittens."

Genni meowed, a soft sound, a sound of compliance.

"You now see, Genni that I am a völva of some consequence, not as your former so-called oracle said, 'a pathetic example of a völva'. You notice I said 'former oracle'. My clever aunt discovered Queen Gunnhild has fled to new shores. She has many sons and has no time left for you. I control your future."

Will and the others stared in awe at this indomitable young woman, secure in her power and new sense of self. The diffident apprentice had vanished. This woman had faced death and her deepest fears, emerging with poise and assurance.

"What are your plans for Gennadios, Annie?" Meg asked.

"I require his assurance that he will stop collecting people. If he gives me that pledge, he may become a man again. He also needs to believe *I will know* if he relapses and then he will be seeking scraps on the Mese. What is your response, Genni?"

Another compliant meow escaped the cat's mouth. She wound her black body around Annie's legs and purred.

"I take that as a yes," laughed Annie. 'As I am also now held in high esteem by the Empress Helena, she has agreed that you should do this important task for me, not as Genni but as the famous and influential Gennadios of Mytilene. Seek out your contacts and find a Viking sword with the name Ulfberht engraved on the blade. Give the sword, as a gift, to Asmud of Novgorod, tutor to Prince Sviatoslav of Kiev before he returns to the north.

"As soon as your guard Dexios returns, we will return to your town house and then I will leave of my own accord after returning you to normality. You will not hinder my leaving in any way, nor will you try to find me. I am now under the protection of the Empress Helena."

89

Narses had outdone himself. All of the low tables in the rooms of Asmud of Novgorod, emissary to Princess Olga of Kiev, groaned under food platters and flagons of wine. Small plates of grilled eggplant with shaved salted mullet roe, dried figs and toasted walnuts, olives in honey, vinegar and thyme, a steaming dish of lamb served with oinogaros sauce and rice pudding garnished with cherries and candied citron. Narses recounted all the ingredients in awe. "The chef made a special effort as he knew the feast is for our famous conjurer, and the wine is from the Peloponnesos and Macedonia," he finished with a flourish.

"It doesn't feel the same without Ivar grumbling away," Annie picked up an olive, "but I'm sure we'll manage to enjoy ourselves."

The four lounged on their respective couches prior to sampling the delicacies.

"That was quite a meal we had last night at St. Mamas," Will reminisced. "Finne and the men really looked after us."

Meg nodded. "Lars looked quite comfortable, didn't he. I'm always amazed at the flexibility of youth. He said goodbye to us and hello to them with no effort at all."

"I think you exaggerate, Meg. I saw tears in his eyes when he hugged you and Annie," said Asmud

The tutor nibbled on a few figs. "Annie, you have had the smuggest look on your face for a while now. You look like Rosamund and Bea after finishing a dish of cream."

"I have no idea what you are talking about, Asmud of Novgorod." Annie leaped off her couch and pirouetted around the room before

coming to a halt in front of the others.

"Okay." she laughed. "I'll come clean."

"You are clean," said Will. "We just came back from the Baths."

"I mean, my darling, I will tell you my story. Do you remember me telling Gennadios that Empress Helene is protecting me? I didn't make that up. Shortly after my amazing visit to the Basilica Cistern, a messenger came to Gennadios' town house. Gennadios was somewhere else recovering, no doubt. The messenger made it clear he wished to see me alone. I met him in the peristyle. He had come from the Empress; she wished me to visit her *at my earliest convenience,* privately. I went immediately to the palace. We entered through a back door and I was ushered into her private rooms. The Empress Helena was alone."

Annie's audience were agog. All thoughts of food and drink had gone. The lamb was cooling; its aroma of rosemary and oregano disregarded.

"What did she want?" Meg leaned forward, not wanting to miss a single word.

"She wanted to know how I did what I did in the Hippodrome. She told me she admires powerful women, just as she is a powerful woman. She said she governs the Byzantine Empire; her husband, the Emperor prefers to be involved with his books and writing."

"What did you tell her?" Asmud's eyes were huge above his beard.

"I told her the truth; all of it. How I travelled through time aided by my aunt, another powerful woman gifted with the skills of a wise woman. I told her of Jorvik and of the despair of the twins' parents. I described the court of King Eiric and of our petition to him. The Empress was most interested in the fact that the King had two wives and wanted to know in detail how they looked. I can tell you her eyes grew wide when I told her of Queen Gunnhild and her history as a sorcerer.

"I shared some of our adventures during the journey from the Baltic Sea to Byzantium. I believe she might hold the Rus traders in even higher regard now. I forbore to share our Olbia experience: I did not wish to push the boundaries of belief too far. She knew of Princess Olga, of course, and delighted in my description of her silken stateroom. The Empress was most impressed when I shared the stories of the many times Queen Gunnhild tried to stop our attempts to find the twins. She remarked that only our love for each other allowed us to defeat her."

"What of the Hippodrome?" Will's face was a mixture of anxiety and pride.

Annie pirouetted again. "I told her I created an illusion. I made everyone see what they wanted to believe—that I, a young woman, in danger of being torn to pieces by lions—could control the beasts, make them bow to my will." She shrugged. "Good versus evil, I guess, God triumphing over the Devil. Anyway, the point is, the Empress was fascinated by the whole story. I have told you before; Greeks love a good story, and our odyssey equals Jason and the Golden Fleece. Moreover, do not forget, Jason was married to the sorcerer, Medea. So while The Greek Orthodox Church doesn't approve of witchcraft, all of the ancient Greek myths are about magic."

"So Empress Helena is not going to have us all thrown to the lions for consorting with witches?" Will's face now reflected only pride.

"In fact, the opposite; as a reward for rescuing the twins and returning them to their parents, she has invited us to spend some time at the Imperial Family's summer home: the Boukoleon Palace. It's only a stone's throw from here, down by the Sea of Marmara, but we will have it all to ourselves, except for our own servants and chefs. The Imperial Family won't be moving there until next week. What a special time it will be, and a celebration before we leave Constantinople?"

Her audience greeted this remark with both delight and then sadness. No one spoke.

Annie looked at each of the faces she had grown to love. She had to help them through this, knowing how painful their parting would be.

"Let us gather our belongings and accept Empress Helen's offer of a few days together in a Royal seaside palace.

90

After packing their bags, the remaining four plus two cats walked
down to the beautiful Boukoleon Palace, summer home of the Emperor and Empress of Byzantium, perched at the edge of the Sea of
Marmara.

Greeted by a beardless one, wearing a heavily embroidered tunic
and a large hat to denote his importance, the special guests were welcomed into more opulence. They ate cuisine of unimagined delight
served on gold plates; the men swam in the warm Sea of Marmara
passing through an archway protected by two stone lions (Annie de-
clined the invitation); slept on luxurious couches and bathed in the
private Royal Baths—all thanks to Empress Helene.

One warm and sultry evening, while the two women relaxed after
dinner on a balcony catching the sea breezes and the men were inside
playing *hnefatafl*, Annie quietly asked Meg what her plans were regarding Asmud.

"It is not a problem for me, my sweeting. I can visit him whenever
and," Meg shrugged her shoulders and smiled, "perhaps it is a romance of this time only. What of you and Will? The question never
goes away, does it?"

"Aunt Meg, I do not know what to do about my feelings for Will.
Nothing has changed. We love one another but I have a life and he
has a life, except that 500 years separate them. I have made my mind
up to go home. I have parents and friends, my sweet cottage, a pro-
fession that I love and, in all fairness—Adam. Will has made it clear
he will not live in my future world."

As Annie lay on their sleeping couch that night, listening to Will's quiet breathing, she remembered her aunt's interesting comment, 'perhaps it is a romance of this time only.' Annie translated that to 'holiday romance.' If only she and Will could regard their love in the same way.

Her mind whirled as she tossed and turned. How could she tell him? The thought was too painful. Perhaps she could get Aunt Meg to tell him after she had left. No, totally a coward's way out. Right from the moment Aunt Meg had brought Will to be part of their search for the twins, she had known deep down that this moment would arrive.

As she tossed and turned, a warm body jumped on the sleeping couch and snuggled up to her. Rosamund began purring. The familiar high sweet voice filled her mind. "Your love for Will is eternal. It will always be there even though you cannot be together. Accept that and move on. Tell Will to do the same. Who knows what the future holds. Have courage."

Annie pondered Rosamund's words. It was true that Will was the love of her life. Knowing that, could she in all fairness, replace him with Adam?

Yes, tell Will he was her eternal love, but to move on with his life. She would go home and resume hers. Let the Arrow of Eros fall where it may.

Annie sat up abruptly. She could not go on for another minute in this agony of indecision. She had made her choice. She was going home. It was the telling of it that was torturing her.

"Will, Will, my darling." She shook his shoulder gently, then harder as he didn't move. "Will. We have to talk."

Will turned over, bleary-eyed, then sat up. "What's wrong?" He rubbed his eyes.

"We need to talk, now." Annie's voice wobbled.

Will took her into his arms. "Annie, my sweetheart, I know what you are going to say. You are going home. We are to be parted again." He kissed her forehead and stroked her hair. "Of course, you must go home, that is where your life is. Me too, back to my inn and my friend Jack."

By this time Annie was sobbing. "But Will, you have to move on with your life, as do I, but I don't know if I can." Now she was wailing.

"Annie, Annie, I will always love you. Now there's a miracle. I never thought I would love a witch, but you have bewitched me."

Will's voice calmed Annie and they rocked together in silent desperation until the need to comfort each other grew stronger.

Early the next morning Annie, with Rosamund clutched in her arms, approached Aunt Meg who was having breakfast with Asmad. "It's time, Aunt Meg. I have to go. I have said my goodbyes to Will. Now I say goodbye to you, Asmad."

Asmad stood and hugged Annie so hard she thought he might break her ribs. And she had thought him reserved!

Meg pulled her niece into her arms. "I'm sure I will be seeing you before long, my brave and clever Annie. Allow Bea and Rosamund a chance to say farewell."

Meg kept her arm around Annie and took her to the archway with lions on either side that led out to the Sea of Marmara. "Just a reminder of how much courage you have, my sweeting. Look at the sparkle on the water. Keep looking. Farewell for now."

Addendum

NORWAY

Did you think I had forgotten about the foolish searchers who caused me so much trouble?

Nevertheless, I had my entertainment at their expense and I still have the gold from Gennadios. I understand he has nothing, no twins, and no völva.

Eiric is long dead; it was only a matter of time before his enemies killed him. I fled to Denmark with my sons, then onto Norway where my son Harald became King and my other sons became lords.

You know me as Gunnhild but I have another name now: *Konungamóðir*, Mother of Kings. I hold much power, controlling the affairs of state in this country.

Perhaps one day when I become old and tire of ruling a country, I will find my former playmates and toy with them again. It might be fun to see if those so-called völvas think they can still outwit me. In the meantime, I have much to do.

Is Annie and Will's romance over? Only time will tell. In Annie's next adventure, *Coventina's Well*, she slips through time to Romano-Britain and meets up again with her Aunt Meg. When they attempt to help a young Roman wife whose life is in peril, Aunt Meg becomes incapacitated, leaving Annie alone to fend for herself except for a new Celtic friend.

What's Real and What's Not...

Jorvik is real. The Viking museum in York has been re-created where it was found – in the mud of York and is well worth a visit. It's not still in the mud!

Eiric BloodAxe was real. He was King of Norway before ruling twice in Jorvic.

Queen Gunnhild is a quasi-historical figure who appears in the Icelandic Sagas.

Queen Iseabail is a name I made up although there are rumours of a Scottish queen, married to Eiric, and a relative of—

Saint Caddroe, a monk and abbot who was real and venerated for his works.

Birka is an Island in the Baltic Sea and an archaeologist's dream. Many grave findings have given light to Viking life.

Princess Olga and her son, Prince Sviatoslav, are real. The Princess and her grandchildren brought Christianity to Russia.

Thorfinn Skullsplitter, jarl of Orkney, Scotland was real but may not have been as ferocious a pirate as I described.

Varangian traders were real and as adventurous and brave as I have portrayed.

The Trade Route of the Varangians to the Greeks was real and is constantly delivering up new artifacts.

Ostia: Ruins of early Greek settlements along the coast of the Black Sea still remain.

Constantinople is real and now known as Istanbul. All my descriptions of the city are as authentic as possible. An exciting place to visit.

Acknowledgements

Writing can be hard and lonely work. What makes it worthwhile is YOU, dear reader. Your comments, reviews and expressed pleasure after reading my story drives me on.

My editor, Carol Ann Sokoloff, keeps me on track; thank you. Thank you to Ekstasis Editions for adopting me.

My three brutally honest early readers show no fear in telling me what doesn't make sense. Thank you, Bruce Robinson, Karen Sharp and Patti Acheson.

Heartfelt thanks to my family who support me constantly.

Lars Eric Larson, a Chiropractor in Sarasota, Florida gave me permission to use his wonderful Viking name. Thank you

My husband, Jim, is my 'wind beneath my wings'.

Research, research, research…

An older book on Vikings, discovered in a second hand bookstore:

History of the Vikings by Gwyn Jones is where I discovered the Varangians and sent Annie on her journey.

The web has many excellent sources on Vikings. My constant 'go to' page was: *www.thevikinganswerlady.com*

Also by the author in
The Annie and Rosamund Series

Tangle of Time